A LOSING BATTLE

"Look at that!" Ethan said tautly.

"I know," Dan'l replied cocking the heavy Heinrich. "The Devil's own French!"

Guns were still making yellow explosions in the new light of dawn and arrows were flying across the compound, but most of the fighting was at close quarters. Heads were being split open by tomahawks, and a few Shawnee were still going down with hot lead in their chests and bellies. But there were too many of them. The defenders were fighting a losing battle, and that was already clear to Dan'l.

The white men who had just entered the fray, the ones on foot, carried Charleville muskets, and one had already killed a defender, exploding his heart like a paper bag. The other one turned to yell up at his commander as Dan'l raised his gun in that direction. They could not hear what the man on foot said, but they distinctly heard the officer's reply.

"Yes, I said all of them!" he shouted. "Kill them all! I want no prisoners!"

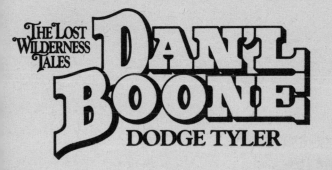

THE LOST WILDERNESS TALES

DAN'L BOONE

DODGE TYLER

A RIVER RUN RED

LEISURE BOOKS   **L**   **NEW YORK CITY**

To Donna

A LEISURE BOOK®

April 1996

Published by

Dorchester Publishing Co., Inc.
276 Fifth Avenue
New York, NY 10001

Printed in the United States of America.

A
RIVER
RUN RED

Prologue

The bearded frontiersman sat on the narrow stoop before his cabin and carefully cleaned the Kentucky rifle that lay across his knees. As he worked, he watched the approaching rider. Gradually the horseman loomed larger, coming through the corn, rocking in his saddle. Finally the rider stopped just a few yards away. He wore a bowler hat and wire spectacles; he gave the impression of being a preacher.

"They told me in town where to find you. Are you really the great Indian fighter and explorer Dan'l Boone?"

The old man set the rifle aside and squinted up at the mounted stranger through clear, penetrating eyes. He was bareheaded; his hair was thinning and almost white. He had a tooth missing at the corner of his mouth.

"What if I was?" he asked suspiciously.

The rider dismounted, retrieved a large notebook from a saddlebag, and came up onto the porch, where the old fellow sat on a willow chair. The musket leaned against the log wall of the cabin beside the frontiersman, but Boone saw no need for it.

"I'm Adam Hollis. I've come all the way from Boston to find you, Dan'l. I'm pleased and mighty proud to finally meet up with you."

"I don't talk to newspaper people." When Hollis smiled, Dan'l liked the eyes behind the glasses.

"I'm just a library clerk. Mind if I shake the riding cramps out on your porch?" Hollis asked.

When Dan'l motioned grudgingly to a second chair not far away, Hollis slumped onto it and stretched his legs. The aroma of cooking food came to him from inside. He looked out past the cornfield to the woods and admired the view.

"Thanks," he said wearily. "People have been coming to me for years, selling me bits and pieces of your life story because of my special interest."

Dan'l grunted. "Most of them is selling swamp fog."

Hollis grinned. "I figured as much. But all those stories got my curiosity up, sir, and I came to realize your own story could be one of the great untold legends of the frontier. So I spent my life savings to get out here, hoping you might talk to me some about yourself."

8

Dan'l Boone #1: A River Run Red

The old hunter regarded Hollis sidewise. "You want to write down all that stuff? Hell, ain't nobody'll want to read about them times. We're in a whole different century, by Jesus. Nobody gives a tinker's damn about that early stuff no more."

Hollis shook his head. "You'd be surprised, Dan'l. You're already something of a legend— even in Europe, I hear. But I think that's just the beginning. If you let me document your life while it's all still in your head, generations to come will know what wild adventures you had."

The great hunter rose from his chair. He no longer enjoyed the renowned robustness or grace of his youth, but he still looked as hard as sacked salt. Dan'l went to the far end of the porch and stared out into the green forest beyond the fields, the kind of country that had been his home for all of his life. He finally turned back to Hollis.

"What would you do with these stories once you got it all writ down on paper?"

Hollis shrugged. "Publish them, but only if you wanted me to. At least we'd have them all down. For safekeeping, you might say."

Dan'l shook his head. "I can't say I'd want them in no book. Not in my lifetime. Not the real stuff. Most of them are too damned private. There's too many people out there who might not want them told. Or they might be moved to correct them, so to speak. Come out with their own versions so they would look better."

A resolve settled over Hollis. "All right. It can

all be hidden away till long after you're gone if that's what you'd like. Then if the stories don't get lost somewhere down the line, maybe they will all come out later, at a better time, and be given over to some book people. That's what I would hope for."

Dan'l thought for a long moment. "You'd promise that in writing?"

Hollis nodded. "I will."

A laugh rattled out of the old man's throat. "I guess you'd want even the bear mauling and the wolf eating and the nasty ways some redskins liked to treat a white man when they caught him?"

"Yes, everything," Hollis said.

"There's treks into the West, the far side of the Mississippi, that hardly a man alive now knows about," Dan'l said, reflecting. "And these eyes have seen things that nobody's going to believe."

Hollis was becoming excited. "I'd want it all."

Dan'l took a deep breath in and called, "Rebecca! You better put a big pot of coffee on! Looks like we got company for a spell!"

As Hollis relaxed and smiled, Dan'l heaved himself back onto the primitive chair and closed his eyes for a moment. Finally, he said, "I reckon we might as well get going on it then."

Hollis was caught off guard. He fumbled in a pocket for a quill pen and a small ink pot, then opened up the thick but empty notebook. Hollis dipped his pen into the ink and waited.

"Most of it happened in about thirty years,"

Dan'l said quietly. "The important stuff. The stuff most folks don't know nothing about. That's when I got this raw hunger for the wild places, the far-off country where no settlers had been.

"I was just a stripling when I first started hearing about the land west of the Alleghenies," Dan'l said, his gaze wandering off toward the woods.

Hollis did not hesitate or interrupt with any questions. As the old man talked, he just began writing steadily in the thick book with an urgency he had never before experienced. He had to get every sentence down exactly as Dan'l said it. He could not miss a single word.

Chapter One

The attack came without warning, in the watery half-light of that foggy morning in eastern Tennessee. Dan'l Boone and his cousin Ethan had stopped over at Scotborough for the night to trade pelts on their long hunt from Carolina. The Shawnee party had come into the fortress the day before, making demands on the settlement. When those demands were rejected out of hand by the tiny six-man British garrison and the elders of the village, Dan'l had sensed there would be trouble.

As the next day dawned, Dan'l stood on the catwalk atop the palisade wall with the British commander. They stared out toward a line of trees rising like ghosts just yards away, but the fog obscured their vision.

"I told you, Boone," the captain was saying

when the attack started. "You exaggerate the danger. There's no sign of the stinking savages out there this morning. If you'll just get on about your trapping and let us worry over the safety of this garrison town, I'm sure all will be—"

In that instant came the familiar hissing that Dan'l knew as well as the sound of a snake striking. A dull thud followed, and an iron-tipped arrow was protruding from the captain. His chest was painted with a crimson that was a deeper red than his uniform. The arrow had broken a posterior rib, then sliced through the officer's heart before thrusting out through his tunic and popping a brass button.

"Damn!" Dan'l whispered, looking past the officer into the fog.

The captain's eyes had gone very wide, he stared down at the bloody tip as if there were some terrible mistake. He looked back up at Dan'l, as if to continue their conversation, then just collapsed in a heap at the hunter's feet.

Even in the raw morning light, Dan'l could see the redskins running across the clearing. He quickly turned toward the interior of the fortress and cupped a hand to his mouth.

"Shawnee!" he yelled down into the compound, where Ethan stood talking with the other British regulars. "Shawnee at the perimeter!"

Boone turned back to the clearing outside the stockade wall and saw the Indians coming in scores. They were yelling bloodcurdling war cries, and as they approached, Dan'l could plainly see the ribbon and feathers decorating their midskull strips of hair and the war paint on their faces. They were the dread Shawnee, all right. At their rear, Boone could just barely make out the blue uniform of a French officer and the buckskins of two other white men. As was usual in that area, the French were responsible for the attack.

"I'm coming up, Dan'l!" Ethan called as arrows began flying.

As a group of Shawnee charge the big gate with a log ramrod, Dan'l raised his ten-pound Heinrich Long Rifle, primed it, and cocked it. "No, defend the gate!" he yelled down to his cousin. Then he fired the first gunshot of the battle, killing a Shawnee trying to scale the palisade.

Then Dan'l paused for a moment. In all his 20 years, he had tried to befriend local Indians. The one he had just killed was his very first. His action gave him an unpleasant feeling in the pit of his stomach.

But then he was rapidly reloading and shaking off the feeling. He tamped powder from a hip flask into the muzzle of the long gun, then dropped a ball in, wrapped in an oiled linen patch, and rammed it home. A moment later he was primed and ready to fire again. A gun roared outside the wall, and a hot chunk of lead tugged at the collar of his rawhide shirt.

Indians were throwing ladders up against the wall and setting fires at its base. Dan'l could hear the big stockade gate cracking under the impact of the ramrod hits. There were almost a hundred Shawnee gathered out there, and their war whoops made a din that drowned out the sporadic crackling of rifles and muskets.

Dan'l aimed at an Indian on the ramrod and fired again. Jerked off his feet, the fellow took another Shawnee down with him. Shot through the heart and lung, he was dead when he hit the ground.

Inside the compound, the soldiers had raised a hue and cry. A couple of them had come up onto the palisade near Dan'l and were firing down onto the attackers. One of them was almost immediately hit with a ball of hot lead in the chest and thrown off the parapet.

Settlers were streaming from their private residences, some half clothed and sleepy eyed, most carrying rifles or muskets. Ethan and the other regulars had knelt before the gate, guns at ready, knowing it was about to crash inward. Settlers came and stood behind them, loading and priming. All along the wall, Shawnee were dropping inside and beginning to fire arrows across the compound.

Dan'l could not prevent the wall-scaling with any effectiveness, so he decided to go down into the compound, where most of the fighting would occur. He was halfway down a wooden ladder when the big gate crashed open with a rending of wood and the Indians came streaming in, yelling at the top of their lungs.

The first through were met with a thunderous

volley of lead, as the Brown Besses of the regulars and the muskets of the settlers exploded brightly in unison. Ethan stood at their fore and brought down a wild-looking Shawnee with a blast in the torso. But in the next moment, the defenders were overwhelmed. They tried to reload, but were attacked at close quarters by redskins wielding knives and tomahawks. Ethan clubbed an onrushing Indian with the butt of his rifle, cracking the assailant's skull audibly; then Dan'l was beside him, thrusting his long skinning knife into a Shawnee who was about to split Ethan right down the middle with a big tomahawk.

Most of the swarm had run on past them, attacking the settlers who had gathered in the compound. The British regulars, lay dead or wounded all around, and the settlers were quickly falling under the onslaught.

Dan'l pulled Ethan aside where they could reload and saw that his cousin had been grazed by an arrow, and there was a big stain of blood along his right side. Ethan was a year younger than Dan'l, and Dan'l felt responsible for him. They reloaded furiously with Dan'l watching to make sure Ethan did it right in his haste. Dan'l was a broadly built young man and his blue eyes focused on his wounded cousin with concern behind them. A bit taller and more slightly built, Ethan was dressed like Dan'l, with a rawhide shirt, leather breeches with leggings, rawhide boots, and a wide-brimmed black hat that sat cockeyed on his head.

"Tamp it all the way in!" Dan'l reminded him.

"I should throw it down!" Ethan said in his excitement. "I could have killed three by now, with my knife!"

"There's too many for hand combat!" Dan'l yelled back.

He was already regretting their decision to stop here at Scotborough to trade off their beaver and buffalo skins. Now they were embroiled in an emerging war between the British and the hated French, and there was absolutely nothing they could do to stop what was happening. All he had done was place his cousin's life in grave danger.

They were finally reloaded, and just then Ethan looked toward the destroyed gate and saw the white men enter, two on foot and the French officer mounted on a white stallion.

"Look at that!" Ethan said tautly.

"I know," Dan'l replied, cocking the heavy Heinrich. "The Devil's own French!"

Guns were still making yellow explosions in the new light of dawn, and arrows were flying across the compound, but most of the fighting was at close quarters. Heads were being split open by tomahawks, and a few Shawnee were still going down with hot lead in their chests and bellies. But there were too many of them. The defenders were fighting a losing battle, and that was already clear to Dan'l.

The white men who had just entered the fray, the ones on foot, carried Charleville muskets, and one had already killed a defender, exploding his heart like a paper bag. The other one turned to yell up at his commander, as Dan'l raised his gun in that direction. They could not hear what the man on foot said, but they distinctly heard the officer's reply.

"Yes, I said all of them!" he shouted in French, which both Dan'l and Ethan understood. "Kill them all! I want no prisoners!"

Ethan had just cocked his big gun. He turned to Dan'l. "Did you hear that?"

Dan'l, though, was too busy taking aim on the Frenchman.

"That son of a bitch!" Ethan said loudly. "That demon from hell!"

The French officer had not even seen them. He now drew a long saber from its scabbard and waved it in the air. "Death to all English!"

Dan'l squeezed the trigger of the Long Rifle, the officer's torso in his sights. But at that same moment, the stallion reared at a nearby explosion of a musket, and its head came between Dan'l and his target. The Heinrich fired loudly and the musketball exploded into the horse's right eyeball.

"Damn!" Dan'l exclaimed in frustration.

The stallion fell like a boulder, its right eye blown out of its socket, its brains all over the blue tunic of the Frenchman.

The French officer jumped clear at the last moment, and rolled free of the big animal, swearing under his breath. He had not seen where the shot came from, nor had his companion. In the next instant he was on his feet again, uttering obscenities and running into the melee on foot, brandishing the razor-sharp saber. He sliced at a settler's head, and decapitated the man in one easy stroke. The head rolled at his feet, the face still contorting in surprise and shock.

"I'm going to get that bastard!" Ethan said fiercely. "He's going to let these savages maul this place!"

"No. Wait, Ethan!" Dan'l cried out to him as his cousin hurled himself into the fight.

But Ethan was gone, out in the center of the compound. A Shawnee immediately tried to kill him with a tomahawk, but Ethan blasted a big hole in him from front to back, and the red man was jerked off his feet as if pulled on a wire. Ethan was then moving on, abandoning the rifle for the knife at his side.

He was already cut off from the French officer, though, by swarming Shawnee, and Dan'l could see he would never reach him, not in that chaos. A tomahawk sailed past Dan'l and thunked into the building wall beside his left ear, and then a musketball chipped wood near his left shoulder. Dan'l fired again, and the hot slug tore through the side of a charging Shawnee, kept going, and struck a second one in the high back, taking them both down.

But Dan'l could see that he and Ethan would soon be dead if they continued the fight. Things were going very badly in the compound. Rifle fire had almost entirely stopped, and the fighting was now hand-to-hand, and deadly. The

French officer had beheaded several settlers, and had sliced off the right arm of a council elder that Dan'l had met on the previous day. The older man lay screaming in the dirt, with nobody to hear him.

Corpses and wounded littered the ground, and there was a lot of blood everywhere, and screaming, and gunsmoke still hung acrid and pungent in the damp air. Women were being dragged from their houses now, and the Shawnee were busy scalping fallen men, many of whom were very much alive. Dan'l saw Shawnee on a couple of young women, their long dresses thrown up to expose their thighs, and they were being brutally raped in the midst of the battle. Dan'l ran to one such encounter near him, and pulled the redskin's head back and cut his throat from ear to ear with his big knife. The woman was screaming uncontrollably.

A tough-looking Shawnee came striding out of a house not far away with a baby, holding it by its feet. Before Dan'l could act to intervene, the red man bashed the baby's head against a hitching post, crushing its skull. Blood and matter went flying.

Dan'l let out a guttural growl from his throat, in complete frustration, that ended in a primeval roar. But it was lost in the noise from the dead and dying.

Dan'l got hold of himself. They had to get out of there. He looked in desperation for Ethan, and could not see him.

"Ethan! Where are you?"

He saw a small group of Shawnee standing over an older woman, filling her body with arrows, Just for sport. He could stay no longer. He reloaded the rifle once more, and headed out into the center of the compound, searching for Ethan. He came upon another rape, and the young woman had already been shot with an arrow, through the side. Dan'l angrily fired the rifle and blew the side of the Indian's face off. The woman, eyes staring upward but seeing nothing, did not flinch.

Dan'l moved forward, the expended rifle in one hand and the skinning knife in the other. A Shawnee threw himself at Dan'l, and Dan'l stepped aside, then drove the long knife into the fellow's ribs. The Indian fell at his feet.

Dan'l could not find Ethan. With great reluctance, he edged his way toward the big gate. An arrow flew past his head, and he moved on to the gate. There was nobody there at the moment. He stepped outside the gate, where the clearing was empty of Indians. A Shawnee in the compound, though, had seen him exit, and now hurtled through the gate opening, eyes flashing fire, his mane on the top of his head looking like that of a wild animal. He hurled himself at Dan'l with a hoarse cry, and swung a tomahawk at Dan'l's face. Dan'l ducked away and it thudded hard into the upright of the palisade beside his head. He thrust the hunting knife into the belly of the savage, and it went in to the hilt, and Dan'l felt the handle slippery in his grasp.

The Indian muttered something inaudible, and collapsed into the arms of Dan'l. He broke free, and went and looked into the compound again. Finally, he saw Ethan.

Ethan had been disarmed on the far side of the compound, with a gash along the side of his face, and he was still on his feet, being playfully harassed by his captors.

"Oh, God in heaven," Dan'l murmured.

There were hundreds of Shawnee between him and Ethan. An attempt to rescue him at that moment would be suicidal. Dan'l stood there aching inside for a long moment, watching the braves poke at Ethan with knives and clubs, having a good time. The killing was over for the moment, and they were beginning a celebration.

Dan'l could not see very well. He hurried to a rough-hewn ladder that still stood against the palisade wall. He climbed it with gun in hand, until he could see over the top of it.

Inside the compound, there was a lot of yelling and dancing. The French officer was walking slowly among the fallen, and administering coups de grace to the wounded, with the bloody saber. He did not hesitate when the victim was a woman, or a child. All around him were women who were being raped and tortured, and he ignored it. One man was being flayed alive, and his screams rent the heavy air of the morning.

The only ones alive were those few, and the half-dozen taken captive, including Ethan.

They would be made examples of.

Dan'l saw men, women, and children lying in bloody pools all over the compound. There were a few small fires set, in homes and at the wall, but none that would destroy the settlement. The Frenchman wanted to loot the storehouses and residences before any final destruction was wrought.

As Dan'l watched helplessly, Ethan was tied to a hitching post, and the other captives were similarly secured, to any post or object handy. Chunks of wood and branches were laid at their feet, and Dan'l did not realize what was happening until the Shawnee were almost set to proceed.

"Oh, holy Jesus!" he grated out atop the wall from his vantage point.

Down in the compound, Ethan understood all too well what was going to happen to him. It was a favorite way to kill for the Shawnee.

"Why didn't I listen to you, Dan'l?" Ethan said, barely moving his lips. He was bleeding badly alongside the face, and from his side. Shallow cuts also caused him pain on his chest and back, from the poking with knives.

I hope you got away, Dan'l. I hope you live to wreak vengeance on these bastards! I hope you're miles away by now.

Ethan thought he had voiced the last thoughts aloud, but they had been only in his head.

In the next moment, a brave touched a torch to the debris and wood at Ethan's feet.

Dan'l had had to reload, and was caught unaware by the suddenness of developments. His face was flushed with anger and fear for Ethan, his breathing shallow. He aimed down the barrel of the gun as the brave leaned forward to touch the wood at another place, and fired.

The Shawnee was hit in the back and thrown against Ethan, and then fell onto the low fire, almost putting it out.

The dancing stopped for a moment, as they all looked around to see where the shot had come from. Dan'l had ducked down, and they did not see him.

"Find where that shot came from!" the officer yelled out in French to his subordinate with the buckskins.

The fellow took two Shawnee and came across the compound toward Dan'l, but not looking up at the wall. They disappeared into a couple of buildings inside.

The dancing and yelling resumed. The other captives had fires set under them too, and the flames began licking high, and they began screaming terribly. A brave came to Ethan and touched another torch to the wood, and Dan'l could do nothing to stop him.

Dan'l closed his eyes. It was hopeless. As the flames licked at Ethan's lower legs, Dan'l could see his cousin stick his chin out defiantly and accept his fate. Tears streamed from Dan'l eyes as he reloaded, primed, and cocked the big gun another time. The flames licked up higher on

Ethan, and soon he would be screaming in ugly pain.

Dan'l aimed the long barrel at his cousin, and put the sights directly over Ethan's heart. Blinking wetness from his eyes, Dan'l squeezed down on the trigger.

The gun exploded a last time, and Ethan was hit dead center. His body jerked under the impact of the fiery slug, and just like that it was over for him. His body slumped in the flames.

A great outcry went up this time, just as the buckskin-clothed underling emerged from one of the houses below. Dan'l was already climbing back down the ladder and dropping to the ground when the French officer finally understood.

"That came from the wall! Jacques, go find that shooter and bring him in here. He will take the hunter's place."

"There were two of them, Colonel Duvall! I think the other may be Dan'l Boone!"

Duvall looked toward the wall. "Boone. The one the Shawnee call Sheltowee. Excellent! Find him and bring him in here! We will show him how his enemies honor their captives!"

Outside, Dan'l was within earshot just long enough to hear the colonel's name spoken. He repeated it several times to himself as he turned and ran as hard as he could for the line of tress under a hundred yards away. All through that run, he kept seeing Ethan's brave face as those flames licked higher and higher.

Out at the edge of the woods, Dan'l stopped

for just a moment and turned to see his pursuers. There they were, coming on fast, just 50 yards away. The man called Jacques was leading two very wild-looking Shawnee.

Dan'l turned and headed into the forest, running easily as an Indian, leaping over fallen logs, ducking under tree branches, splashing through watery, swampy sloughs. Birds went dead silent with his passage, but there was almost no sound as he made his way into the deepest part of the woods, holding tight onto the rifle, the knife back in its sheath.

Dan'l came to a small, narrow stream, and leapt over it, landing downstream on the far side, so his trail would be hard to pick up. In another several hundred yards, he came to the place where the small stream emptied into a wider one. He leapt in and ran down the length of the stream, kicking water up, avoiding boulders and holes underwater. Then he was out again, on the far side, racing on through the dense forest.

Behind him, Jacques had deferred to the tallest Shawnee who accompanied him, and that expert tracker kept on after Dan'l in the lead, with Jacques coming after him, and then the shorter brave bringing up the rear. Both Jacques and the tall Shawnee had brought muskets, and they were primed, cocked, and ready to fire once Dan'l came in their sights.

The tall Shawnee was good. He found Dan'l's trail on the far side of the small stream immediately, almost without breaking stride. At the larger stream he took a bit longer, but just ran up and down the far side of it until he saw a broken twig where Dan'l had passed, and then a confirmatory imprint in the mud.

"This way!" he said in Shawnee.

Jacques was a mountain man and trapper himself, so he had no trouble keeping up with his tracker. Dan'l, up ahead a quarter mile now, could hear them coming, and he knew that the Shawnee were like bloodhounds from England when they were after a man. They never gave up, and they never lost a trail.

He would have to use strategy.

After he had stretched the distance to just over a quarter mile, Dan'l began circling back. In a wide circle he went, remembering a bear that had done that to its pursuers when Dan'l was just learning about hunting in Carolina. Silently, like a panther he moved. Sheltowee, whose hunting and shooting exploits were already legend among the Shawnee and Cherokee. Sheltowee, who could track like the best of them, and who could hit a flying grouse at a hundred yards with the long rifle, with a crosswind.

Dan'l ran back parallel with his pursuers now, and could even hear them from time to time as he circled back on them, dark images of Ethan crowding his fevered brain. I had to do it, he kept repeating over and over in his head. He would have burned alive. But the awful feeling was high in his chest again.

Duvall, he said as he ran. Colonel Duvall.

He would not forget that name.

In just short moments, Dan'l was back on his own trail, lying in deep brush at the side of it. The tall Shawnee had already passed that spot, and now, from cover, Dan'l could see the man named Jacques come running past, bearded and looking dangerous, holding his musket at ready. Dan'l let him pass on by, and then heard the short Indian approaching.

Dan'l moved forward through the ferns and brush, until he was at a place where the Indian would pass within a few feet of him. He could see the Shawnee now, running hard to keep up with the others, a tomahawk gripped tightly in his hand.

Dan'l crouched very low, like a stalking wolf. The Indian came even with him, having no hint he was there. Dan'l hurtled from the brush with a low snarl, swinging the butt of the heavy rifle against the Shawnee's head. The blow was a savage one, exploding the Indian's right eardrum and fracturing his skull inward. There was a short grunting sound from his throat as he plummeted forward onto his face. He jerked a leg spastically there, kicking at the leaf-strewn forest floor, and was dead.

Dan'l stood over him, breathless. He looked ahead, and the others were almost out of sight. He put his hand to his mouth, and made the sound of a hawk in flight, one of the woods signals of the Shawnee.

He heard the man named Jacques stop, and turn back. Dan'l had stepped behind the trunk of a white oak tree. He saw the Frenchman squint toward him, and fail to find his second Shawnee. He heard Jacques call to the tall one.

"Go on! I'll take a look!" he said in Shawnee, which Dan'l understood perfectly.

Jacques came back cautiously. Dan'l hoped he did not take too much time, since the tall brave would now be making the big turn on his trail, and realize Dan'l had doubled back.

Jacques approached to within 20 feet of the fallen Shawnee, staring hard at the body now. He was squarely built, like Dan'l, but many years older, which meant he was very experienced at all this. He held his Charleville musket tightly in both hands as he approached, knowing now what had happened. He scanned the trees with his eyes, but Dan'l was well hidden. He came on up to the body.

Dan'l had laid his gun aside, and held the big hunting knife loosely in his right hand. He stepped from behind the tree now, and showed himself boldly to the Frenchman.

"He's dead, you French son of a bitch!"

Jacques's bearded face showed surprise. He thought Dan'l had gone on into the forest, after this small success. But he did not yet know his adversary.

"You little sow udder!" the French hunter growled at Dan'l. "You think you play with the big men, yes? Now I take your scalp back to Duquesne!"

In that moment he raised the muzzle of the Charleville, and aimed it at Dan'l's chest. But

Dan'l had anticipated the move. He was already hurling the knife in a quick, underhand motion. The big blade turned over twice in midair and then buried itself in Jacques's center chest, breaking skin through his back.

Jacques just stood there in disbelief for a long moment; then the big gun went off and kicked up dirt at Dan'l's feet. Jacques then fell forward onto the corpse of the Shawnee.

Dan'l looked around. The other brave would be on his way back now, and the shot would hurry him. He knelt over the Frenchman and withdrew the skinning knife, wiping its blade clean on the Frenchman's rawhide shirt.

Then he headed off along his original trail.

Dan'l knew the Shawnee who had tracked him so well would not give up the hunt because the others were dead. He could not return to Scotborough without Dan'l or his scalp. He would lose face, and be disgraced among his people. It was only moments later, therefore, that Dan'l heard the Shawnee coming after him once again, and closing the distance between them.

Dan'l had not had time to reload the Long Rifle, and realized there would be no time now. He would have to depend on his ability in up-close fighting, and he was certain the Shawnee was good at that.

There were only a couple hundred yards between them as Dan'l made his way through the dense woods again, and he could hear the Shawnee back there, coming fast. Dan'l knew he had to think of something very fast, or he would have a tomahawk buried in his middle back.

As Dan'l ran, he spotted a depression in the ground to the left of him, filled with leaves. He slowed and looked it over, then ran on for several yards, stopped quickly, and leapt away from his trail to his left, so that his tracks stopped abruptly and did not continue. He heard the Shawnee coming.

Dan'l dived into the depression beside his trail, and quickly raked leaves up and over him, with both hands. He buried his Heinrich in the depression with him.

A half moment later, the Shawnee came running past him, and then slowed to a walk up ahead a few yards. Then he stopped completely.

He was a big man, Dan'l saw from the leaves. Well muscled and lean, the kind of warrior Dan'l had admired when growing up in Virginia years ago, when he had thought he could befriend all red men, and live in peace with them. Then he had met the Shawnee and their allies, the French. And war had come to the frontier.

The Shawnee was turning back, puzzled by the trail's ending so abruptly. He began circling, moving about, trying to decipher what the ground was telling him.

Dan'l waited. The Indian turned his back on Dan'l, just a few feet from where Dan'l lay covered with leaves. Dan'l savagely sprang from the ground, leaves flying, and hurled himself onto the Shawnee. The tall man turned at the last second, tomahawk in hand. Dan'l shoved his knife into the Indian's side, violently.

The thrust was a glancing blow, and the blade was deflected by the Indian's floating ribs, and the wound was shallow. He did not go down, but now was grappling with Dan'l, trying to break the tomahawk free to use against his suddenly found enemy.

The Indian had 15 years on Dan'l in experience, but Dan'l had the extraordinary strength of youth, and of deep anger. They grunted and strained against each other, and the Shawnee had a hard smile just barely showing in his long face, since he was confident of victory. He would take Sheltowee's scalp back to his people, and he would be honored for his great deed in killing this young but great white hunter from Carolina.

Dan'l felt the great strength of the Indian, and his resolve, and knew he could not just use strength against strength in this death struggle. He stuck a foot out behind the Shawnee and shoved, and they went down hard together, rolling and rolling on the ground, into the depression Dan'l had laid his ambush from, and out of it again, leaves flying in their wake. The tomahawk came down close to Dan'l's throat, and he just barely managed to keep it at bay. The Shawnee gave an unexpected twist of Dan'l's wrist, and his knife went flying.

Now he was unarmed, and knew the odds were going against him. The smile widened on the redskin's face as he rolled onto Dan'l, his well-muscled arm shaking with the effort of bringing the hatchet blade down onto Dan'l.

"Sheltowee, you are dead!" the red man grated out.

Dan'l met the fellow's hard gaze. "Not yet!" he replied in equally good Shawnee. Then he kicked upward into the Indian's crotch, with all his strength.

The Shawnee cried out in surprise and pain, and in that moment Dan'l grabbed the wrist of the hand that held the weapon with both of his own, and twisted his whole body away from the Shawnee.

Dan'l could hear the wrist bones fracture as he fell away, and then the tomahawk was suddenly in his hand. While the Indian recovered from the new injury, yelling again in renewed pain, Dan'l swung the red man's own weapon against his long face, and split it wide open.

The Shawnee fell in agony beside Dan'l, grabbing at his face. But he was dead and just did not know it yet. Dan'l could look into his head, past his nose and cheekbone, and it was not a pretty sight. The Shawnee writhed on the ground for a long moment, making guttural noises in his throat, and then finally lay lifeless.

Dan'l rose slowly, standing over his enemy somberly, trying to get his breath back.

"Go to your ancestors with honor," he finally said in a low voice. "You were killed by Sheltowee."

He then retrieved the long gun from the leaves, reloaded it wearily and slowly, and

headed on through the forest, toward Carolina.
They would send nobody else after him.
There would be no more fighting this day. But
the conflict was not over.

Chapter Two

When Dan'l arrived back home, on his family farm near Salisbury, the news of his cousin's death was received with deep mourning by Dan'l's family and that of Ethan, who lived at the far end of the Yadkin Valley. Dan'l did not tell of the way Ethan had actually died, though, until his father took him aside privately that evening of Dan'l's first day back.

"Did you let that boy burn?" Squire Boone asked his son as they sat alone on a low front porch of their log cabin. Squire was in his 40s, and had the beginning of gray in his hair, but was a tough-looking man, broadly built like Dan'l.

Dan'l ran a hand through his own sandy hair and squinted his blue eyes down into somber slits. "I couldn't."

Squire nodded slowly, looking out into a growing darkness. "I figured."

"I had to do it, Paw."

"I know. I'm sorry, boy."

Dan'l felt a tightness in his throat. He and Ethan had done a lot of hunting together, and had a lot of good times.

"I can't seem to get his face out of my head," Dan'l said quietly, and the elder Boone looked over at him. "There was a French colonel. Name of Duvall."

"Oh, that son of a bitch," Squire Boone said heavily. "He done the same thing up north in Pennsylvania. The settlers up that way are scared to death of him, son. Henri Duvall. A very ambitious Frenchman. Says he'll run us all out of the west country. But the English got Braddock at Fort Cumberland now. He says he's going to Fort Duquesne."

"I heard. One of Braddock's officers going to be in Salisbury in a couple days. To recruit a militia here." His father regarded him closely as Dan'l said, "I'm joining up, Paw."

"What!"

Dan'l met his surprised look. "I know you need me around here. The trapping done helped the family income some, I know that, Paw. But you got young Squire, and the other kids. I'm going after that butcher, Paw."

"Who, Duvall?" Boone said curiously. "Why, this ain't no personal matter, Dan'l! This is war. That Duvall will be got to, you can count on it. The English hang the likes of him."

36

"There ain't no guarantee on that," Dan'l said. "Anyway, even if I don't get to shoot that French devil myself, I'll feel better just being a part of them that bring him down. No, I give it a lot of thought. I'm going to Duquesne. With or without Braddock."

His father looked into Dan'l's face and saw the resolve written on it. He let out a long breath. "Well. I didn't have to do what you done. I reckon you got the right."

Dan'l rose, and looked out into the night. "I wish you wouldn't mention Ethan's way of going to the others."

Squire Boone rose too. He laid a hand on his son's shoulder. "It ain't nobody's business but yours, Dan'l."

"I'll try to bring some skins in," Dan'l said. "Before I go. The beaver is thick as fleas on a hound, down by that creek that runs into the Yadkin."

"Well, if you go down there, take somebody with you," his father warned him. "Remember old Atkins."

Dan'l knew what he referred to. There was a killer bear roaming the woods in that area, and just six months earlier it had mauled and killed an experienced hunter.

"I remember," Dan'l said.

Dan'l did not sleep much that night. He kept seeing Ethan tied to that hitching post, raw fear sagging his young face as the Shawnee danced around him and piled wood at his feet. And the blood and death in the compound, and Duvall shouting his orders to take no prisoners. And the bizarre sight of his dead white stallion, lying near the big open gate, shot through the head by Dan'l's musketball.

The next morning he tried to get young Squire, the spitting image of his father, to go out with him, but the boy, only 16, was committed to take some trade items into town. So Dan'l saddled up a plow mare and rode off into the woods alone, which is the way he liked to hunt best.

He was only ten miles from home when it happened. He had been pulling traps down by the creek, and paying little attention to the woods around him, still replaying that awful scene at Scotborough in his head. He was quite surprised when the fetid smell of the animal alerted him, and when he turned, the bear was there, just paces away, the primordial power of it suddenly overwhelming him with its terrifying proximity.

It was the killer bear.

It had been a day something like this one when Atkins had passed this same way, and had been horribly mauled by this same big grizzly. Atkins, it was believed, had fired a ball into the brawny predator's chest, but then the savage animal had come past the gun, ignoring the musketball in its innards, and tore the hunter's head off his shoulders, then sat down and ate his guts out of his abdominal cavity. His comrades had heard the shot, and then awful screaming, but by the time they arrived on the scene, the bear was gone, and Atkins lay in bloody pieces on the ground, turning the brush crimson.

Still healing from that other encounter with firearms, the bear now reared onto its hind legs, its red eyes flashing anger and hatred at Dan'l, and roared its deafening challenge into the intruder's face.

Dan'l rose slowly from the beaver trap he had been bending over, one of a string he had set along the creek bed. He very slowly brought the Heinrich up with him, the gun that had killed with such efficiency at Scotborough. It was primed already, and he needed only cock it. He did so very cautiously, and the metallic clicking brought forth another hair-raising roar from the rampant bear, which stood a head taller than Dan'l on its back legs.

Dan'l could see the dark spot on its chest where it had been hit by Atkins, and realized immediately what animal he was confronting. This bear had a reputation that went back beyond Atkins. It was believed to have carried a small child off from a campsite almost a year ago, and the child had never been seen since.

Dan'l clutched the rifle in both hands, his eyes glued on this primeval opponent, an animal that would have considered any of Dan'l's adversaries at Scotborough a puny challenge to its sovereignty. This bear despised all humans, and welcomed any opportunity to rid his territory of them.

Towering over Dan'l, it looked eight feet tall to him, almost at arm's length. It snarled menacingly in the new quiet, intending to make short shrift of this invader. Dan'l tasted an old parchment taste in his dry mouth as he recalled his father's warning to him, which he had ignored.

In a final blast of noise that shook leaves on the trees, the bear hurled its last thunderous challenge at Dan'l, and he felt the wind from the bear's throat against his body, and in that moment he was thrilled with the majesty of this beast of the forest, and as it had in Shawnee and others before him, the feeling of wonder overpowered his fear in that timeless moment.

He raised the muzzle of the Long Rifle and aimed it calmly at the bear's nose.

"You going to just talk about it, varmint, or really do it?" he said breathlessly.

In the next instant the bear lunged at him, a mountain of bone, muscle and fur, razor-sharp claws extended, enormous fangs bared.

In that same moment, though, Dan'l squeezed the trigger on the big gun, firing directly into the bear's gaping mouth. The gun exploded like a cannon in their ears, and the .54-caliber ball smashed through the bear's skull like a branding iron and blew the back of its head off.

The momentum of its charge, though, combined with its will to kill, carried it on forward, and then its enormous weight was on him, knocking him over, the musky, iron smell of its pelt heavy in his nostrils, the claws ripping, the jaw working spasmodically. It fell like a tree beside him, kicking and jumping, Dan'l still trying to protect himself with the barrel of the gun. He finally slid out from under its foreleg, with a deep bite on his left arm and shallow claw wounds on his side and leg, all through ripped-open rawhides.

Dan'l scrabbled awkwardly to his feet, weak and dazed, breathless and shaky suddenly, and fumblingly reloaded the gun, standing well away from the bear. He never presumed a bear was dead until he had it skinned and its pelt hung on a wall. Dan'l stood there with the gun aimed again at the bear, waiting. The bear kicked out once more, and was lifeless. Dan'l sighed wearily, already sober inside about the bear. It was not a villain, like some men. It had been doing only what bears do—hunting, and protecting its territory. Dan'l would rather have a hundred killer bears in the woods than one Henri Duvall, he thought, standing there. He found himself wishing his shot had torn through the brainpan of the Frenchman, instead of this four-legged predator.

Dan'l examined his wounds, and found that his arm was bleeding steadily. He took a cloth from a belt bag, and tied it around his arm, above the wound, with his right hand and his teeth.

Only then did he think of the horse he had ridden there on, which was tethered downstream a hundred yards. He squinted to find it, and it was still standing there, a little skittery, but making no outcry. The bear had come from the opposite direction, and the mare had simply ignored it. Domesticated animals were strange, Dan'l thought. The horse should have warned him of the bear's approach.

Dan'l knelt over the bear, and inspected the pelt. The head was no good for mounting, but the skin would serve as a blanket later, and he would cut off some meat, and a little tallow for wagon grease.

"You should of killed me first, then told me about it," he said to the bear.

Dan'l put the gun down, finally, and drew the long skinning knife, the one he had killed with in Tennessee territory, just a few days ago. He stared at the blade briefly, and saw Ethan's face in the polished metal for a moment, and the thickness came back into his throat.

He quickly went to work on the bear. A long slit along the belly, and then each leg, then the sticky cutting and slicing and scraping. It was a job Dan'l had come to accept as routine. Buffalo took the most time, and were the hardest work. But you usually had a horse, and you could peg the nose to the ground after making your cuts, then let the horse tear the hide off in one long pull.

When Dan'l had scraped the pelt fairly clean, he cut some lean meat off the carcass, and some slices of fat, and packaged it all in small hides from the mount's saddlebags. Then he threw the bundled hide over the mare's rump, got aboard, and headed back home.

Unfortunately, Dan'l's trouble on that crisp spring morning was far from over.

He was still several miles from home, and in deep woods, when he heard the wild turkey call that he knew instinctively was not a turkey. Dan'l himself knew many Indian ways, and could imitate the sounds of deer, owls, and turkeys so well that experienced hunters could not tell the difference. But this sound he had just heard was not done as expertly as he himself would have done it.

He had just emerged into a clearing, and he now scanned the opposite side of it, past a berry bush into the trees. This was familiar country to him. He had come here many times to gather walnuts or gooseberries, or take down a ruffled grouse or rabbit.

The sound came again, and Dan'l tied the reins around the saddle pommel and dismounted. He studied the trees and saw nothing. He felt the hair on the nape of his neck. Very quietly he reached to a saddle scabbard and withdrew the rifled musket, and began repriming it.

Then the two Shawnee strode boldly into the clearing.

Shawnee and Cherokee often lived in mixed groups in this area near his home. The white settlers had always gotten along well with the latter, until the Shawnee had come. Now they caused some occasional trouble, even here in

Carolina, where British troops watched over many settlements.

Dan'l had never seen these two before, and figured them for renegades, who lived outside the laws of the local tribes. These two looked very tough, and somber. They both wore rawhides, like Dan'l, and had eagle feathers dangling from their shock of scalp hair. They came on into the clearing, studying Dan'l's horse, and the pelt on its rump.

If this fortuitous meeting had occurred before Scotborough, Dan'l would have presumed these Indians would leave him in peace. But Scotborough had changed him. He no longer presumed any Indian could be befriended. That innocence had died in that fortress massacre. Now every redskin was suspect, and especially every Shawnee.

The one closer, who was a bit taller than his companion, raised his hand casually, in a deferential greeting. When he spoke, he spoke arrogantly, and in Shawnee.

"You are greeted, white face. You come to our woods with a gun, we see."

Dan'l knew that local Indians, at least some of them, resented the white man's use of firearms in hunting. Most Indians had none, unless they were given to them by Frenchmen.

Dan'l did not respond to the hand gesture. "I did not know that these woods belonged to the Shawnee," he said deliberately. He finished priming the long gun, nonchalantly.

The Indians watched him. The shorter one

came around to the far side of the mare, looking it over, and putting him off to one side of Dan'l. The tall one came a bit closer, narrowing his dark eyes down on Dan'l.

"You are Sheltowee."

Dan'l glanced sidewise at the other one. "I am called that by some Shawnee."

"You have killed our bear, white face," the tall one added.

Dan'l felt the anger rising inside him. In his head he saw those other Shawnee, dancing around Ethan, building a fire under him.

"This bear has killed a white man, maybe more. It tried to kill me. I have made it my bear. When it roamed free, it belonged to no one." All in Shawnee.

The taller fellow came closer again, and a little to the other side of Dan'l. They had him flanked. Dan'l cocked the big gun and held it loosely in his hands.

"The white face does not make the forest his by building a cabin on it, or killing a bear. This forest belongs to the People. You may make a gift to us of the pelt."

Dan'l stood unmoving.

"You may make any protest to Chief Yellow Eagle's council," the Shawnee added to him.

Dan'l raised the level of the gun's muzzle. "I make my protest to you. With this."

The tall one grinned, and drew a long war knife from his side. Dan'l could see the other Indian, just past the mare's head, do likewise.

"We will take the pelt, and the mare. You can

only shoot one of use with that gun. Or maybe neither."

"My rifle is ready for firing," Dan'l told him. "And you will go down first."

The grin evaporated. "My knife will be in your chest before you can pull that trigger device!"

"Maybe," Dan'l said firmly.

The tall Indian was suddenly angry. "You think you cannot die, Sheltowee? If you wound one of us, we will make you wish you had never heard of this bear! We will eat your liver for our evening meal! We will cut your skin away and wear it to ward off evil spirits! Your scalp will decorate our belts!"

Dan'l held the gun ready. "I won't wound you, Shawnee. You know my way with guns. I will shoot you through the heart. No matter what happens then with you companion, you will die. All for the skin of a bear."

It was his companion, though, that made the move. He grabbed the reins of the mare, and pulled on them. The horse, sensing all the excitement, suddenly reared and stepped backward, exposing the shorter man to view. Flustered and embarrassed, the fellow now drew back to hurl his knife at Dan'l.

Dan'l turned in a fluid motion, and fired the big gun from the hip. The lead smacked the Indian in mid-chest, ripping his aorta and blowing a rib out of his back. He went flying off his feet, the mare now rearing wildly. In that chaotic moment, the tall Indian threw himself bodily at Dan'l.

But Dan'l was already turning back toward him. He swung the barrel of the Heinrich, and it cracked loudly against the side of the Shawnee's head, and then he was hitting the ground near Dan'l.

Dan'l threw the gun down and knelt over the dazed Indian with his own knife in hand. He poised it over the redskin's throat. The Shawnee's eyes widened as Dan'l stuck the tip of the sharp blade up under his chin, to drive it home into his skull. Dan'l's hand trembled with new rage as he held the knife there, his face flushed with emotion.

"Use the knife," the Shawnee said. "Otherwise, I am dishonored."

That made Dan'l think a moment. He hesitated. "Where are you from, thief of bear pelts? You are not of Yellow Eagle's tribe."

The Shawnee glared into his face. "From the north. I fight in many brave battles with the French, who are blood brothers to the Shawnee."

Dan'l removed the knife from his throat, and rose to stand over him. "Get on your feet."

The Shawnee looked at him curiously, then rose. He was very groggy from the blow to the head.

"You will live with your shame," Dan'l said slowly, so the Shawnee would understand. "Bury your comrade. Then go north, to Fort Duquesne and your French friends. Tell them Sheltowee is coming."

The Shawnee glowered at him, but said nothing.

Dan'l grabbed the reins of the mare, led it across the clearing, and then looked back at the Indian.

"Tell them," he said. Then he headed on home.

Chapter Three

In an area claimed by Pennsylvania Colony, fifty miles south of Fort Duquesne, Colonel Henri Duvall halted his troops on the edge of a woods. Stationed at Duquesne, which was the largest French garrison outside of Fort Detroit, Duvall had been terrorizing British colonial settlements for some time before the massacre at Scotborough to the south, and was intent on furthering that career of terrorism on this tiny settlement that now lay before him, at the far side of a wide clearing, called Eben's Place.

This was an even smaller settlement than Scotborough, which Duvall had sacked just days ago, and where his Shawnee warriors had tried to burn Dan'l's cousin Ethan at a stake.

On this bright, sunny morning, Duvall commanded not only a contingent of Shawnee, but

30 regular French troops, in their blue uniforms and brass buttons. The French were all mounted, but all the Shawnee, except for a young chieftain called Blackfish, were on foot. That well-muscled, rather handsome red man sat his unsaddled mount beside Duvall now, studying the partially erected stockade wall that was being built around the few dozen houses that was referred to as Eben's Place, after the Virginia farmer who had brought the group there, on the very edge of what the French were calling Louisiana.

"They do not even have a wood fence to defend them, Colonel," Blackfish said to Duvall in excellent French.

"If we had waited a week, it would have been finished," Duvall replied. His long face featured a Roman nose, piercing blue eyes, and a wide, sensual mouth. He and his officers were wearing shako caps that made them look very regal. "That is why I persuaded the general to let us come now."

"It will be like shooting beaver at a dam," Blackfish said almost to himself. There was no excitement in his voice. He was merely stating a fact, a rather unpleasant one to him.

"Good. We will not lose many men," Duvall told him. He was now riding a roan stallion, smaller in stature than the horse Dan'l Boone had shot from under him at Scotborough, and not as fast in a gallop. Duvall rode it grudgingly, because there was nothing better at his disposal at Duquesne.

"What about non-combatants?" Blackfish said. He knew Duvall's reputation for annihilation, and did not particularly care for it. Duvall's attitude in battle encouraged the worst traits in the Shawnee to come out, and Blackfish did not like that.

"What about them?" Duvall said with a hard look.

Blackfish shrugged. "There is no point killing women and children," he commented blandly. "They will only do it to us then, later. It is preferable to capture them and take them back as slaves. Our tribe has adopted a white child on occasion. Some make good warriors."

Duvall looked over at Blackfish as if he must have gone insane. His horse neighed under him, catching the excitement. "Capture them!" Duvall said angrily. "To hell with capture, Blackfish! You put them out of their misery, they can't come back at you later. And I recommend you do not admit to General Beaumont that you are training English boys to wage war!"

Blackfish held the Frenchman's hard gaze. "I do not answer to the French general," he said pointedly. "You do."

Behind them, mounted soldiers were restless in their saddles, unable to hear what the two were discussing. Mixed in with the blue-coated French were about 70 Shawnee, war paint heavy on their faces, ready to go in.

A crow cried out loudly from a tree behind them, as Duvall considered how to respond to the Shawnee's arrogant remark. He could not

51

lose the goodwill of the Indians of the area, if he wanted to drive the English out of the Alleghanies.

"You answer to me when you are under my command," he finally said to the young chief. "Just prepare your men to go in there and kill English settlers."

Blackfish sighed slightly. "They will do their job, Colonel," he said.

The Shawnee were brought up to the front then, and Duvall drew his saber, the one he had wielded so wickedly at Scotborough. He raised it high in the air. Before them lay a sleepy village basking in an early morning sun, unaware of what was about to happen to it. There was no gate to crash this time, only a 20-foot gap in the wall to rush through, unimpeded.

"Send them in!" Duvall shouted.

Blackfish yelled a command in Shawnee, and the Indians raised a loud cry and raced across the clearing, as the mounted French held back, waiting for the first onslaught to occur.

The Indians steamed into the fort, and Duvall could see settlers emerge to defend themselves, just as at Scotborough. Except that this village did not even have a garrison of British regulars, only farmers with rifles.

The French soldiers rode in after another command by Duvall, and the air was soon wracked with gunfire and yelling.

It was worse than at Scotborough. The settlers surrendered after just brief moments, and then Duvall had them lined up and shot down in cold blood. Shawnee scalped live children, and women had parts of their bodies sliced off. Blackfish stopped a few of them, but they were out of control, because of Duvall.

It was over very quickly. The French had slashed off heads and limbs, never getting off their mounts, never getting their boots dirty. A couple of them would not participate, and Duvall made a mental note of who they were. When it was over, Duvall walked his stallion to the center of the compound, and raised his bloody saber high.

"A great victory! I'm proud of all of you!" he said in perfect Shawnee. Then, to his men: "Well done, soldiers!"

Blackfish stood to one side, silent. He had killed three men of the settlement, then stopped and watched. There was no honor in killing babies. Many of his people seemed to have forgotten that. But they were paid good wages by the French. As a response to Duvall's bizarre compliment, a young brave screamed out a reverberating cry, holding the severed head of a woman in his bloody fist.

"Victory! Victory!"

A short time later, they all filed back out of the burning village, carrying their loot. And their scalps.

Later that same day, Duvall arrived back at Fort Duquesne. His troops were quiet now, the flush of battle gone, and a few of them were ashamed. They had not ridden with Duvall until very recently, and some did not like the way he fought a war. The Shawnee were gone, returned to their nearby village, where Chief Blackfish had just replaced his father as head of their rather large tribe. In their village, they had already heard, through the forest drums, that a relative of the great young hunter Sheltowee had been killed in the south country, and that Sheltowee would ride north for revenge.

It was almost high noon when Duvall was finished cleaning up from the expedition, in his quarters at the end of the large compound that was Fort Duquesne. Duquesne was primarily a French military fort, with only a few residences, of persons who serviced the garrison. The compound was a parade ground, with a flagpole in its center, where the tri-color of the Republic flew from morning till night.

Duvall was just about to walk over to the mess hall for a midday meal, then report back to the general, whose name was Georges Beaumont. But a Beaumont aide, all spit and polish, met Duvall outside his billet.

"Colonel Duvall, the general would like to see you."

Duvall furrowed his light brow. "Oh? Well, I will meet with him just after my meal." Arrogantly. Duvall was highly regarded by Beaumont's superior in Canada, because he was an aggressive officer, and he did not defer to the general, even though Beaumont was in charge.

"Uh, Colonel. The general suggested you come now. Sir."

Duvall made a face. "Oh, he did!" He scowled. "That damn rabbit!" he said in a low voice. "All right, all right. I'll be right there."

Duvall took a detour to a barracks, to congratulate his officers, and to make the general wait a bit. Then he walked down to the general's headquarters building, at the end of the compound. Beaumont was waiting in his office.

Beaumont rose from a polished mahogany desk when Duvall entered. "Ah, Duvall. Please come in and take a chair."

Duvall nodded. "General."

Duvall sat down on a French provincial spindle chair that faced Beaumont's desk. Beaumont went and sat behind it, on a high-backed chair he had brought from Paris. Whereas Duvall was young, slim, and athletic-looking, Beaumont was gray-haired, potbellied, and flaccid-appearing. He picked up a fancy quill pen and rolled it between his fingers.

"I understand your assault on Eben's Place went well," Beaumont said to him in Parisian French.

"*Oui, General,*" Duvall said dryly. "*Tres bien.*"

"Where are your prisoners, Colonel?" Beaumont said.

Duvall shrugged his shoulders, making his gold shoulder epaulets move slightly. "The Shawnee may have taken a few, I don't know."

"You didn't take any prisoners," Beaumont said darkly. "Did you, Duvall?"

Duvall eyed his superior icily. "The French contingent took none, General."

Beaumont was dark-visaged. "What the hell are you up to, Colonel? We want the British out, but we are civilized men!"

Duvall's face went very straight-lined, and his cold, blue killer's eyes looked diamond hard. "Do you remember Detroit? Did they not wipe out an entire company of our countrymen?"

"Those were soldiers they killed!" Beaumont said loudly. "And there was no flag of surrender!"

"You make fine distinctions, General," Duvall said sourly.

"Fine distinctions! Distinctions, *certainement*. Between soldiers and women. Between armed men and babies."

"The children grow up to aim guns at our brave men," Duvall said. "They are all potential assassins."

Beaumont shook his head slowly. "If I were staying on here, we would have this out, Colonel. Unfortunately, I must leave Duquesne."

Duvall's face changed. This was better news than he could ever have anticipated.

"I am being relieved of command here, and sent to New Orleans," Beaumont added.

Duvall tried to hide his pleasure. "Congratulations, General. That is an important command."

"I leave later today," Beaumont went on. "I have a long journey ahead of me, down the Ohio to the Mississippi."

Duvall nodded. "At least it is all through French-held territory."

Beaumont's heavy face looked weary. "Fort Pontchartrain du Detroit has named my successor, Colonel. They have put you in charge of Fort Duquesne."

Duvall could not believe it. He had thought it could be years before he had a command. He could not hide his surprise. "Well. I'm very pleased, General."

"I recommended against it," Beaumont said flatly. "I do not think you are ready for command."

Duvall's eyes narrowed down on Beaumont. "This does *not* surprise me, *monsieur*."

"My judgment was overruled by people who do not know you, Colonel. I think you require assessment. I am not at all certain that you are worthy of any command."

"That opinion is mutual, *mon general*," he answered gratingly.

Beaumont ignored the insult. "I am to advise you also that you will be promoted to general."

A repressed grin came onto Duvall's narrow, aquiline face. "Well, well."

"You will be just one rank below me," Beaumont added, as if the notion disgusted him. "But it was felt that the responsibility here demanded a promotion."

"A wise decision," Duvall commented.

Beaumont eyed him. "I can't tell you how to run things here, Duvall. You will be watched from Detroit. But I recommend you begin behaving like a civilized Frenchman."

Duvall grunted in his throat. "Like Charlemagne's army, which pillaged, raped, and massacred?"

Beaumont frowned heavily. "Your tactics unnecessarily arouse the enemy, Duvall. General Braddock has been sent from England to mount an attack against this very fort. You will have to defend it if that happens. The word is that resentment is strong in the South about what you did at Scotborough. The Indians say some woodsman called Dan'l Boone has vowed personal revenge against you."

"I know that story." Duvall laughed. "Am I to concern myself about the hurt feelings of one backwoods hunter?" The laughter dissolved into a quick sobriety. "Anyway, I welcome this hunter's vitriol. The bastard shot my Arabian stallion out from under me. I have instructed Blackfish to bring his scalp to me, to hang on a post here at the fort. The Shawnee respect that sort of thing."

"Only the ones you have carefully trained, Colonel," Beaumont said. "I am not speaking of one man who has a grudge against you. Boone's hatred of you is very nearly universal among the English colonists. Your methods generate hatred. It may all catch up with you one day. You give your enemy resolve. You feed his emotional fire."

"I don't think you need concern yourself about my methods, General. Since you won't be here to assess their results anyway, *oui?*"

"*Merci Dieu,*" Beaumont murmured. "I will be leaving the fort at mid-afternoon, with a guard of two platoons. Most of them will be sent back to you in two days. As of the moment I leave, later today, you will be officially in charge. Try not to lose the fort to Braddock, *s'il vous plait*. Meeting a real army may not hold quite the same pleasure for you as executing settlement women."

Duvall's face reddened slightly, but he held his temper in. "Don't lose any sleep over the manner in which I give an account of myself, General. You have your own career, such as it is, to nurture."

"You are such a bastard, Duvall," the general said.

Duvall grinned a brittle grin. "Why, thank you, General."

It was about that same time, back in Salisbury, when Dan'l Boone rode into town to find a recruiting sergeant named Medford. The sergeant was supposed to pass through Salisbury at about noon, stay around for an hour or two, and head on north for further recruiting into the Carolina Militia. He was to hold fort either at the local British garrison headquarters or at the Meeting Hall.

The word had spread around Salisbury and the valley about Dan'l shooting the renegade Shawnee to save his bear pelt, and that story on top of the Scotborough one had made Dan'l the subject of many conversations at the local provision store and the public house. Dan'l already had a considerable reputation as a woodsman and hunter, and now he was held in even higher regard by most citizens.

There were a few, however, who resented this growing community respect for this very young trapper who supposedly could talk to wolves in their own language, and speak to either Shawnee or Cherokee in their native tongues.

Corey Ruskin was one of the latter group. Corey and Dan'l had shared one school year when Dan'l's family first came to the valley from Virginia, and Ruskin had always treated Dan'l as an outsider. Now that Dan'l was being talked about locally as a great marksman and woodsman, Ruskin's resentment had grown into real dislike, and was heightened by the fact that Ruskin considered his own skills at shooting and hunting to be quite extraordinary.

Every time Dan'l came into town, therefore, Ruskin and his young cronies would find some opportunity to harass Dan'l, joking about his Quaker background, or his early friendship with red men. Dan'l was different from others in town, and that made him an easy target for jokesters.

Dan'l had tolerated Ruskin with patient good humor, but lately Ruskin's comments to him had become harsher, and with less humor behind them.

Consequently, when Dan'l found Sgt. Medford at the Meeting Hall that early afternoon, signing up several local youths and men for the Militia, he was not pleased to see Ruskin appear in the short line just behind him, with a couple of friends.

"Well, looky here!" Ruskin said loudly as Dan'l waited for his turn at the recruiting table. "The Boone kid is going to try to be a soldier! I thought they only let grown men in the Militia."

Ruskin was a year older than Dan'l, and 50 pounds heavier, and he never let Dan'l forget he was Ruskin's junior.

Dan'l turned to him dispassionately. "I thought they only wanted fellows who can shoot a gun, Corey. Don't that leave you out?" He wore new buckskins, because the old ones had been ripped up and bloodied by the killer bear, and he had a bandage on his left arm, under the clothing. He had left his wide-brimmed Quaker hat on his horse's irons, and his sandy-hued hair was wild-looking.

Ruskin's grin slid away at Dan'l's remark. "The big hunter," he said caustically. He had always used his size and muscle to push other youngsters around. But for some reason he did not understand himself, he had never physically challenged Dan'l, and that bothered him more and more too. Ruskin was a farmer who knew little of the woods, but practiced with a Brown Bess musket regularly in all of his spare time. He thought all Indians should be exterminated, to make way for white settlers, and had always derided Dan'l's efforts to know and understand the tribes. Ruskin knew that friendly Cherokee had stopped at the Boone farm often for trading, and that Dan'l was always in on the negotiations because the Indians wanted him there. All of that irritated Ruskin, who was easily irritated anyway.

"You think these people will really take a Quaker?" Ruskin added now. Two comrades stood behind him, whom Dan'l knew as Little Red and Nick. Both Ruskin and Nick were bigger than Dan'l, but Little Red, feisty and wiry, was a rather small young man.

"They won't take no Quaker," Nick declared. He was not very bright, and he always echoed Ruskin's sentiments.

"Hell, who'd want one?" Little Red said.

"All right, you're next," came Sgt. Medford's voice.

Dan'l moved up to the table with the big ledger sitting on it, and Medford glanced at him. "Oh. You're the Boone kid, ain't you?"

Dan'l nodded. "Yes, sir."

Medford grimaced. "I ain't no sir, Boone." He was a hard-looking militia non-com who was a veteran of several skirmishes with the French over territory. He had a square, jutting jaw and shaggy brows, and his big hands wore callouses from blacksmithing, which was his regular work. He looked Dan'l over. "I heard some about you, lad. You can really handle that Long Rifle, they tell me."

Ruskin and Nick exchanged sour looks behind Dan'l.

"It's what I hunt with, Sergeant," Dan'l said.

Medford grinned. "They say you can hit a shilling at two hundred paces in a windstorm."

"Oh, God," Nick said audibly.

"Most of that's just swamp fog," Dan'l said, embarrassed.

"Well, I reckon you'll do to march with," Medford told him. "Sign your name right there, boy."

Dan'l signed the big book, while Ruskin and his friends looked on.

"You'll report to Fort Cumberland tomorrow," Medford said when he had finished. "You better get started right soon."

Dan'l returned the sergeant's grin. "I'll be there."

As Dan'l turned and passed the other three, on his way out, Ruskin spoke to him. "Two hundred paces in a windstorm?"

Dan'l ignored him, and went outside. A few minutes later, when Dan'l had just returned to his plow mare from a quick visit to the local store, Ruskin and his comrades were just emerging from the recruiting station.

"Hey, there's the big soldier!" Ruskin said loudly as the threesome came up to Dan'l where he had just slipped a small bag of sugar into a saddlebag. "Looks like I'll be going to Cumberland too, Quaker." He had not been able to persuade his cronies to join up.

"Good for you, Corey," Dan'l said noncommittally. He was preparing to mount the mare, but Little Red came and stood between him and the saddle.

"You think maybe you can take Fort Duquesne all by your lonesome, Quaker?" Ruskin badgered him.

"I'd like to get at my mount," Dan'l said. "I got packing to do, back at the farm."

"Hell, wait till this evening, and you can travel with me," Ruskin said acidly. "I can protect you from varmints in the woods on the way."

"I think I'll just travel alone, like usual," Dan'l told him. The last person in the world he wanted to go with, or be with at the fort, was Corey Ruskin.

"Hey. The Quaker thinks he's too good to go with you, Corey," Nick said. "Ain't that a hoot?"

Ruskin came up close to Dan'l, and he stood three inches taller than Dan'l, who was a couple inches under six feet. "We don't believe them stories you been spreading about killing no mammoth bear, Dan'l my boy."

"I bet that wasn't no bear at all," Nick said lightly. "I reckon it was just some poor scared rabbit with dark hair."

"I hear Quakers run from bears," Little Red added.

Ruskin's voice was more menacing. "You think you can be a real soldier 'cause you shot a couple of Injuns at Scotborough?" He was angry because Dan'l had rejected his offer of traveling together so casually, even though the offer was not a genuine one.

Dan'l felt the proximity of Ruskin, and resented it. He was aware of all the young men Ruskin had bullied and beaten senseless in recent years, but Dan'l had never shown Ruskin any deference.

"You think you could hit a Shawnee if he was tied to a post right in front of you?" Dan'l replied in a hard, low voice.

The mare whinnied softly in that moment, sensing the new excitement in the air. Little Red backed away from Dan'l, leaving Dan'l and Ruskin standing face-to-face. Just as Dan'l started to grab at the reins on the horse, suddenly Corey Ruskin hauled off and threw a big fist at Dan'l, without any warning.

The blow caught Dan'l completely by surprise. It struck him full on the jaw, and knocked him down. He hit the ground hard, beside the horse.

He was suddenly breathing shallowly, holding a hand to his face. His eyes narrowed down on Ruskin, as hot anger flooded into his chest.

Several passersby on the board walk fronting the public buildings stopped to look when Dan'l was knocked down, and a young woman let out a little cry.

"Hey, boys!" a man called to them. "No need for that."

"Keep out of it, old man," Nick warned him.

Dan'l just sat there in the dirt for a moment, as something crawled up out of his insides that he had never noticed before Ethan's death. It was like a wild animal in there, straining to get out. His eyes changed, and the others saw it, and Ruskin had a moment of doubt about what he had just done, as Dan'l rose to his feet. Little

Red glanced quickly at Ruskin, to see his reaction to the look in Dan'l's eyes.

"Damn you!" Dan'l said in a voice none of them had ever heard before.

Ruskin backed off a step, not even knowing he was doing so. "What's the matter, Quaker?" He licked his lips. "Want us to fetch you a bear to shoot?"

The other two laughed uncertainly. Several townspeople had gathered now, watching soberly, and Sergeant Medford had stepped out into the midday sun, and saw what was happening. But he made no move to break it up. Dan'l wiped blood from the corner of his mouth.

"You shouldn't have done that," he said in the new voice. Soft. Deliberate.

"Ha!" Nick shouted. "Maybe you better pray, Dan'l. Ain't that what cub-shooting Quakers do? Pray for help?"

Dan'l drew the long hunting knife from his side, and all three of them stepped back quickly away from him, their eyes wide. Dan'l's reputation with a knife was almost as big as with a gun.

"What the hell!" Nick whispered, suddenly scared.

Ruskin eyed Dan'l warily. "So that's the way it is, Quaker! Get into a real man's fight, you pull a weapon to settle things! It's a damnable coward you are!"

Dan'l said nothing, but turned and hurled the knife savagely into the upright of a nearby hitching post. It thudded hard there, just beside Little Red, and he jumped visibly.

"I removed the knife to show you I won't use it," Dan'l said gratingly.

Over near the building, Sergeant Medford nodded knowingly to himself.

Ruskin was momentarily relieved, but then doubt flooded back into him. "So what will you do?" he said with false bravado.

Dan'l stepped closer to Ruskin, and Ruskin threw his fists up in front of him defensively.

"Get him, Corey!" Little Red urged quietly.

But in the next instant, Dan'l threw a lightning-fast fist into Ruskin's face.

It came so fast that Ruskin had no chance to deflect it. He was hit on the cheek and nose, and with an explosive force that shocked him. He stumbled backwards, and then was falling to the ground. He hit there hard, a look of complete bewilderment on his thick, beefy face, blood running from his nose.

There was quite a crowd in the street now, and most were suddenly laughing boisterously. Medford stood there smiling, wishing he had more like Dan'l on his recruitment list.

"Thataway, Dan'l!" somebody yelled out.

"Give him what for, lad!"

They all knew Ruskin for a bully, and were happy to see him put down by a young man who was already becoming a kind of Yadkin Valley hero, since Scotborough.

Ruskin struggled to his feet, breathless. Little Red and Nick were dumbfounded, and sullen.

"We'll all take him!" Nick said gutturally.

"The hell you will, boys," Sergeant Medford said.

They glanced toward the militiaman, and stayed put.

"I don't need no help," Ruskin growled. "I'm going to mash you, Quaker!"

Ruskin came in again, throwing both big fists. Dan'l deflected most of the blows, but in Ruskin's desperation, he finally landed another right to Dan'l's head. Dan'l fell up against the mare, and the animal almost knocked him down. Ruskin came in again, throwing a vicious right fist at him. Dan'l ducked under it, and brought all of his broad-coupled, hard-muscled strength into a driving blow to Ruskin's mid-section.

Ruskin's eyes exploded wide, and he doubled over, the wind gone from him. He staggered around in a small circle, trying to get some air in, like a fish out of water. When he came past Dan'l on his mindless turn, Dan'l hit him a last time, swinging a powerful blow against the side of Ruskin's head. The whole watching audience heard the crack of fist on bone, and then Ruskin went down again.

This time he could not get up. He scrabbled there like a crab for a long moment, then lay on his back sucking air into his lungs, half-conscious. Blood ran from his nose and ear, and he looked awful.

There was a heavy silence now in the street.

After a long moment, Little Red said, "Jesus in heaven!"

The heavyset Nick came and stood over Ruskin.

"Get up, Corey, for God's sake!"

But Ruskin was unable to. Nick reached down, and grabbed him, and pulled him to his feet. Ruskin could hardly stand. He could focus now, on Dan'l, and the look in his eyes was still bewilderment.

"He'll be at Cumberland too," Nick hissed out to Dan'l. "You better watch your back, Quaker!"

Ruskin shook his head. "Hell, come on. Let's get out of here."

As the threesome left, Sergeant Medford smiled again, and returned inside, and several town men joined in light applause for Dan'l. Dan'l wiped the blood from his mouth, nodded to those present, and climbed aboard the mare. A moment later, he was on his way home.

He had just crossed over an invisible line, from a growing-up period into another, deadlier kind of life.

Now he would be a soldier.

Chapter Four

Dan'l had never seen Fort Cumberland, a long day and a half to the north. When he arrived there on the same dun mare he had taken into town for recruitment, he was surprised at its size. It was a real fort, even bigger than Duquesne, with a tall stockade wall around it and many log and tent dwellings outside its walls. Inside, clapboard and log buildings lined its perimeter, as at Duquesne, with the compound used for a parade ground. At this moment in time, there were tents thrown up on one side of the big area, where recruits were billeted, in training. There were also rows of tents outside the fort, to its rear, where the rest of the local militia and British regulars billeted, in separate companies.

Wagons rolled in and out of the fort regularly,

and militia were marching in formation most of the time, learning discipline from colonial and British officers. General Braddock's headquarters was off to the right as Dan'l rode in that late day, and he saw several red-coated officers confering on the steps of that rather sizable building.

It all looked very military.

Dan'l reported to a recruits' barracks, and the mare was taken from him and he was paid a small sum for its confiscation. Corey Ruskin had arrived an hour ahead of Dan'l, and Dan'l saw him outside a tent in the compound, when Dan'l was taken to his own tent, which he shared with three other men. Ruskin just glared at Dan'l, not speaking to him.

Dan'l had been put in with three real characters, all from Carolina. Slim Buford was a dealer in rifles and handguns from Raleigh, a slow-speaking, narrow-faced man. Sam Cahill was a farmer from Salisbury, built leaner than Dan'l and with an ugly face. The third fellow was John Findley, a man just over 30 who had served as a guide for a couple of groups of settlers going west, and had done some exploring in a place known as Kentucky, where Dan'l had never been.

Sergeant Medford, it turned out, was going to be in charge of Dan'l's company of militia, and Dan'l liked that, because he had liked the looks of Medford. Medford stuck his head into their tent just after a light evening meal had been served to them in mess kits, and recognized Dan'l immediately.

"Gentlemen. Ah, Boone. Good to have you here, Dan'l."

"Thanks, Sergeant," Dan'l said.

"The general says we're heading out for Fort Duquesne tomorrow," Medford said. "That won't give you newcomers much training. But he wants us to see how you shoot. There's still a couple hours of light in the sky. Let's all gather on the target range for some shooting practice, and to see how you qualify. Out in back of the fort."

They all trailed out there, in groups of four and five, talking and joking. A brassy bugle blared out a call for a gathering company of regulars, and as they left the inside of the fort, a drum and bugle group was playing a march tune. It was all very exciting to Dan'l.

Out on the range, behind the lines of tents out there in the meadow, was a long firing range, with straw bales at the far end, all lined up in a row, and soldiers with markers huddled behind earthwork bunkers below each target, whose bull's-eyes decorated each bale.

Up at the firing line, there were five groups of British regulars and five of militia. The redcoats were veterans from Europe, and scoffed derisively at their colonial cousins, who they believed would make terrible soldiers. Dan'l's group of four from his tent gathered to fire at one target, and the British groups started on their left. On their right was another militia group which included Corey Ruskin. Ruskin saw Dan'l immediately, and seemed to have gotten over his embarrassment at Salisbury. He was pretty much as arrogant as ever.

"I guess the bragging time is over, Boone," he said from his shooting position a few yards away. "It's time to fish or cut bait."

Dan'l looked over at him. "Good to see you too, Corey."

"All right, you laddies," Sergeant Medford was saying to the five groups of colonials. "Let's show these regulars how we use a real weapon." He was referring to the fact that most colonials owned rifled muskets, now called rifles, whereas the British Army still adhered to the Brown Bess muskets. They all began loading, all along the firing line, and most colonials were finished ahead of their young British counterparts.

Medford was in charge of all the colonials at the line, and a tough-looking Brit was over the regulars. Behind them both strolled a British lieutenant named Arnold, looking stiff and formal in his red coat and gold epaulets.

"Prepare along the firing line!" he called out in his Cockney accent.

"All prepare along the line!" yelled both Medford and the British sergeant major.

Each grouping of men, firing at a specific target, lined up to take turns firing at their own target. The British soldier first in line in his group, next to Dan'l's group, turned and grinned at the colonials.

"They should have give you lads bigger targets!" he called over to them. "You'll never hit these now, will you?"

Dan'l and his people turned but said nothing.

"Where are your plows, farm boys?" another Brit yelled out.

Private John Findley, standing behind Dan'l in his line, shouted back. "You sure you Brits ain't missing your tea time?"

"All right, lads," the British lieutenant said. "All ready on the firing line!"

"All ready on the firing line!" Medford echoed him.

All along the line, in ten different positions, aiming at ten different targets, the men first in their line raised their long guns and cocked them.

"Ready!"

"Ready!"

In unison. "Fire!"

Ten long guns exploded loudly across the meadow, and tiny holes were punched in the targets down the way. Soldiers sprang out from their bunkers and spotted the hits with long markers on rods. Five was a bull's-eye, and when the cards went up with numbers on them, there were three fives among the colonists, and just two among the regulars.

The British lieutenant was not pleased, as he saw the colonials had beaten his seasoned troops. "Come on, lads! We can do better than this, by blessed King George! Let's go again!"

The second man in each of the ten lines, half

British and half colonials, stepped up to shoot. Dan'l was up to shoot now in his line. He took careful aim, and noted that Ruskin was also shooting now, in his line, not far away. The command came again to fire, and the big guns boomed out a second time, almost in unison. When Dan'l's marker put the circle on the hole his ball made, it was dead center in the bull's-eye. Ruskin's was also a bull's-eye, but on its edge.

This time there were three bull's-eyes again among the colonials. The British had just one.

Lieutenant Arnold took note of Dan'l's dead-center shot, and then was yelling encouragement again to his own troops, who had fallen silent now that the colonials were outshooting them. When each group had fired once, down to the last man in it, the colonials had far outshone their British colleagues.

"How do you like farming now, London boy?"

"You want to trade them Besses off for some real guns?"

Lieutenant Arnold, frustrated by the performance of his veterans, dismissed them, and kept the colonials there for another round through their ranks, because they were "green recruits." The Brits moved off sullenly, while the colonials started all over again. When Dan'l came up again, both the lieutenant and his sergeant came and stood behind Dan'l and Ruskin, and watched them shoot, much to Medford's pleasure. Dan'l put another shot in mid-bull's-eye, and once again Ruskin hit the edge. The other colonials did not do as well as before. When each man had taken his turn a second time, Arnold came over to Sergeant Medford, with his own sergeant major by his side.

"Who are these two, Sergeant?" he asked, indicating Dan'l and Ruskin.

"A couple of hotheads from Salisbury," Medford said with a grin. "Not bad, eh?"

Arnold nodded. "Dismiss your men, Sergeant. All but these two. You say they're hotheads?"

"They seem to be village rivals," Medford explained.

Medford dismissed the other colonials, and told Dan'l and Ruskin to stay on. "This could prove interesting," Arnold said. "A little competition, maybe?"

Medford looked over at Dan'l and Ruskin, who were wondering why they had been detained. Ruskin glanced over at Dan'l, guessing it had to do with their excellent shooting. He hated it that he had gotten the idea to join up first, but that now this Quaker had ended up here at Cumberland too, and in the same company. Ruskin had killed his first Shawnee six months before Dan'l's trek to Tennessee and Scotborough, and figured that had made him a man, and had gotten quite a lot of recognition from the feat, because it had happened on a retaliatory raid by settlers on a small Shawnee village. But since Scotborough, Dan'l had once again stolen the acclaim from him. All of that was beginning to bother him a lot, especially since Dan'l had knocked him down in their home town and embarrassed him.

"I'd like to see you lads keep on shooting for a bit," the lieutenant told them. "Markers, hold at those two targets there!"

Dan'l gave the British officer a sour look. He figured this was foolishness. None of this had much to do with actual killing.

"Do you think this is a good idea then, Leftenant?" Medford said to him doubtfully.

Arnold looked slightly nettled. "I obviously do, Sergeant. Get your men loaded and primed, and we'll see if they can keep hitting bull's-eyes."

Medford sighed slightly. "Very well, Leftenant," he said.

Medford gave the orders, and Dan'l and Ruskin followed them. Ruskin was certain in his own mind that he could shoot every bit as well as Dan'l Boone, and resolved now to take this chance to show everybody.

They shot a first round, and both men put their slugs in the center of the bull's-eyes.

"By Jesus, they're good!" Arnold muttered.

Medford grinned with pride, and the sergeant major looked disgruntled.

Dan'l and Ruskin were standing very close to each other. Ruskin turned to Dan'l, full of himself suddenly, with his great success. "Now it all comes out, Dan'l Boone. There ain't no locals to cheer you on now. It's just you and me. And I'll show you who can shoot straighter, by God!"

Dan'l eyed him soberly. "You have to keep

making a fool of yourself, Corey? Even here at Cumberland?"

That remark made Ruskin seethe with anger. They were ordered to fire again, and Dan'l hit dead center as if it were automatic. Ruskin fired, and it barely hit the edge, but was in.

"I see your blind luck is holding, Quaker," Ruskin sneered.

"I hope the sun didn't boil that tiny brain of yours, Corey," Dan'l said, now angry himself. "You'd be left to picking wings off'n flies again, like you used to done."

Arnold turned to Medford and grinned. "I told you this could be pleasant, Yankee."

Ruskin was red in the face. "I'll show you, you bastard!"

"All right, one more time!" Arnold called out. "You Yankee Doodle farmers!" He and his sergeant laughed softly.

Dan'l and Ruskin took no notice of the remark as they reloaded, but Medford knew the insult well. Yankee Doodle was a fictitious colonial made up by the Brits in the 1600's to denigrate their American cousins as stupid buffoons. Medford gave the lieutenant a hard look, and the laughing stopped.

On the last shots, Dan'l hit just off center in the bull's-eye, and Ruskin went to pieces, missing it by a couple of inches. When he saw the marker put the disc on his hole, he suddenly exploded in rage, and threw his rifle down.

"Goddamn you, Boone! You made me miss!"

"You sure that Shawnee you killed weren't

tied down?" Dan'l said levelly. He had had quite enough of Ruskin.

"Why, you son of a bitch!" Ruskin yelled at him. He could not take it that Dan'l was embarrassing him again here at Fort Cumberland, where Ruskin had hoped to make his mark. He suddenly drew a long knife from his belt. "Let's see how you are with one of these!"

Sergeant Medford started forward, but Arnold restrained him. "No, Sergeant. Let's see how they handle themselves."

Medford hesitated, then backed off. Arnold was in charge. As the Brits always were.

Dan'l saw they were not going to stop it. So he drew the big skinning knife from its rawhide sheath, and took a stance facing Ruskin. "It's your call, Corey."

Medford stepped forward and picked up the two long guns and got them out of the way, and the soldiers marking targets came in toward the firing line, to watch. Arnold and his sergeant anticipated the fight with much pleasure, since knife fights between colonials were legendary.

Ruskin did not wait for an invitation. He figured his bigger size would give him the advantage he needed to put this Quaker down once and for all. He lunged forward savagely and struck at Dan'l's belly. Dan'l deflected the blow with his own blade, but the knife still sliced along his rib cage and made a shallow wound there. Dan'l felt the thing crawl into his chest in that moment again, and his eyes got that deadly look in them that Ruskin had seen in Salisbury.

He thrust the knife at Ruskin's midsection, and Ruskin grabbed at his wrist and caught it, and a hard grin came onto his beefy face.

Dan'l pulled away, and they circled, looking for an opening. Medford saw some blood on Dan'l's side, and looked over at Arnold, but Arnold shook his head. Ruskin came in again, and his purpose had turned deadly, just as Dan'l's had. He thrust at Dan'l's chest, hard, and Dan'l caught his arm and held it, then made a wide swipe at Ruskin's belly, and caught flesh on the end of the swing. Ruskin sucked his breath in as the blade sliced him open along his hip.

"Damn you, Quaker!" I'll cut you in little pieces!"

They came together again, each holding the other off with a straining, trembling hand. Ruskin's weight forced Dan'l backwards, and then he stumbled over uneven ground and lost his balance. He went down heavily, with Ruskin on top of him, thrusting the knife downward toward Dan'l's right eyeball. Dan'l used all his strength to defend against the thrust, and still the knife came closer and closer. Eight inches. Three. Dan'l kicked upward and knocked Ruskin sidewise, and then Dan'l rolled on top of Ruskin, in an instant when Ruskin was defenseless. Dan'l raised the knife to plunge it into Ruskin's chest. He had lost all emotional control.

A strong hand came and grabbed at his wrist, and held it. He focused on Sergeant Medford, who had come and stood over them, not caring anymore what the British officer wanted.

"That's enough, Dan'l. You made your point."

Dan'l hesitated, then relaxed the arm with the knife. Ruskin looked surprised by the sudden turn of events, and it was just dawning on him that Medford had saved his life.

Dan'l got up off Ruskin clumsily, the emotion draining out of his young face.

"Why in bloody hell did you do that, Sergeant?" Arnold complained loudly. He had wanted to see the end.

"Because we both need that man for Duquesne," Medford said in a hard voice. "Or had you forgotten why we're here, Leftenant?"

Arnold glared at him. He did not like being lectured by a colonial, and in front of a non-com of the king's regiment.

"I haven't forgotten, Yankee. Just don't you forget when we get to Duquesne."

Ruskin was still sitting on the ground, holding the bloody place at his hip. Dan'l stood over him. "You're one lucky farmer, by Jesus," he grated in a low, husky voice.

Ruskin was finally convinced. He decided not to respond to that comment. He got clumsily to his feet. "Can I leave now? I need some doctoring."

"Yes, of course, Private," Medford told him.

Ruskin moved off without giving Dan'l another look. The others were dismissed too, by Arnold. Just Arnold, Medford, and Dan'l remained on the firing line. Arnold walked over to Dan'l. He had just gained a lot of respect for the young woodsman.

"So you're Boone. Aren't you the fellow that shot Duvall's horse out from under him, at Scotborough?"

Dan'l just stood there.

"He's the one," Medford answered for him.

"I wouldn't mind seeing you in a red tunic, Private," Arnold said to him.

"Yes, sir."

"How would you like to stay on here and train recruits in the use of firearms, lad? I could talk with the general."

Dan'l met his gaze. "No, sir. I want to fight the French. I got a score to settle."

Arnold regarded him curiously. "Very well, laddybuck. I think I see your point."

"Come on, Dan'l," Medford said to him. "We'll go get that scratch attended to."

"Hell, I got bear digs healing that's worse than this," Dan'l told him. Then he headed off toward the compound.

Arnold and Medford looked after him. "I hope you can keep that one, Sergeant."

Medford nodded. "So do I."

That same evening, General Braddock lined all the troops up in the fort, regulars and militia, and addressed them in a loud, pompous voice. It was dusk, and difficult to see his face, but he looked rather soft to Dan'l, and out of shape. He had been sent over to the colonies from the Coldstream Guard, handpicked by William Penn to meet the French challenge in the New World for territory.

Braddock was one of those Britons who felt the English Army was superior to any other in the world, and was certain he would make short shrift of the French and their Shawnee allies, with his seasoned British regulars. He announced that they would march the following morning, and head along well-traveled trails to Fort Duquesne. There they would meet the enemy head-on in open, direct combat, and would win the day.

"I know that some of you militiamen have little military experience," he told them in a loud, firm voice. He wore a powdered wig and gold braid, and sat stiffly aboard a white horse, not unlike the one of Duvall that Dan'l had shot.

"You may learn much from your British counterparts. Watch what they do, how they behave under fire, and emulate them."

Dan'l had noticed that several British officers also sat mounted on horses behind the general, along with a militia officer with a blue tunic and a tri-corner hat, who looked very dignified and sober.

Oil-fed lanterns on posts shed yellow light on all present that caused shifting patterns to fall across their faces and clothing.

"We will engage the French in force at Duquesne. As you may have noticed today, we have brought in over one hundred supply wagons and many animals for this campaign. We'll have a regiment force to march with. We will smash the enemy at Duquesne, and drive him from the area!"

It all sounded so easy, the way he put it, Dan'l mused, standing at attention in the long lines of soldiers. The redcoat regulars stood out front in their lines, with the militia behind them, which irritated the militia officers.

"Now, I'll let Colonel Washington say a few words," the general concluded.

Dan'l watched the colonial officer step his mount forward a couple of paces. George Washington was an aide-de-camp of Braddock, but also the colonial officer in charge of the militia, which had gathered mostly from Carolina and Virginia.

"I have just a few words," Washington told them, sitting easily in his saddle. "Fight hard, fight well, fight smart. The French are good. The Shawnee are good."

All present saw Braddock turn and give Washington, a surveyor from Virginia, a sober look.

"If we are to defeat them in battle, we will have to give everything we have. We are hundreds, but we will still be outnumbered. Do not be over-confident. Good luck to us all. God save the king!"

Dan'l was impressed. The words rang with much more realism than those of Braddock. After a few more words from Braddock, assuring the troops of a quick victory, the troops were dismissed for the night. Dan'l returned to his tent at the side of the compound, only to find Medford there waiting for him.

"We're going to take a few of you out of the

foot regiment and put you on wagons," the sergeant said to him outside the tent. "Think you can drive a wagon, Dan'l?"

"That shouldn't make no problem, Sergeant," Dan'l said.

"Well, four wagons are going to carry munitions and explosives. Very dangerous work. We want all those drivers to be volunteers. Your home-town boy Ruskin just signed on for that duty, egged on by his new friends. Maybe you wouldn't want to do it because of that."

Dan'l thought a moment. "We'd be on separate wagons?"

"That's right. Each driver will be responsible for defending the wagon he drives. So all have to be good shots, and good soldiers. I think you both qualify."

Dan'l nodded. "I'll drive a munitions wagon, Sergeant."

Medford grinned past his shaggy brows. "That's my boy. Tomorrow morning, soon as you've eaten, you'll muster out in back of the compound, by the corral. All the wagons will be gathered there. The munitions vehicles will have a red stripe painted on the buckboard."

"I'll be there," Dan'l told him. He was very excited about being involved in this momentous campaign against the French, and the hated Duvall.

"Listen for the muster call," Medford said.

The next morning was warm and muggy, and all the platoons and companies headed out at early light, the soldiers on foot and all officers mounted. Several militia privates were put out front as scouts, because they knew the terrain better than the British soldiers. Then came two companies of regulars in their full battle dress; red coats, polished shoes, and shakos. The companies were alternated then, between militia and regulars, with the supply wagons at the end of the column, and the munitions wagons at the far end, with just a platoon of militia coming up behind them.

It was all very splendid, with Braddock on his white horse near the fore, and red-jacketed regulars all around him. The militia soldiers had no uniforms, but came in their regular clothing, which varied from cotton and muslin shirts and trousers, with open shoes called shoepacks, to rawhide shirt and leather trousers like Dan'l wore. A few wore the dark, wide-brimmed hat of the Quaker, like Dan'l, but others wore bowlers, tri-corner hats, and even coonskin caps, such as John Findley wore, who had been billeted with Dan'l.

The colonials were a ragtag lot, therefore, with their several kinds of guns and unusual clothing, and most regulars figured them for poor soldiers.

It soon became quite clear, though, as the march progressed that morning through dust and heat of the wilderness, that the colonials had more stamina than their soft-living cousins in the red tunics. Their spirits were buoyed somewhat by the fifes and drums that led the march, playing such traditional tunes of glory as the Grenadier's March.

Dan'l brought up the very end of the column, on his wagon, except for the few militia that brought up the rear. Two wagons ahead of Dan'l was the munitions wagon of Corey Ruskin, who had not spoken to Dan'l since their last physical encounter, nor even looked at him. Each of their wagons, and those of two other drivers, were loaded with musketballs, cannisters, and mostly black powder in various kinds of containers. Braddock hoped to have a cannon brought up to meet them about halfway, but it never got there. In fact, if not for the efforts of one Benjamin Franklin, a politician from the north, Braddock would not have had the wagons and horses needed for the campaign. But Braddock had never acknowledged the financial support of Franklin or the colonies.

It was only midday when the first excitement occurred. The whole column had stopped for rest and food, and then had headed out again, over a well-worn trail leading north. In the confusion of leaving, the rear guard got ahead of a couple of the munitions wagons, because a horse on the team ahead of Dan'l got its traces crossed. That trouble was on Ruskin's wagon, and Dan'l decided to wait until it was all resolved, and maintain his position as dead last. When Ruskin pulled out, therefore, and Dan'l coaxed his team after him, they were both removed from the column by several hundred yards.

That was when it happened.

Suddenly there were loud cries from the forest around them, and the sounds of crackling gunfire from the trees, and then arrows began sailing through the air, all around Dan'l and Ruskin. A moment later the Shawnee came charging from the cover of the woods, attacking the last two munitions wagons.

Both Ruskin and Dan'l were ready, with rifles loaded and primed, and in the first seconds they both brought down a charging Shawnee. Dan'l's shot hit a wild-looking savage full in the face, and his legs ran out from under him as his torso was hurled backwards. Ruskin had killed an Indian trying to board his wagon.

Arrows were flying everywhere, some carrying firebrands. One of the latter stuck in the buckboard beside Dan'l's leg, and he quickly pulled it out of the wood before it could set the wagon afire.

"Corey!" Dan'l yelled. "We're isolated! Drive on up to the troops! Fast!"

Corey Ruskin turned for just a brief moment, and a grin crossed his meaty face. "Let's go, Quaker!"

In that moment, Dan'l knew, Ruskin had grown into a man. Ruskin was now whipping his two-horse team, and the wagon jerked into a plummeting plunge to safety.

Dan'l goaded his own team into action, and both wagons were moving. A Shawnee jumped onto the buckboard beside Dan'l, and Dan'l jammed a fist into his face, and the redskin went flying off the vehicle, hitting the dirt of the track.

The rear guard had now seen what was happening to the straggling wagons, and were hurrying back along the trail, trying to get their guns into play. But they had not fired a shot yet. Up ahead, someone had signaled for the column to halt. This attack was obviously by a small, independent force separate from that at Fort Duquesne, up ahead. But it required the attention of all officers on the column, because of the importance of the cargo the wagons carried.

There was no way either Dan'l or Ruskin could reload through this turmoil, so both would have to rely on themselves and the knives at their belts. Dan'l saw Ruskin thrust his blade at a Shawnee, stabbing the Indian in the belly, and the red man fell off his wagon. But it was clear now that the attackers' main purpose was to set the wagons afire, because more and more arrows tipped with flame were hitting the canvas and wood of the vehicles. Ruskin's wagon was flaming suddenly, both the wood and the canvas cover, and Dan'l was busy slapping at fire on the canvas just behind him, all this while the wagons were jerking and bumping along the narrow trail.

"Corey, your bed is on fire!" Dan'l yelled out to Ruskin, referring to the box of the wagon.

Ruskin turned toward him, over his shoulder, as the wagons slowed down to meet the foot soldiers of the militia. "I know. Thanks, Quaker!"

Now the militia was firing into the attackers, who were a rather small force, and the Indians were going down all around the wagons. The wagons had ground to a stop now, and were surrounded by Indians and militia, some in hand-to-hand combat. Dan'l saw soldiers go down with arrows in their chests and backs, and one man's head was split open with a tomahawk. But the Shawnee were getting the worst of it, and some were already retreating into the woods as they saw a company of redcoats arriving now, to reinforce the militia.

Ruskin's wagon was blazing brightly, but Ruskin was still wrestling with a last Indian who had tried to get aboard. Dan'l had left his buckboard to slap out fire on his canvas cover, and now soldiers were aboard helping him. When he turned and saw Ruskin still aboard his flaming vehicle, he yelled again at him.

"Get off, Corey! Get off the wagon! It's going to—"

In the next moment, there was a violent explosion that hurt Dan'l's ears, and knocked him off his feet, behind his buckboard. He saw Ruskin's figure thrown wide off the wagon and hit the ground, and then there were more explosions that knocked soldiers down, all from Ruskin's wagon, and then it was burning wildly just yards away from Dan'l. The Indians were now running back to cover of the forest, and the soldiers still on their feet were firing after them, both redcoats and militia.

Dan'l looked to where Ruskin had fallen, and saw to his dismay that Ruskin was aflame.

"Holy Jesus!" Dan'l whispered to himself.

He jumped off his wagon as several militiamen completed dousing the fire on it, and ran over to Ruskin. Ruskin was just struggling to his feet, dazed, and now he was enveloped in flame.

"Get down, Corey!" Dan'l screamed out at him.

But Ruskin was beyond hearing instructions. His arms waved wildly about, and he began running and screaming. Dan'l threw himself at him, and knocked him down, and felt the flames on his own face and hands. In the next moment he was on his feet, looking about for something to throw over Ruskin. But two pairs of hands pulled him back, away from the flames.

It was too late.

Corey Ruskin lay inert on the ground, the flames consuming him.

Dan'l stood there with two militiamen restraining him, his own hands burned, his hair singed, staring in revulsion at what had been Corey Ruskin.

"You can't help him," somebody said.

"Jesus in heaven," Dan'l grated out.

Other British troops had arrived now, and were firing some shots at the woods, hoping to still kill a Shawnee or two. There were some young officers with them, prancing their mounts arrogantly around the wagons.

"You bloody fools!" a young captain yelled out at Dan'l and the militia. "Keep the bloody wagons up with the troops! We can't afford to lose munitions! And get that corpse off the trail and move this last wagon forward!"

Dan'l hurled a blistering look at the officer, and started toward him. But the nearest militiaman grabbed at his arm and stopped him.

"Let it go, Boone," he said quietly.

The officer moved off on his chestnut horse, and several of the militia glared after him. The one holding Dan'l's arm sighed.

"Are they any better than the damned French?" he said almost to himself. Then, "Come on, Boone. I'll help you bury the poor bastard."

Chapter Five

After a long additional march that day, they encamped in a wide meadow, with Braddock setting sentries out all along the perimeter, to watch for renewed attacks. The only tents set up were for senior officers, with a special, fancy one for Braddock himself. Colonel George Washington rejected such civilized sleeping quarters, and made up a groundsheet near his colonial troops, and went among them after they had had their evening meal and asked how things were going.

Near the end of his little tour, with campfires glowing all across the big meadow, Washington found Dan'l Boone, huddled away from the rest of the troops, staring into the blackness. Sergeant Medford was with the colonel.

"Well, here's our munitions driver," Washington said to Dan'l as they approached him.

Dan'l rose quickly to his feet, and saluted. "Pleasured to have your company, Colonel." But his face did not reflect pleasure.

"That was a terrible thing that happened to Ruskin," Washington told him. "I'm sorry you had to see it."

"It's all right, Colonel," Dan'l said quietly.

"This is the lad that almost killed General Duvall," Sergeant Medford told Washington. "In Tennessee."

Washington grinned broadly. He was tall and rather handsome, with dark hair tied back in a pigtail, like most colonials, including Dan'l. He had a face that Dan'l immediately liked. "Ah. You're *that* Boone. I hear you're originally from Virginia too."

"Yes, sir," Dan'l said, trying a smile. "We only been in Carolina a few years."

"A farming family?"

"Yes, Colonel. We have a farm near Salisbury."

"I hear your father has quite a brood."

Dan'l widened the smile. "I guess he does."

"What were you doing out in Tennessee, Boone?"

"Trapping," Dan'l said. "And buffalo hunting, sir. My cousin and me just stopped at Scotborough overnight, for supplies, when the French come at them."

"I see. Then you must be the Dan'l Boone that the Shawnee call Sheltowee."

"The same, Colonel."

Washington was impressed. "You've earned a lot of respect among the red men, young fellow."

Dan'l looked down, embarrassed. He got a vision of Ethan, with that fire licking up around him, and Ethan's face was mixed in with that of Corey Ruskin. "I used to like the Shawnee," he said. "Now . . ."

"I'm sure they're not all cruel savages," Washington said to him.

"I reckon not," Dan'l said. Now he saw Duvall on that white horse, waving the saber, and his face showed anger in it.

"Well, we're glad to have you with us," Washington said. "The sergeant here says you're an excellent shot. We need people like you in the militia. It could be a long fight with the French. We can use good marksmen."

"He's better than good, Colonel," Medford said. "I never seen nobody shoot like he does."

Washington nodded.

Dan'l looked into his blue eyes. "Colonel, it's going to take more than good shooting. With all respect, Colonel, we're going about this all wrong."

Medford looked suddenly embarrassed.

"Go on," Washington said.

"Our tactics is European, Colonel. Braddock's got us all lined up in a row, marching like there ain't no enemy out there. Walking on the big trails, using scouts that ain't had no experience and don't even know the terrain. We ought to put Shawnee or Cherokee scouts out front, and use them as sentries."

Washington turned to Medford and grinned.

"That's just what the colonel's been telling Braddock, soldier," Medford told Dan'l.

"Oh," Dan'l said. "Well, then. Why ain't he listening?"

Washington took a deep breath in. "The general has his own ideas about how a war ought to be fought, Private Boone. And he isn't disposed to take advice from a colonial militia officer. But he is the general, and don't you forget it. What he says is the law. We'll do our best to defend our column, within his orders. You understand?"

"Yes, sir," Dan'l said slowly. "But I just think we're going to be ripe pickings for them Shawnee, when we get closer to the fort."

"That may be. But what we have to do is give a good account of ourselves regardless. The British officers will be watching us to see how we perform."

"All right, Colonel," Dan'l said.

Then Washington moved on, to move among the ranks.

It did not take long for Dan'l's concerns to become hard, cold fact.

It was early afternoon of the following day, and they were getting closer and closer to Fort Duquesne. Braddock figured Duvall would defend from inside the fort, or just outside it, after Braddock had had a chance to form up his battle formation before the fort.

But at Duquesne, Duvall was thinking very differently.

Duvall was sitting in his office, the one vacated by Beaumont not long before, when the runner came in, accompanied by Duvall's aide.

"News of the British, sir," the aide said.

Duvall rose from the long desk, and frowned at the sweaty, breathless runner. He had just ridden 30 miles at top gallop to bring the latest to Duvall.

"Well, speak up, man," Duvall said impatiently. "Where are they?"

"They've just crossed the South Branch Creek, General," the runner said excitedly. "There are hundreds of them. A full regiment. Wagons, horses. I saw no cannon."

Duvall let a slow smile move his aquiline face. "Are they still on the road, out in the open?"

"Yes, sir. They have two scouts out front, but they aren't making any sorties into the trees. They seem to have no Indians with them."

"The damned fool!" Duvall hissed out. "Utter British arrogance!"

"Yes, sir," the blue-coated runner replied.

Duvall turned to his side, a captain. "Are the Shawnee here? Did you reach Blackfish?"

The young officer nodded. "We have close to a thousand Shawnee, including Chief Blackfish's braves. The ones we trust are armed with muskets. And we have ten companies of regulars in the fort now, after the arrival of reinforcements from Detroit. We'll have them outnumbered."

"Excellent," Duvall said, rubbing his hands together. His tunic was unbuttoned down the front, and his dark hair was mussed, from the long morning of conferences with his staff. "I want to meet them at Gaston's Fork, where they'll be most vulnerable to surprise, surrounded by woods. Tell my officers to be ready to move out within the hour."

The aide nodded.

As an afterthought, Duvall said to the runner: "Is that damned woodsman with them? The one called Sheltowee?"

"My information is that he drives a wagon, General."

Duvall had not forgotten the loss of his best horse. He nodded. "Don't forget to tell Blackfish. I want his scalp brought to me. No, wait. Make it his head. I'll put it on a pole in the compound."

The runner frowned slightly. "Yes, General."

"Now get ready to march!" Duvall said loudly.

It was later that afternoon when the two armies met.

Because they were getting close to Duquesne, Braddock had brought the munitions wagons up to the fore, so ammunition and powder could be distributed quickly if the need arose, and extra powder had already been given to each soldier. Dan'l was driving up ahead of most of the regiment, just behind redcoat advance troops, Braddock's best and most experienced regulars. As the column moved along, kicking up dust on the narrow road that ordinarily was used only by wagons and carriages, Braddock halted it at Gaston's Fork, where the column was obliged to take the left fork in the road to reach Fort Duquesne. Braddock wanted to confer briefly with his officers before moving the troops on toward the fort, and make certain the regiment was ready to fight.

But in those moments of pause, the attack came.

Braddock did not even know it was happening at first. The Shawnee fired arrows only, from the trees on either side of the column, and they started at the rear end of the mile-long formation. British regulars and militia began going down all along the formed lines, hit in the side, chest, back—and for a few minutes there was only the sound of muffled outcries from the stricken men. Then, when one of the officers saw the flurry of arrows from the Shawnee longbows, and the hurled lances, he called out the alarm that went up and down the long column.

"Shawnee! Shawnee! We're under attack!"

Up near the front of the line of four-abreast troops, driving the lead munitions wagon, Dan'l realized immediately what was happening. The French and their Indian allies were using their time-honored tactic of ambush to cut down their enemy from cover.

Now the attack came all along the column,

with arrows first, thudding into one soldier after another, and then came the crackling of gunfire from the trees.

"Take cover!" Dan'l cried out, trying to rein in on his team as the horses reared and whinnied, catching the excitement.

Braddock was just 20 yards away, up near the front of the column. He turned red-faced, seeing his men going down, some now kneeling and cocking their long guns. Those ready to fire could find no targets to shoot at, the Indians were so well hidden by the dense forest at either side of the roadway, just a few yards off it.

Now the Indians had accelerated their gunfire, and Dan'l could get glimpses of blue tunics in the forest, also firing at the column. It was the Fort Duquesne regiment, all right.

Braddock rode along the line of frightened and bewildered soldiers. "Return fire! Return fire! Hold your positions! Keep your formations and return fire!"

Washington was now riding along the column too, calling out to the colonials. "Get down! Find cover if you can! Get into the trees with them!"

The colonial militia began running for the trees, to get off the deadly roadway and the hail of arrows and lead. Soon most of them were out of sight, shooting Indians from cover, mingling with the enemy. In contrast, Braddock's regulars merely knelt or stood on the road surface, trying to return fire to an enemy that was invisible, following their general's orders. They were being cut down mercilessly.

"Stand and fight!" Braddock was yelling now, seeing the colonials running for cover. "Stand your ground, damn you!"

Some of his own men were following the lead of the militia, and that enraged Braddock. He galloped up and down the line of soldiers, roaring his commands, knocking a couple of men down who were breaking for the woods.

"You damn cowards! Hold your ground! Fire back from the road! Maintain your formations!"

"We can't see them to fire back, General!" a young officer complained. It was Lieutenant Arnold, who had been in charge at the firing range. "They're all—"

His left ear suddenly exploded off the side of his head, and Braddock could see brain matter inside. Arnold flung his musket away in a spasmodic jerk, and plummeted to the ground.

Washington rode up to Braddock, his face flushed. Now the Shawnee were coming out of the trees, and rushing the column. "We must take cover, General!"

Braddock looked at him as if he had gone crazy. "Take cover, by Jesus! Are you out of your mind, Colonel? Get your men back on this road immediately! We need them to protect our flanks!"

"Our flanks are decimated!" Washington replied. "We must get out of this hail of fire!"

"Damn you! Obey my orders!" Braddock fairly screamed at him.

Then Braddock wheeled and rode back toward the front of the column. Washington, knowing his orders were impossible to carry out, just shook his head in disgust, then began galloping off in the opposite direction.

Dan'l had reloaded twice, and was in the act of killing his third advancing Shawnee. He aimed carefully from the buckboard of the wagon, and an onrushing Shawnee yelled and went face-down. The wagon ahead of Dan'l had already overturned, because of the rearing and plunging of its team, and the driver was now being scalped by a tall Shawnee. Dan'l's wagon looked like a pin cushion, with all the arrows in it. Gunfire crackled and boomed heavily in the air, and the smoke from it was acrid in his nostrils.

Dan'l grabbed the reins of the team, whipped them into movement, and drove the wagon off the road and into nearby trees, where it would not be such a target. Then he cut the leanest horse loose from its harness, and mounted it, using shortened reins. Riding onto the road like that, he saw that the French bluecoats were now swarming into the ranks of the British. There was deadly hand combat, and the confused and wounded British soldiers were being annihilated. Dan'l rode among them, brandishing his long knife like a saber, stabbing and cutting at the hated French. Two went down under his knife, and a third.

He looked around, and realized there was almost no firing coming from the trees now. The few colonials who had not been shot were now making a covert retreat in the woods, escaping from the slaughter

Dan'l jumped his mount over the carcass of a dying horse, and then stopped short. There, only yards ahead, wielding a saber like a madman, was Henri Duvall, mounted on his new stallion.

"You son of a bitch!" Dan'l muttered. He kicked his heels into the wagon horse's sides, and it leapt forward.

Duvall saw him coming at the last moment, and a tight grin creased his long face. "Sheltowee!" he grated out.

Then Dan'l was there, swinging the long knife. It came down toward Duvall's shoulder, but Duvall blocked the blow with his longer saber. Dan'l stabbed at Duvall's chest, and Duvall blocked the blow again.

"You arrogant farm boy!" Duvall yelled at him. "I will have your liver for supper!"

He swung the saber at Dan'l's head, to decapitate him, but Dan'l caught the blade on the back of his skinning knife, and deflected the blow.

"You'll pay for Ethan, damn you!" Dan'l croaked out.

Duvall had no idea what he was talking about. He swung again, and Dan'l ducked away, and the saber slashed into his horse's neck shallowly. Dan'l had a light bandage on his right hand from his attempt to save Ruskin, and it hampered his dexterity. He stabbed toward Duvall's gut, but Duvall's horse reared and Dan'l missed completely. In the next second, a Shawnee hurled himself at Dan'l bodily, and knocked him off his mount.

Dan'l hit the ground hard, and the horse almost caved in his skull with a hoof; then it was running off. Dan'l looked for Duvall as the Shawnee regained his feet, and Duvall was now busy with a wild-looking militia soldier. The Shawnee threw a tomahawk at Dan'l's head. Dan'l rolled away, and hurled his knife into the Indian's stomach. A moment later he was retrieving it, smeared with blood, but Duvall was not in sight now.

A musketball tore through Dan'l's collar, narrowly missing killing him. As at Scotborough, though, the gunfire was diminishing as hand-to-hand fighting heightened in intensity. Even British regulars were now running for cover, trying to ward off tomahawks with bayonets. Many, though, were cut off from the woods, and it was clear no prisoners were being taken.

Dan'l knew he had to find cover to survive. But as he started for the woods, he saw Braddock on the fringe, leaning on his saddlehorn. He was injured.

Dan'l ran over to him, and yelled up at the general.

"General! The day is lost! Get out of here!"

Braddock was holding his side, where crimson showed between his fingers. He looked at Dan'l dully. "What? What did you say?"

"They're cutting us down, General! Get into the woods!"

Braddock just looked at him. A Shawnee came running crazily at Braddock's mount, and Dan'l met him with a quick thrust of his long knife. The fellow went down grabbing at his violated inwards.

"Damn!" Dan'l muttered. He found Braddock's reins, and jerked them from the general's hands. "Come on," he said.

Dan'l led the horse to the closest trees, and suddenly they were in deep cover, with nobody following.

"Hey! Bloody hell, what's going on?" Braddock suddenly asked.

"I'm getting you out of here, General," Dan'l said, not caring if Braddock understood or not. He led the horse directly into deep woods, away from the action on the road. The general just sat on his horse in a daze, wondering what had happened. In moments they began catching up with retreating troops, colonials and a few redcoats, straggling back toward Fort Cumberland. The colonials had fought from the woods, then had given up when they were overwhelmed.

Back on the road, Dan'l could still hear the screams of men being scalped, and the unnerving war whoops of the Shawnee, celebrating victory.

Dan'l was devastated. It was Scotborough all over again, only on a much larger scale, and against a real army.

He led the general's horse through the trees until they came alongside a sergeant major of

105

the British regulars. Braddock looked down on him quizzically.

"Sergeant! Where are you going? You should be out on the road, killing Shawnee!"

The redcoated soldier gave him a hard look. "Give me a thousand men, General, and I'll bloody well go back!"

Braddock was outraged. "That's damned insubordination, Sergeant!"

Dan'l caught Braddock's attention. "General."

Braddock looked down at him again, weaving slightly in his saddle. It did not appear, though, he was hurt badly. "Who are you?"

"The battle is over, General Braddock. I took a last look. There's nobody left out there to fight."

Braddock looked toward the battle site, and his face seemed to go white. "Oh, God!"

"We're headed back to Fort Cumberland," Dan'l added.

The sergeant nodded to Dan'l, took the reins from him, and led the white horse on into the woods, away from Fort Duquesne.

Dan'l was glad to be relieved of the responsibility. He did not like Braddock. Braddock, through his European arrogance, had gotten a lot of good men killed, British and colonial. And for nothing.

Dan'l unwrapped the bandage from his right hand and threw it onto the ground. He saw some colonials ahead, trudging through the trees, and he caught up with them and walked up alongside several. One was Sergeant Medford, and he had blood running from his head. He turned and saw Dan'l.

"Well. The hunter survived."

"Are you all right, Sergeant?" Dan'l asked.

Medford stepped around a dead colonial, who lay in a pool of crimson among fallen leaves. "I'm middling good, Dan'l. Glad you got out alive."

"It—was awful," Dan'l said.

"I wouldn't give a tinker's dam for that redcoat general," Medford said bitterly.

Dan'l nodded. "I reckon he larned something at our expense, Sergeant." He looked ahead, and saw another small knot of colonials in the trees. "I'm going to try to find Findley and the others."

"Watch yourself," Medford advised him. "They know some of us escaped."

Dan'l hurried onward, passed through several mixed groups of Brits and colonials, and finally found John Findley struggling through the underbrush, limping. He was the soldier who had worked as a guide into Kentucky and Tennessee, and who had shared Dan'l's tent at Cumberland.

He saw Dan'l approach. "Well, looky here." A big grin. "I wondered if you made it."

"Good to see you, John," Dan'l told him, walking along beside him.

"Sam Cahill's up there ahead somewhere. But our other tent comrade didn't make it. I saw Slim Buford go down under three Shawnee. They really cut him up. Had his scalp off while he was still fighting back."

"Sorry to hear that," Dan'l said heavily.

"The colonel is right up ahead there. See, on his horse? He stayed on that road till the very last time he could get out."

Dan'l looked through the trees and saw Washington, walking his mount in the middle of several militiamen, a white bandage wrapped around his head.

A third colonial came up beside them, looking very fatigued. "Either of you have water?"

Dan'l started to reply in the negative, when an arrow came hissing past them and thumped into a tree beside Dan'l's head. A second one pierced the newcomer's neck and came halfway out the other side.

The man grabbed the arrow at both ends, and just stood there, his jaw working. Dan'l propped him up, and pushed him against a nearby tree.

"We're being attacked!" Washington was yelling. "Over there!"

Dan'l stared toward the trees on his right, toward the trail they had come to Duquesne on, and saw a redskin dodging behind a thick hickory tree. He glanced back at the soldier he had propped up, and the man's eyes were glazing over.

"Go seek them out, lads!" Washington was calling out. Then an arrow thudded into his right thigh.

Dan'l saw the American colonel grab at his leg and make a face, wincing in pain. Dan'l turned and ran toward the trees and the Shawnee he had seen there, joining several other able-bodied soldiers who were doing the same.

As he ran toward their assailants, Dan'l saw one of the running colonials hit in the chest with a Shawnee arrow, and tumble forward onto his face. Dan'l went into thick trees, and saw a red man running back toward the trail. Dan'l drew his big knife and threw it after the fellow, and it turned over several times and sank into the Shawnee's back. There was a dull outcry, and he went down. Dan'l ran up to him, and saw he was dying. He grabbed the knife and looked around. Another colonial had run down a second Shawnee and was killing him in hand combat. The other attackers seemed to have scattered back to the trail. Dan'l turned and headed back toward the retreat column, and had gone just a few yards when the still-hidden Shawnee hurtled out from behind a thick tree. He came at Dan'l like a madman, tomahawk raised above his head, warpaint making him look like a demon from hell.

"You will die, Sheltowee!" came the high-pitched scream as he threw himself on Dan'l.

Dan'l sidestepped the charge deftly, and the tomahawk split the wood of a sapling beside him, instead of his skull. Then he was grabbing the Indian by his brush of scalp mane, and yanking his painted head back, and thrusting the knife into the brave's back, over and over again.

Emotion spilled out of Dan'l in that moment that he did not even know was boiling inside him. The brave tried to fight back, but Dan'l was on him now, on the ground, and shoving the knife home over and over, cutting and slicing.

When the Indian was lifeless, Dan'l did not quit. He turned the dead man over, and made a big, long cut across the painted forehead, and around past the ears, and then peeled the scalp off, neatly, and held it above his head.

He let out a bloodcurdling cry then, and it echoed through the forest.

Several other returning colonials stopped, and looked toward him, surprised.

"I am Sheltowee!" Dan'l screamed out to any Shawnee who might still be within earshot. "And I will be back!"

His right hand was slick with the blood of the badly cut-up Shawnee, and his young face was flushed with emotion.

He heard a quiet voice behind him, and it was Sergeant Medford. "It's over, Dan'l. They're gone."

Dan'l looked over at him fiercely.

"They got Braddock," Medford went on. "A Shawnee rode right in on us and put a lance through him. It was him they was looking for."

"He's dead?" Dan'l said.

Medford nodded.

The anger crawled back out of Dan'l's chest, and it was replaced by an overwhelming depression.

"Let's get out of here," Medford said. "They won't be back now."

A moment later, they moved off into the woods.

Chapter Six

As at Scotborough, Duvall seemed to go a little mad on that road outside Fort Duquesne when he sensed a complete victory. He rode up and down the dirt road, his mount leaping wounded and corpses, urging his people to kill, and himself murdering in cold blood redcoats and militiamen who had made clear their intention to surrender. Heads were bashed in while the victims hands were up above their heads in submission, and torsos were cut in half, many by Duvall's own saber.

Not all French officers or soldiers embraced these inhuman tactics of their young general, though. Some watched the slaughter in dismay, while others even made objections to their superiors. A few Shawnee felt the same way about it, but were pushed aside by those with blood lust.

When it was finally finished, on that bloody roadway, corpses were strewn along a mile-long path, and in some places there were pools of blood that covered low-cut shoes and boots. Many bodies were not whole, and many more had lost their scalps. The taking of scalps was an honored tradition now with the Shawnee and other area tribes, but even among the Shawnee it was considered in bad taste to take a scalp from a live enemy. On this battle day, many had been taken in that manner, and Chief Blackfish had not tried to stop it. There was a great hatred at this time among his people for the British soldiers and settlers, whom they feared would drive them from their traditional hunting grounds. The French, who were primarily hunters and trappers and not settlers, played on those fears of the Indians, and aroused their baser instincts. For Chief Blackfish, it was politically expedient to go to war against the British, because it united his people in a great cause, and gave him a leadership role he would not have enjoyed otherwise.

Actually, the ones who lay dead on that road at day's end were the lucky ones who could not escape the battle. The Shawnee took a dozen prisoners for purposes of celebration, another Indian tradition, and Blackfish approved it. Eight redcoats and four colonials, most of them wounded in some way, were marched back to the fort, and as at Scotborough, were tied to whipping posts and flagpoles there. While the sun settled behind distant hills, but with light still in the sky, the Shawnee began dancing around the compound in preparation for killing their prisoners, with bluecoat French soldiers standing by along the perimeter of the long parade ground, watching somberly.

Duvall stood on a raised platform that was used for parades, grinning broadly as Shawnee warriors brought red-hot branding irons to the prisoners and seared their bare flesh until the air stank with the smell. The screams of the prisoners were unbearable for some French soldiers, who left the compound rather than view what was going on. Blackfish and Duvall stood together for a short time on the platform, together with a few French aides and one of the chief's sons, and watched the rituals proceed.

The branding-iron death was a very slow one, and it required a number of deep burns to make a victim pass out from exquisite pain and, finally, deep shock.

Other prisoners were cut open slowly, skin flayed, innards exposed, until they too succumbed from the shock of mutilation.

Duvall enjoyed every minute of it.

Blackfish did not. He watched solemnly, with the Indian's lack of real empathy, adjudging that these enemies were deserving of a dishonorable death, and knowing that if they tolerated it with some degree of dignity, they would receive honor from their ancestors. He neither enjoyed the horrible spectacle nor disliked it. It was part of living and dying, in his culture, and nothing more. The participants were just ordinary men taking justified vengeance on a particularly despised enemy.

One French soldier who had stayed to watch turned away from the ritual ceremony, near its end, and vomited onto the dirt of the compound.

When it was almost over, Duvall invited Blackfish and a couple of Duvall's colonels into his private office with him, at the end of the compound, while the Shawnee were allowed to begin a victory feast before returning to their villages.

In the office, which was nicely furnished, some furniture left by Beaumont, Duvall poured champagne all around, and seated his guests on tall-back chairs, while he heaved onto his upholstered desk chair. Duvall wore a bandage on his left arm where a colonial musketball had grazed him, and one of his underlings was limping from a leg wound. His name was Bethune, and he wore a deep scowl on his angular face. The other colonel present was unwounded, and appeared pleased with this celebration.

"To the death of all English!" Duvall toasted.

The unwounded colonel, named Sarti, repeated it. "Death to all English!"

Blackfish, who knew both French and English well, smiled and drank the champagne in one long swig. He had refused a chair, preferring to stand. He was eager to get his people back to their villages, where they could celebrate in their own way.

Duvall leaned back on his big chair. "We have accomplished more here today than Beaumont did in his entire tenure at the fort!" Duvall beamed. "But we could not have done it without our Shawnee allies!"

Blackfish bowed his head slightly. "My people do not shy away from a just war," he said.

"The English will never come here again!" Sarti proclaimed loudly. He did not have the taste for blood that Duvall had, but he was a very ambitious young colonel. "We should take this opportunity to drive them from Cumberland!"

Duvall nodded, and swigged some more champagne. Then he noticed that Bethune was not drinking. "Bethune? You do not like our champagne?"

Colonel Bethune hesitated before speaking, his face still sober. "The champagne is fine, General."

Blackfish looked over at him.

"Then what is it?" Duvall said, more seriously now.

"I didn't like what I saw out in the compound, General. Or on the field of battle."

Duvall's expression sagged into hard, straight lines. "Ah. You refer to the celebration of our friends the subjects of Chief Blackfish."

"And our own soldiers," Bethune said. "You let them get out of control, General. One must fight a war honorably."

Duvall rose from his chair, red-faced. "You tell me our fighting is without honor, damn you!"

Bethune came and set his full glass of champagne on Duvall's desk. "You will have my resignation on your desk tomorrow morning, General. I'll be returning to Quebec."

Duvall was fuming. "Fine! Get out, damn you! We do not need weak-kneed officers at this fort who faint at the sight of blood! You are not a soldier, Bethune, you never were! Get back to Quebec, and let us who can fight keep you safe and sound!"

Bethune did not comment further. A moment later, he was gone, and an embarrassed silence had fallen over the assemblage.

Finally Sarti spoke up. "That damned coward!"

Blackfish looked at him somberly. "I do not think so, Colonel. I saw him out there. He did not shirk his duty."

"To hell with him," Duvall said, pouring himself more champagne. "The more of his kind we can weed out, the better our men will fight."

They all settled down. Sarti swigged some champagne. "Our soldiers and braves can outfight a man like Braddock ten times out of ten, General. Without the likes of Bethune."

Blackfish set his empty glass on Duvall's desk. He was middle-aged, and sagging in places, but still heavily muscled. He wore his hair in the traditional scalp brush, but two eagle feathers dangled from its back end, and he wore a beautiful fur cape over his broad shoulders, making him look very regal.

"The English are not all like Braddock," he said slowly. "They will send somebody else. I saw it in a dream. A younger man, and a more clever one."

"Let them come," Duvall said loudly. "Let the whole damn British Army come!"

"It is not the English regulars who trouble me," Blackfish said quietly. "It is their new habit of using colonial militia."

Duvall frowned at the older man.

"These farmers fight for their land, not for King George," Blackfish said slowly and clearly. "We Shawnee do not believe in ownership of land, but they do. They believe they are defending their right to plant crops and colonize the wilderness. It is a religious thing with most of them. A stupidity, to be sure, but a strong belief. They will fight hard wherever they are taken. Men like Sheltowee."

"*Mon Dieu*, there is that name again!" Duvall cried out. "I met the hunter in the battle. He tried to kill me! I had him dead with my saber, when the battle intervened!"

"He is well known by my people," Blackfish said.

"He killed my Arabian stallion!" Duvall complained as if to a judge in a court.

"Sheltowee tracks better than my own braves, and can kill a buffalo at five hundred yards. He gives an example to us. Of what we can expect from colonial soldiers."

117

Duvall waved a hand as if to dismiss Dan'l.

"He has vowed to return and defeat us," Blackfish added.

Duvall looked up at him. "This is a private soldier we're talking about! What do I care what he's vowed!"

"His oath has something to do with you personally, General."

Duvall held his gaze with a more serious look. "He shouted something at me. I think we killed someone close to him at Scotborough, or were about to. One captive was shot from outside the fort, before your braves could finish with him. I suspect this hunter did it."

"Sheltowee was in my dream also," Blackfish said to him.

Duvall studied the older man's face closely.

"What is all this about dreams *du minuit*, for God's sake!" Sarti complained finally.

"Go on," Duvall said to the Indian, ignoring Sarti.

"I saw Sheltowee come for you, General. I saw you two in mortal combat."

Duvall leaned forward. "Yes?"

Blackfish shook his head. "I do not know. I did not see the end of it."

Duvall made a sour face.

"Enough of dreams, General," Sarti said. "Let us deal with reality. The English have shown they cannot fight us on even terms. In a year, they will have their backs to the wall."

Duvall hesitated, trying to forget the visions

of Blackfish. "Yes," he said distractedly. "Of course."

It was late the following day that the straggling British column arrived back at Fort Cumberland.

The retreating soldiers had mustered under the pennant of a Braddock colonel whom Dan'l had never met, a brash young man named Jameson. He was now in charge because both Braddock and his top colonel had been killed in the campaign. Nobody thought he was competent to take command, especially the officers who now had to serve under him for the time being.

Dan'l helped tend Washington's leg wound. They had a private conversation about the way things had gone, and the colonial colonel found he enjoyed the woodsman's company. He confided to Dan'l that he had tired of fighting under the British, and was hoping for independent command for the militias. In fact, Washington figured that might come whether or not the British wanted it, since relations with King George were slowly deteriorating, because of differences over such issues as quitrents and taxes. If there were a real break with England, Washington knew, the colonials might be fighting these same people they served under.

When Colonel Jameson finished with a meeting of his officers, including Washington, and the big compound was empty but for sentries, quiet fell on the fort. Rows of tents still lined the east side of the area, some with lamps lighted inside, because the militia had not been dismissed. Jameson invited Washington then to take a short walk around the compound, to work out the stiffness of wounds, and Washington agreed. He walked with a stick, and still had a bandage across his forehead. Jameson wore one on his right arm, and carried it in a sling. Jameson, the same age as Washington, assumed a superior air with him at the outset.

In the meeting just before their walk, Jameson had been explaining that the defeat had been bad luck, that Braddock's orders had not been carried out and that had caused the defeat. Jameson had not come to terms at all with the real reasons for the rout. Now, as Washington walked side by side with him in the darkness, with oil lanterns flickering in places around them, he turned to Washington soberly.

"You disobeyed Braddock's direct orders today, Colonel." He walked with his hands clasped behind him, in the European way. His tone was arrogant.

Washington looked at him. "Colonel, the militia is trained to fight in a certain way. The red man attacks from ambush, from trees and other cover. He kills quickly, from hidden positions."

"Bloody cowards!" the young Englishman said.

Washington gave him a sidewise glance. "They don't know the European way of fighting, Colonel. They think it's foolish to attack frontally, on open ground. Frankly, many of our militia agree, and have adopted their tactics. To take the cover that their enemy already enjoys. And fight from that cover."

"Your men ran," the Briton said evenly, as they made a big circle in the compound. "They deserted their ranks, the impudent scoundrels! Left us flanked when we needed their support, by God! There's no excusing it!"

"They fought the way they know," Washington said coolly to him. "And I should add, in doing so, they killed a lot of the enemy. Shawnee and French soldiers who would have wrought even greater havoc on us. Braddock should have ordered troops off that road immediately, Colonel, in my opinion. In failing to do so, he abdicated his responsibility of command. It was his tactics that brought disaster on your men, and ours."

The Englishman stopped before a row of darkened tents, and turned to Washington, his face straight-lined with anger. He had never had anybody speak to him like that about a general of King George. Braddock had been a personal friend of the great William Penn, and was considered one of Europe's finest military leaders.

"You take too much on yourself, Colonel!" he said in a grating voice. "Your behavior here, and at Duquesne, will be reported to our superiors!"

Washington held his dark look. "I'm sorry if I offended you, Colonel. But I felt certain things had to be said. If you want to make an issue of it, so be it. But we are what we are, Colonel.

Products of the New World. The Crown must recognize that fact one day soon."

"You even challenge the King?" Jameson said incredulously.

"We must challenge any authority that is wielded without regard to realities," Washington told him earnestly. "Most of us feel that way, on this side of the Atlantic."

The English colonel shook his head. "It's a black day when a subject of the Crown utters such sedition," he said. "I thought it was a mistake to incorporate colonials into our command, but I was overruled. Now, this fiasco at Duquesne will be reported to London, you may be certain. And as for you, I promise you that your commission is in the gravest jeopardy. You may not command again under the name of the Crown."

Washington smiled. "I'm resigning my commission in the militia and returning to my home in Virginia, Colonel. I don't enjoy this mix of command. I'll be going back to surveying."

"Perhaps that will suit your temperament better, Colonel. You're dismissed."

Washington nodded. "Incidentally, Colonel Jameson. The militia soldier who tried to save Braddock's life at Duquesne. Did you want to commend him?" he asked sourly.

The Englishman frowned. "What soldier?"

"His name is Boone. Dan'l Boone. One of the best natural soldiers I've ever seen, but I suspect he has little interest in a military career. He took your stunned general off that deadly road at Duquesne, at risk of his own life, to try to get the general back safely. It's the kind of action you might want to encourage."

"Oh, yes, I heard of the incident. His action was in direct violation of the general's orders, but Braddock was too wracked with pain to stop him. This was just another example of the anarchy that obtained there at the battle site."

Washington sighed. "I see."

"Isn't he the wagon driver from Carolina?" the Englishman said. "Who spent his younger days with savages, the one the Shawnee call Shel-towee?"

"That's the man, Colonel."

"Yes, it comes back now. Unfortunately, young men like that one are commonplace in your colonial militia. Fellows seeking individual recognition, and glory. Wanting to stand out among their peers, to win the gold cup, as it were. We are trying to build a real army over here, where there is no room for glory-seeking and reputation-building, such as Boone seems bent on. Our soldiers work and fight together, without thought for personal acknowledgment. They fight for their common good, for the unit as a whole, without regard for personal considerations."

"Even so," Washington said. "A word from a British officer would not only assure the soldier's loyalty to your cause, but would give the entire militia unit a lift when they need it badly. That should be good for the whole army."

The Englishman smiled wryly. "Now, you see,

that's where your lack of formal officer training shows itself, Colonel. A basic rule is that you never reward a soldier for insubordination. No matter what result may come from it. Discipline is everything, you see. Armies cannot survive without it."

Washington gave up. "Very well. If you feel that way."

"In this instance, however, I won't insist on punishment for his actions, nor will I recommend it for the rest of your men. They absolutely must receive further training, though, before participating in any future actions."

"You're too kind, Colonel," Washington said acidly, the sarcasm heavy in his voice.

The English officer eyed him narrowly. "I think we're finished with this conversation, Colonel Washington."

Washington saluted smartly, and turned and disappeared into the darkness, without another word.

Not far away, down at the edge of the flickering campfires, Dan'l Boone and John Findley shared a tent again; only this time they were the only ones in it. The militia had received heavy losses while trying to defend their British cousins at Duquesne.

They had an old oil lantern lighted in the tent, and it fluttered some in a slight breeze from outside, and made shadows move on their faces. They had had a small evening meal since arrival, and had visited the hospital tent to look for soldiers they knew casually, but found only strange faces. Now they sat cross-legged on ground mats, looking very tired.

Findley was an older man than Dan'l, and had a rugged, outdoors look. He was the one who had been west on a couple of explorations for potential settlers, and all of the men in their company who had met him seemed to like him.

"That was a damn fiasco yesterday at Duquesne," Findley was telling Dan'l as they sat there quietly in preparation to turning in for the night. Findley was smoking on a corncob pipe, which he was never without.

Dan'l nodded. "It was just pure hell out there."

Dan'l could not get Duvall's face out of his head. Filled with anger, trying to kill him, Dan'l had been so close, and then the opportunity was gone. If he had killed Duvall, the whole fight might have gone differently. But just as importantly to him, Ethan's death now went unavenged. Dan'l knew he would not rest until Duvall had paid the ultimate price for what he did at Scotborough.

"I won't be doing this again," Findley was telling him. "I'm getting out, Dan'l, and try to get backing for another trip to Ken-ta-ke."

Dan'l looked over at him. Findley had briefly mentioned that western land to him, on the way to Duquesne, and it had sounded wonderful to him.

"Sounds like a fellow could hunt and trap all day and not move from his camp, if what you're saying is true," Dan'l said with a small smile.

"I'm telling you, lad. It's all out there, even better than Tennessee. Green meadows as far as you can see on a clear day. Rushing streams, by Jesus, and game everywhere. Beavers so thick you can catch them in a net. Buffalo herds so big they stretch to the horizon, and they multiply faster than you could ever shoot them. Birds—why you can't believe it. Eating birds you ain't never saw before. Songbirds that fill the sunny air with music. There ain't no place like it nowhere in the world, Dan'l."

Dan'l's eyes had clouded over, and he stared blankly into the night outside the tent. "Damn. That sounds like my kind of place," he said softly.

"Why, you and Ken-ta-ke would be like two lovers!" Findley grinned. "With your know-how in the woods. Say, what happened to your Long Rifle?"

"Lost it at Duquesne," Dan'l said. "I'll have to trade some pelts for another, when I get home. I hear we're being mustered out tomorrow. Put on leave."

"Well, it'll be a permanent leave for me," Findley told him. "I'm exercising my option. I'm hungry for the woods."

Dan'l looked into his face. He liked John Findley, and would have liked very much to join him in a western expedition.

"Of course, the Shawnee are right ornery out west of here," Findley went on now, looking down at his hands. "On my last trip, a partner of mine got hisself captured by some of them.

126

We looked for them for three days, but never caught up with them. About a week later, we come upon old Mike."

There was a long pause, and Dan'l looked over at him.

"They'd put him on a spit, over a low fire. Like a goddamn hog. They'd cooked him slow-like, so it would take a long time. I couldn't hardly recognize him."

Dan'l shook his head.

"They'd cut pieces off him too. Probably ate a few, to take on his powers. I buried him in a cool, shady place, to take that fire out of his soul. He was just a kid."

Dan'l sat quietly, thinking about that.

"That kind of thing scares the settlers away," Findley concluded. "And the Shawnee know it."

"I heard they were worse west of here," Dan'l said.

"I heard a rumor," Findley told him. "That Chief Blackfish is going recruiting in that direction pretty soon now. If you stick with this, you might run onto some of them later."

Dan'l looked at him, and smiled at the warning.

"My idea is, get out of this soldiering and come with me on my next trip west," Findley said. "Then you won't have to worry over what you run into at Duquesne if they go back."

Dan'l shook his head. "I won't give up on this, John. Not till I run that son of a bitch down. I can't. He's in my craw."

"Hell, the French will still be around to fight,

even if you take a year or so off," Findley said. "You don't have to be so damn eager to lay your life down again for these London dandies."

"It ain't for them," Dan'l said. "It never was."

Findley leaned forward. "I know a couple of men in your area down by Salisbusy, would jump at the chance to finance a trip to find and stake out good farm land. We'd get part of the profit, Dan'l. A man could make hisself some real money, for his old age."

Dan'l smiled again. "Never had no need for money," he said easily. "Probably never will."

Findley sighed.

"I can't take a year out," Dan'l went on seriously. "Much as I'd like to, John. I got me a mission to complete, and it comes down to Henri Duvall. They could send him to New Orleans next month, and I'd never see his evil face again. I don't want that to happen."

Just at that moment, a figure appeared in the open tent entrance, and Sergeant Medford ducked down and came in.

"Boys," Medford greeted them.

"Evening, Sergeant," Dan'l said.

"Do either of you require further medical treatment?" Medford asked them.

They exchanged glances. "I don't think so, Sergeant," Findley replied. "We got us our little bandages, and is wearing them like good boys."

Medford grinned. "Consider yourselves lucky. We got a couple boys ain't going to make it."

"Sorry to hear that," Findley said.

Medford took a dark hat off and scratched at his head. He looked very tough, standing there. Dan'l was pleased to be associated with him.

"There will be wagons to take some others home. The rest of you will be on your own, I reckon. You can get back the best you can."

"When are we going back to Duquesne?" Dan'l asked.

Medford met his gaze, and grinned. "By God, Boone. Ain't you had enough for a while?"

"Not as long as Duvall is alive," Dan'l told him.

"Well, he's alive, all right. And the local friendlies tell me he's invited the Shawnee to bring your head to him."

That surprised Dan'l. "He knows who I am?"

Medford nodded. "Through the Shawnee. He also knows you're the one that tried so hard to kill him at Duquesne."

"Good," Dan'l said. "I want him to know!"

Medford grinned and shook his head. "I could use a couple more like you."

"He made me . . . kill my cousin. At Scotborough," Dan'l said.

Both Medford and Findley's faces went sober for a moment. "I heard," Medford said.

"What he did there, it was awful," Dan'l said.

"I reckon he did a lot more of it yesterday," Findley said.

"He has to be stopped," Dan'l concluded.

Medford shoved big hands into his belt. "I think we'll go back," he said. "You may get another chance at him."

"If we don't, *I* will," Dan'l told him.

"I hope you understand," Medford said, "that if you return with us later, the Shawnee will all be looking for you. I suspect there's a bounty on your head."

Young Dan'l thought about that for a long moment. But then he looked Medford squarely in the eye.

"I don't fear the Shawnee," he said evenly.

Medford liked the reply. "I didn't think so," he said. "Anyway, just hold yourself available in Salisbury, Dan'l, and I think you may see some changes in the situation very soon."

"What kinds of changes?" Findley wondered.

Medford hesitated. "In command," he finally said.

Findley and Dan'l exchanged a look. "Now that sounds like a development all of us might welcome," Findley said.

"Incidentally, Dan'l. You still got that Shawnee scalp?"

Dan'l nodded defensively.

"My captain asked me to tell you to get rid of it before you muster in again," Medford said, rather apologetically.

"It's going to hang in our barn," Dan'l said. "As a reminder, till Duvall is dead and buried."

"What a nice thought." Medford grinned.

Chapter Seven

When Dan'l and the few other surviving recruits
arrived back in the streets of Salisbury, there
was no welcoming committee or bunting decorating the buildings. Everybody knew the campaign had been a disaster, and there was only
mourning for the dead and injured. Besides
Corey Ruskin, three other area men had been
killed, and one young fellow who came back
with Dan'l had lost part of his leg.

War, it seemed, was hell.

Dan'l's couple of shallow wounds were healing up nicely, and the most trouble he still had
was from the place where the killer bear had
bitten him on the left arm, in its death throes.
When Dan'l arrived back at the Boone farm, the
several younger children ran to him and smoth-
ered him with affection, which he did not know

he needed until it happened. The younger Squire wanted to know all about the campaign, down to the most minute details, and that took a couple of hours. His mother Sarah just embraced him for a long, long moment, her eyes filled with tears, and Squire Senior sat at a kitchen table he had hewn with his own hands, and grinned a lot. After a while, he ordered the children out, and Dan'l sat alone with his parents.

"I hope thee did not have to take human life, Dan'l," Sarah said soberly to Dan'l then.

"Sarah—" the elder Boone put in.

"It's all right, Paw," Dan'l told him. He looked around their parlor, at the hooked rugs on the floor, the samplers on the walls, and realized Sarah's world was a very different one from that of the British generals.

"I took life," Dan'l admitted. "To save my own."

"Oh," she said softly, in dismay. She rose from her chair. "I'll pray for you, Dan'l."

She disappeared into a bedroom, and Boone touched his son's knee. "She'll understand, Dan'l. Give her time. She's still adjusting to the frontier."

"I know."

"Civilizing the wilderness is God's will," Boone went on. "You're on His side, Dan'l. That's what's important. Don't you ever forget that."

Dan'l sighed. "There's this other thing, though, Paw."

Boone regarded him curiously.

"I'm going to kill Duvall. If it comes to it."

Boone smiled slightly. "I don't know if the Good Lord would approve of you making it personal, Dan'l."

"Maybe not. But that Frenchman made me do an awful thing. Something I won't never forget. I can't live with that eating me. Not with him alive, and leaving death and misery on his trail. I hope somebody else takes him down, Paw. I hope if I meet him, he's armed and ready to do battle. But if he ain't—I'll kill him anyway, Paw."

Boone looked down at the floor. "Well. This man seems an agent of the Devil himself, Dan'l. Who can say that God ain't directing your hand, if you put him to death. He has done it before. 'God hurled the Great Dragon down, the original Serpent, the one called Devil and Satan, who was terrorizing the entire Earth.'"

Dan'l was not particularly religious. He had always preferred hunting on Sunday mornings to church. But he was glad his father understood.

"Thanks, Paw," he said.

"I think you ought to know, Dan'l, that things have changed around here since the French victory at Duquesne."

Dan'l furrowed his brow. "How?"

"Well. The Cherokee and Shawnee in these parts were always pretty friendly. You know how they've been with us. Trading. Swapping stories. Eating our food. Well, that's all changed."

"Not just since Duquesne?"

"No, not all of it. I seen the direction it was heading last year. You ain't noticed, 'cause you ain't around that much. But things is getting stirred up. The Indians ain't coming around no more. I think the French has got them all riled. They think maybe they can get this land back somehow, I guess. Some half-breed down from the north has got Chief Yellow Eagle's ear. He goes by the name of Saucy Jack, and he comes into Salisbury regular. The local Cherokee and Shawnee think he's some kind of great warrior, I reckon, 'cause he fought with the French up at Detroit. He's supposed to be good with a long gun."

"Never heard of him," Dan'l said.

"I hear he's made some friends in Salisbury, boys that don't know what he's about. He sucks things out of them, like about the militia and so forth. Then he goes back to Yellow Eagle and fills him in."

"Saucy Jack," Dan'l said, rolling it over on his tongue.

"A couple of them friends of Ruskin been cozying up to him lately," Boone went on. "I reckon they don't know no better."

"You think there's going to be trouble here, Paw?" Dan'l asked him.

"I'm praying to God there ain't," Boone said. "But just a few days ago a bunch of Shawnee rode up to a valley farm on horseback and just sat there and watched the place for a long time. Got them people real nervous."

"Maybe I'll just ride over there and ask a few questions," Dan'l said, "when I get a chance."

"You ain't no soldier now, Dan'l. You're back home. You don't have to take none of this on you. Not till you're called back to duty."

"If there's trouble here in the valley," Dan'l reminded his father, "every manjack in the valley will have to take up the gun. You know that, Paw."

"Well. I just hope this all blows over," Boone concluded.

Dan'l let a long breath out. "I reckon we might be a long way from the end of it."

In town that same day, at the local public house, Corey Ruskin's old sidekicks Nick and Little Red had come in for a few drinks.

They both had complained loudly about Ruskin's death, talking about joining the militia themselves to avenge Ruskin's killing. But neither of them had made any real move to do so. They were young men without political beliefs or positions, and cared little about the welfare of their community or the colony.

The sky had clouded over about noontime that day, and by the time the twosome arrived at the public house, thunder rumbled across the landscape and some rain came down briefly. Nick and Red came into the place damp from the rain and cold, and wanted some whisky to warm their insides. There was a big potbelly stove at the rear of the building, with wood burning in it, but little of that heat got to the other corners of the room. There was a counter where an innkeeper had his shelves of bottles, and several tables set with chairs. A dart board hung on an end wall, unused, and there was a locally done painting of the royal monarch on the wall behind the counter, with a carefully printed inscription beneath it, *"God Save King George."* The floors were rough planking, and there were hand-rived rafters overhead. Sawdust had been sprinkled on the wood floor.

There were just three customers in the place on that rainy afternoon: Nick, Red, and Saucy Jack. Jack was standing at the short counter, ordering an ale from the heavyset owner, and the two farmers sat at a nearby table, sipping whisky.

Nick and Little Red had had no real feelings about Corey Ruskin's death. None of the three had ever developed any deep relationships, with each other or anybody else. So Ruskin was now already forgotten by them, and they were already talking about Dan'l Boone's arrival home, and how the locals were treating him like a hero.

Big Nick was facing toward the front door, which was open, and he looked glumly toward the drizzle of rain that was still coming down outside.

"I got to get out of this place," he was saying to Little Red. "Get me a horse and go to Boston. I got a cousin there. This damn farming ain't for me."

"You're supposed to be butchering hogs today, ain't you?" Little Red said, sipping at his drink.

"I sneaked off." Nick grinned. He looked a lot like Ruskin, except that he was not as big, and his eyes were shifty. "They think I'm down at the barn, up to my elbows in guts." He laughed and shook his head.

"Hey, you see who come in? Ain't that Saucy Jack?"

Nick glanced toward the counter. "Yeah, I seen him. That crazy redskin's going to get drunk again."

"I heard him telling somebody yesterday what a good shot he is. Can you fathom that Indian bragging about something like that?"

"Hell, if Corey was around, he'd show that breed what real shooting is," Nick said.

"Even that Quaker might beat him, if it come to it."

Nick caught Red's eye, and stared hard at him for a long moment. "Damn."

"Huh?"

"You just give me a big idea."

"I don't know what you're talking about," Little Red told him.

Nick jerked a thumb toward Saucy Jack, who had just turned toward them. "Boys," Jack said, in perfect English. He walked over to their table holding a mug of dark ale. He wore buckskins, a lot like those Dan'l wore, and moccasins on his feet. His hair was long and black, unlike the shaved mane of the full-blood Shawnee, and he wore a small dark hat on his head, with a hawk's feather in its brim. His face was full and square, and he looked more Indian than white. His mother had been a captured white woman, but he never admitted those circumstances of his birth to anyone who did not already know.

"Sit down, Jack," Nick said genially. "We'll buy your next ale."

Jack nodded and took a chair, setting his drink down. "Good to see you boys." Because of the dampness in the air, he had a woodsy odor about him that was rather unpleasant because it was mixed with sweat. "Was it you that did a rain dance and caused this?" He laughed in his throat.

Nick returned the laugh—and rather loudly, Little Red thought. Red regarded Nick quizzically.

"You're one jolly fellow, Jack," Nick said.

"That's what I miss in my Shawnee brothers," Jack said. "They don't laugh a lot."

"Well, it evens out," Little Red told him. "Other folks get to laugh at them."

Saucy Jack scowled at Little Red for a moment, and Nick hastily interjected his own comment.

"What Red means is, us white folks laugh at just about anything. Ourselves too."

Red was chagrined, and a little afraid of Jack. "Yeah. That's what I was trying to say."

"My tribe has a proud history," Jack said stiffly. "We just whipped you boys at Duquesne."

"Why, you ain't no Shawnee, Jack," Red said. "You got good white blood in you."

"Will you drop it, Red?" Nick said in a harsh undertone.

Little Red looked hurt.

"Folks say you're an awful good shot, Jack," Nick said quickly to him.

Jack caught his gaze. "There's no better," he said, gulping down some more ale.

Nick motioned for the innkeeper to bring Jack another glass, and the fellow complied. Jack started right in on it without thanking Nick. It was well known that Jack could get dead drunk on two large mugs of ale.

"What about Dan'l Boone?" Nick finally added.

Jack looked at him. "Boone? You mean Sheltowee?"

Nick nodded. "Everybody says he's the best shot in the valley," he said slowly.

Red began to catch Nick's plan. "Yeah. The best in the valley. Everybody says so."

Jack laughed gutturally. "That was before I got here."

Nick took a breath in. "I talked to Dan'l just yesterday, and he mentioned you," he lied.

Saucy Jack's hard eyes narrowed down on Nick. He was considered Yellow Eagle's counselor for the area's Shawnee, and he was therefore given a wide berth in town.

"Yes?" Jack said.

Nick hesitated. "Dan'l says he can outshoot you on any day of the week and twice on Sundays. That's what he said."

Jack frowned deeply, and Red grinned behind his hand.

"He said that?" Jack said angrily.

"And that ain't all," Nick lied. "He said if you don't quit talking about how good you are, he's going to come after you, Jack. You know how many Shawnee he's killed, don't you?"

"That son of a bitch!" Jack said, his eyes wild.

"I heard him too," Little Red put in. Nick gave him a hard look.

"I wouldn't told you," Nick concluded. "But I thought you might want to be careful, coming into town for a while."

"Careful!" Jack bellowed. "Careful! Why, I'll put that damn fake Indian out of his goddamn misery! The next time I see him in town here, he's a dead man!" His cheeks were flushed, his eyes a little maniacal.

"I just thought he might be dangerous to you," Nick added, not being able to let it go now.

Little Red could hardly contain his glee. He suppressed a wide grin behind his cupped hand.

"Dangerous to *me!*" Jack said in an odd voice. "By the blood of my Shawnee ancestors, that damn white face better worry about how dangerous I am to him! I might even ride out to that damn farm!"

"I wouldn't do that, Jack," Nick said hastily. "You'll catch him here in town easy. He'll be in regular for his family. You can take him on then."

"I'll blow his goddamn heart out through his ribs," Jack promised them. "I'll challenge him in open combat, by God! I don't want nobody saying I ambushed the son of a bitch!"

"I think that's smart," Nick said. He could not believe the success of his scheme. He was, in fact, a little afraid of what he had begun. He hoped the innkeeper had not overheard any of it.

"Jesus," Little Red said, wide-eyed.

The grin was gone.

Dan'l tried to find out more about the plans of the militia from some neighbors that evening, but nobody knew anything. Locals were more concerned about an uprising of the Indians around their valley than they were about whether the militia returned to Duquesne.

The next morning early, he took his younger brother Squire out hunting for rabbits, so the family would have table meat. Young Squire, named after his father, was leaner than Dan'l, and not as broadly built, but he was going to be an athletic-looking young man. There was nothing he loved more than to hunt and trap with his older brother, and in fact, had pleaded with the family to go on Dan'l's Tennessee trip, but Boone Senior had denied him that pleasure. Dan'l was glad now he had stayed home, because he could have died at Scotborough too, like Ethan.

It was just past dawn that morning when they headed out on foot to an area a few miles south of the farm, where game was more abundant. The trouble was, there were also wolves prowling the area presently, so Dan'l knew they had to be more wary than usual.

They hiked for over an hour without speaking much. Dan'l was not a big talker in his own home, but he was even less inclined to conversation when on the hunt. Animal predators found no need to verbally communicate when tracking down some prey, he reasoned, and nothing hunted better than a puma, or a wolf.

By the time they had reached the woods where Dan'l wanted to do the shooting, he had already shot two large rabbits, and Squire had one, and they were hung from their belts along with their powder horns and bullet bags. Dan'l had traded skins for a new rifle, and he was trying it out, and so far he liked it very much. It was called a Kentucky Rifle, and its colonial makers claimed it could outshoot the Heinrich and the Charleville, which were already better than the Brown Bess musket the British soldiers used. It weighed about ten pounds, and had superior rifling, so that its projectile flew to its target with even more accuracy than before. Its calibre was bigger, though, at .72, and this was more than needed for hunting. But Dan'l had more than hunting in mind when he chose it. He hoped to be back in the war soon.

They hiked along a stream bed for a while, and got a glimpse of a red fox, but could not get a shot in. Dan'l was not pulling any traps that morning, because he had not set any after he had signed up with the militia.

A few minutes after the sighting of the fox, Dan'l stopped and held his hand up for Squire to halt behind him. Dan'l scented the air, and the hair raised on the back of his neck.

"Wolf," he said quietly to his brother. "A lot of them."

Squire nodded, and swallowed hard. "I heard there's a pack down here that's almost starved."

"I know. Come on, we're getting out of here."

Dan'l turned and headed north, away from the creek. No longer was his stride casual. He was hurrying, trying to put some distance between them and the wolves. He knew how dangerous they could be if there were a lot of them and they were hungry. Squire struggled to keep up with him, moving along quickly through the underbrush, brambles scratching at him and branches pulling at his clothing.

"Ain't we—far enough?" he finally said, out of breath.

They had emerged into a wide clearing. Dan'l stopped again, and listened. A crackling of a twig, and another. The sounds coming from different directions.

"They caught us," he said quietly.

Squire squinted into the woods. "You sure, Dan'l?"

In the next moment his question answered itself. A dark form moved through the trees, not yet showing itself. Dan'l did a wide turn and spotted several more. They were already surrounded, and there appeared to be about ten of the animals. They looked lean and dangerous.

"Back to back!" Dan'l said loudly. Silence was no longer important, or even desirable.

"What?" Squire said.

"Back to back, damn it! Quick!"

Squire understood, and shoved his back up tight against his brother's. The wolves were now appearing boldly at the edge of the clearing, coming into full view. They were big and very wild-looking, and they had blood in their eyes. They obviously saw Dan'l and Squire as their next meal.

"Cap off your powder horn!" Dan'l said. "Ramrod ready! We'll have to reload faster than we ever have!"

"All right," Squire replied.

"Put three balls in your mouth!" Dan'l added. "So they'll be ready to drop in!"

Squire obeyed, tasting the acridity of the lead. The wolves were beginning to growl, low in their throats, and now they were circling the hunters, out in the open, only yards away. Dan'l had been right. He counted ten. Enough to overwhelm them, to eat them alive.

"Pick out the closest animal," Dan'l said breathlessly. "Then I'll take one out. They'll have to recover from that. I'll cover you while you reload."

Squire nodded, his hands trembling. One very large gray wolf, slanted eyes fiery with excitement, came in closer, snarling out his challenge.

Squire fired his lightweight Ferguson rifle in

the next moment, and the big wolf jumped into the air, hit in the chest, and then hit the ground dead. A second explosion came from Dan'l's rifle, the heavier one, and a second wolf was punched off its feet, yelling just briefly, then became motionless.

The others reacted violently to these deaths, and began circling even more rapidly, looking for an opening. As Squire reloaded furiously, fumbling with powder and ball, a lean female came in on him silently, leaping for his throat. Dan'l saw the move, and swung his rifle like a club, meeting the wolf with a deadly blow to the head. The animal fell at Squire's feet, kicking and jerking, but it was dead.

Squire was now ramming the ball home, but another wolf now leapt at him, and again Dan'l met it, fracturing ribs. It still bit into Squire's leg, but only shallowly. As Dan'l was administering a death blow to its skull, another wolf hurled itself onto his back, and yet another grabbed at his left leg, biting into his thick boot.

Now Squire was loaded and primed. He first fired at a wolf just coming in, and it went down, howling. Then he threw the gun down and drew his skinning knife, and shoved it into the wolf on Dan'l's back. Dan'l had discarded his gun too, and was slicing the throat of the one on his leg, getting bitten on the arm in the process.

Suddenly there were just three healthy wolves left, and they saw now what had happened, and looked very bewildered at the change of circumstance. They gave ground, retreating to the edge of the clearing again, as a couple on the ground whimpered and died. When Dan'l shouted at them, they turned tail and ran back into the woods.

"Get out of here, you devils!" Dan'l yelled.

Squire screamed out something unintelligible, and the combined racket drove the remaining survivors off into the woods. Then the two of them were standing there, still back to back, dead wolves littering the ground around them. One was still alive, and Dan'l stuck his knife into its neck behind the ear, and silenced it. They were both breathless and shaken.

"Good Jesus in heaven!" Squire whispered, looking around him at the carnage.

Dan'l turned and grinned weakly at him. "You did just fine, brother. I won't be afraid to take you anywhere."

"I was scared to death, Dan'l," Squire admitted.

"Hell, so was I," Dan'l said. "Scared is good. Long as it don't get the best of you."

It was over, and Dan'l was relieved that Squire had not been hurt. Or worse. He would have been responsible.

It took them a couple of hours to take the skins. Squire was clumsy at it, so Dan'l did most of the work. Then they were hauling them back through the woods with them, on their way home.

They passed through Salisbury on the way back, and when they got there, they found their sister in town with a wagon, and they loaded the skins aboard and Squire went on home with her. Dan'l decided to stay on and walk home, because he wanted to relax with a mug of ale, and buy some black powder at the local store.

He bought the powder first, and was just on his way to the public house when he heard the voice calling to him from across the dirt street.

"Hey, Boone!"

Dan'l turned and saw Nick and Little Red standing over there, not far away. He had not come across them since his return from Duquesne. "Boys," he said.

"I hear tell you turned tail at Duquesne, and let old Corey get his head blowed off," Nick said.

Oh, God, Dan'l thought. He started to move on.

"You was both driving wagons. I thought militia was supposed to look after each other."

Dan'l turned back to them. "I see you ain't recovered from that diarrhea of the mouth, Nick. How does that taste when you get through blowing off like that?"

Nick became red-faced, and Little Red stuck his jaw out. "We heard you tell your sister about them wolves! Damn near got yourself eat this morning, didn't you? What happened to that rifle you're so good with?"

"Are you really that short, Little Red, or are you standing in a hole over there?" Dan'l responded.

Now both of them were flustered. Nick pointed a finger at him. "Corey outshot you at Cumberland! He sent a note back! You better quit shooting off your mouth about how good you are, Quaker! You got Saucy Jack fit to be tied!" He gave Red a smug look.

"Saucy Jack?" Dan'l said. That was the second time in as many days that he had heard that name. "The breed that Yellow Eagle is listening to nowadays?"

"The same!" Nick said. "He don't like the things you been saying about him. He's laying for you, Quaker!"

Dan'l looked bewildered by all of that. "I ain't said nothing about him. I never heard of him till yesterday. You got your facts mixed up, like usual." He started to turn back toward the public house.

"Tell him that!" Little Red yelled at him happily, pointing toward the entrance of the public house.

Dan'l looked, and saw Saucy Jack descending two steps to the street. Jack had seen Dan'l already, and a dark scowl had etched itself on his heavy features. He had been drinking, and he had poor judgment with a little alcohol in him.

"There you are, you son of a bitch!" Jack called out to Dan'l.

Dan'l felt heavy inside him. He was worn out from the fight with the wolves, and worrying over Squire, and had wanted only to have an ale, relax, and go on home. Now he squinted down on Jack, who was standing in the street facing him. He was taller than Dan'l, and he carried a Heinrich rifle under his right arm. Dan'l had his Kentucky rifle and as usual, it was fully loaded, carried upright on his shoulder.

"I guess you're Jack," Dan'l said easily, studying the half-breed's face. He looked slightly inebriated, and Dan'l wondered why Yellow Eagle would depend on the advice of a man who had to have alcohol in him before midday.

"And you're Boone. Or should I say, Sheltowee?"

Dan'l shrugged. "Whatever you want."

Jack brought the long gun up into position. "What I want is your ass, by the holy spirits!"

Dan'l eased his rifle off his shoulder, and held it across his chest. "You got some argument with me?"

"I heard what you been saying! I'm the high shaman for Yellow Eagle's tribe, by the Great Wolf! I've killed fifty buffalo in one shoot! My parfleche pouch contains a fetish from Chief Blackfish himself! I killed better men than you at Detroit!"

Dan'l had no idea what had caused this outburst, but he had not missed the reference to Blackfish. "You fought with the French," he said slowly.

"It was my honor! With Beaumont, Duvall, and many others."

Dan'l's face went very somber, and he felt the edge of renewed anger rising inside him.

"What do you think of that, Quaker?" Nick's voice came to him. He ignored it.

"I don't know what you heard," Dan'l said. "I ain't said nothing about you 'cause I don't know you. But if you fought for Duvall, and you're filling Yellow Eagle's head with poison from that bastard, you deserve more than talking about."

Nick and Little Red exchanged excited looks, while Jack's face clouded over even further. "I won't shoot you down like a yellow dog, Sheltowee. I will turn and walk fifty paces, and then I will fire on you. I advise you defend yourself."

Dan'l could not believe the man. Jack turned and began walking away, loading the gun as he went. Dan'l called after him. "You're breaking the law, Jack!"

Little Red punched Nick in the ribs, and laughed under his breath. But Nick was holding his breath, realizing he had initiated this whole thing, and wondering what to do about it, if anything. He just watched, doing nothing.

Jack had reached the end of his walk, and was finishing loading and priming. Dan'l primed his own rifle, and readied it for firing. "The council won't abide this, Jack!" he called out to the half-breed.

"To hell with the council!" Jack yelled. "This is Yellow Eagle's hunting ground! And I'm part of his council!"

"How about that, Quaker?" Little Red said.

Dan'l did not even look toward him, but in that instant he knew who had caused the trouble here on this quiet Salisbury morning. Several citizens had stopped to watch now too, and had heard most of what was said.

Jack raised his long gun and aimed it at Dan'l. "Now we'll see how good you shoot when it counts, Great Hunter!" Jack called out as Dan'l raised his own rifle to his shoulder, the Kentucky with its big-caliber ball. "Now we'll see who's the real soldier!"

Dan'l's eyes were as sharp as an eagle's. As soon as he saw Jack's finger whiten over the trigger, he aimed carefully and returned fire an instant after Jack's shot.

The small street reverberated with the double explosion, and Little Red jumped visibly. Dan'l felt a tug at his right sleeve as Jack's shot narrowly missed him. In that same moment, Dan'l's slug struck Saucy Jack like a club, in center chest, tearing through his heart savagely and blowing part of it out through his back. He was picked up off his feet bodily, and hurled onto the ground, dead when he hit.

There were several gasps of shock along the street, but all present understood that Dan'l's shot was a purely defensive one. Most were very pleased to see Jack down, because they knew he was trouble for them.

Jack exhaled one long breath, staring unseeing at the blue sky above him, his buckskin trousers became wet at the crotch, and that was it. He lay in a perfect spread-eagle on the dirt, his rifle still in hand, but looking as if he were staked to the ground.

An older man came over to Dan'l. "Are you all right?" he asked with concern.

"Tell the elders to send Yellow Eagle my condolences," Dan'l said to him.

The fellow nodded. "We seen it all. We'll tell it the way it was."

People were crowding into the street now, from the several buildings along it. One woman took a look, and collapsed. She had to be carried back into her residence. Dan'l went and examined Jack, and verified the kill. Nick and Red had come up behind him silently. Nick's jaw was slightly open.

"I guess you thought it might be me," Dan'l said acidly, gesturing at Jack.

Neither of them replied.

Dan'l came up very close to them. "I want you two to steer clear of me, you understand?"

For the first time, they both showed real fear of him. "Oh, hell, Boone," Little Red managed.

"I mean, if I'm in the store, don't come in till I'm gone. If I go into the public house for a drink, and you're there, I'll expect you to leave. If you see me coming down the street, you cross to the other side."

His voice had been low, and hard. They both looked into his eyes and saw the seriousness there.

"Now, look—" Red said weakly.

But Nick, who was a bit smarter, stopped him. "It's all right. Yeah. We get it, Quaker."

"Don't forget," Dan'l advised them.

Then he turned his back on them and Jack, and climbed the steps to the public house to get his drink before returning to the farm.

Chapter Eight

Will McAfee leaned against a support post on Squire Boone's porch, removed his hat, and took a long sip of the lemonade Sarah had fixed for him. Boone was sitting on a stool near him, and Dan'l was up against the cabin wall, beside the front door. The three men were alone out there.

"That ride out here was hot today," McAfee complained, looking into the glass of cool liquid. "This goes down real easy."

"Glad you like it, Will," Boone said. "I understand you come out here to talk to Dan'l. You want to be alone with him?"

"No, that's not necessary," McAfee said. "There's just a couple of things, and you both ought to hear them. First off, Dan'l is cleared of any culpability in the Saucy Jack shooting."

Boone nodded with a smile. "I could of told you that, Will. My boy ain't no murderer."

"We all know that, Squire," McAfee said. "That Jack caused some kind of trouble about every other time he came to town. He just had all that vinegar in him."

"I heard," Boone said.

"I saw Yellow Eagle on the trail north the other day," McAfee continued. "With a couple of his people. He wouldn't even speak to me. And I think that's the doing of Saucy Jack. And that other Shawnee he brought down with him from the north, called Medicine Eye. They got the Shawnee all worked up hereabouts, Squire. Some Cherokee too. They're having combined palavers, both tribes. I don't like it."

"Jack fought under Duvall," Dan'l finally spoke up. "Maybe the other one did too. That puts them in a whole other category, for my money."

McAfee sighed. "I heard that. I guess you have some personal feelings about General Duvall, Dan'l?"

Dan'l held his gaze. "You could say that."

"His cousin Ethan was killed at Scotborough," Boone said.

"I know how you must feel," McAfee told Dan'l. "I hear there's going to be a second try at Duquesne one of these days soon, and I suppose you'll be going back."

"I will," Dan'l said.

"The thing is, we may have ourselves a war right here, before that ever happens," McAfee went on. "A wagon passing through the valley was attacked yesterday, and the young married couple was killed. We think it was local Shawnee."

"Damn!" Dan'l said.

"My purpose in coming out here is to ask you to help us in this," McAfee said, addressing Dan'l. "We know how good you are with the red man, and how much they respect you. The council wants you to go talk with Yellow Eagle."

Dan'l dropped his gaze to the porch floor, thinking about that. The request had come as a complete surprise. He looked over at his father, and Boone caught his eye, then turned to McAfee.

"Will, there ain't a man in Yadkin County that can talk to the Indians like my Dan'l can. Yellow Eagle used to send him little presents when he was younger. But did you know there's a death warrant out on Dan'l in the Shawnee nation? Issued by that devil Duvall?"

McAfee was shocked. "Hell, no!"

"I ain't rightly sure it would be safe for my boy to go to Yellow Eagle now," Boone said.

"Don't repeat that to anyone, please," Dan'l said to the councilman.

McAfee sighed. "All right, Dan'l. But I guess that does change the picture some."

"You have to understand, Will. Yellow Eagle don't have control over every manjack under him. Dan'l might not get out of that village alive."

Dan'l lifted himself off the wall, and went and

stood looking out over the fields before them. "I'll go," he said.

"What!" Boone said.

Dan'l looked down at him. "It's something ought to be done, Paw. And I'm the one to do it."

McAfee was embarrassed. "I wouldn't have asked, Squire—"

Boone got to his feet. He was the same height as Dan'l, but heavier, and with lines in his face and the big hands of a farmer. "Damn it, Dan'l! We got to talk about this!" But he knew that Dan'l had taken over his own life, and would probably soon be out of the house for good, and that he expected to make his own decisions about his future.

"There ain't no talking to be done, Paw," Dan'l said gently. "I know I got to do it, and so do you."

Boone turned away angrily, afraid for his favorite son. "Damn!"

"Maybe you ought to give it some thought," McAfee suggested. "I might be able to get—"

"Just set it up, Will," Dan'l said to him.

"All right. I'll get back with you."

"I'll be ready."

By midday that same day, a runner had been sent to the village of Yellow Eagle with four armed guards, delivered a message at the perimeter of the tipis, and brought the chief's reply back. Yellow Eagle would receive Dan'l today only.

Dan'l was surprised by the response, but in

early afternoon he rode out to the Shawnee village, alone and without his rifle. It was a two-hour ride on horseback, and his mount was lathered when he got there. He was met by braves carrying guns and taken into the village like a prisoner.

Dan'l was surprised by the enlarged size of the village. He had not been there for a while, and it was teeming with new activity, and there were a lot more people than he remembered. There were a lot of men, and they regarded him very somberly as he passed among them under guard. He was surprised to see a number of Cherokee there too, from a nearby village.

There were over a hundred tipis in the village, and some more permanent-looking wickiups, and naked children running about, playing. Women went about daily chores, and several brown dogs yelped at Dan'l's horse. There were a few Indian mounts tethered to a hitching rail, and one wore a buckskin saddle stuffed with buffalo hair. The saddle was highly decorated and fringed.

There were several dung fires about the place, and some had cooking pouches hung over them, made from the stomachs of animals.

Dan'l was met by a very dignified-looking young man, a son of Yellow Eagle named Iron Fist who was also a counselor to the chief. Dan'l dismounted and they greeted with the raised arm, a sign of friendship, but there was no smiling with the act. Iron Fist wore a beautifully trimmed scalp brush along the top of his shaved head, with three eagle feathers tied in its tail at the back. He wore only trousers of rawhide, with a porcupine tail hairbrush hanging at the waist, where he had tied a red-dyed deerskin sash. Also prominently hanging from the sash was a blondish scalp, taken from some white settler. Dan'l ignored it.

"Greeting, Sheltowee. You honor our village with this visit."

"The honor is mine, Iron Fist," Dan'l told him. He knew that this son of Yellow Eagle had been very receptive to the aggressive ideas of outsiders, and guessed that Saucy Jack and Medicine Eye had persuaded him that the time was ripe to retake lands in the valley from the white settlers, and drive them back east, to Richmond and Charleston.

"My father the chief awaits you," Iron Fist said, gesturing toward the nearby large wickiup that was used for palavers. Iron Fist dismissed the guards who brought Dan'l in.

Dan'l followed Iron Fist into the wickiup, stooping to get through the low entrance that was cut into mud and wattle.

Inside, Chief Yellow Eagle sat cross-legged on a ground mat, with an elder of the tribe on either side of him. Over further toward a corner sat a fourth man, looking a lot like Iron Fist, but thinner, and wearing the paraphernalia of a shaman: a deer-head headdress, and an ornate robe of ermine and rabbit. He held a smoking pipe, with an effigy of a cougar carved on its bowl, and fancy cloth ribbons hanging from the long stem. Before the shaman on a buffalo robe lay a beaded buckskin tobacco pouch and a quilled tamping stick.

Dan'l did not speak. It was rude to do so until the chief had spoken first. Smoke rose from a small fire between Dan'l and the chief, and the white stuff rose straight up to an opening in the roof. The shaman sucked on the pipe, and then handed it to Yellow Eagle. Yellow Eagle puffed on it, and handed it to Dan'l. Dan'l followed suit, and handed it back.

"You are greeted, Sheltowee, Great Hunter, warrior of the long gun, brother to the bear and wolf." Yellow Eagle was middle-aged, and had lost some of the muscle of his youth, but his back was ramrod-straight, and his eyes were clear and piercing. He had a broad nose on a wide face, and wore ear and neck decorations of teeth, bones, and beads. Seven eagle feathers trailed down his brown back, all from golden eagles.

"My presence in your Great Shelter is an honor to be cherished, Defender of the People, Great Warrior of the Yadkin, slayer of the dread puma."

The pipe was passed to the elders, who were older men and more simply dressed. "Please make yourself comfortable, Sheltowee," Yellow Eagle told him.

Only then did Dan'l and Iron Fist sit down across the low fire from the chief. Dan'l guessed that if Saucy Jack had not challenged him in Salisbury, he might also be attending this meeting. He also guessed that the shaman was Medicine Eye.

"You have slain one of my people in personal combat," Yellow Eagle finally said, getting right to the heart of things. He had always been direct.

Dan'l nodded admission. "Yes, great chief, and I mourn your loss." He had said all in his very best Shawnee. At only 20, Dan'l was fluent in Shawnee, Cherokee, and Algonquin, and was fairly good with French. Yet he could barely write his name. "Jack challenged me to a death fight, and I could not refuse to participate. The great spirits were with me."

Yellow Eagle laughed softly. "Perhaps I should not have given you your first weapon when you were but waist-high, Sheltowee." When Yellow Eagle had first become chief, he had done a lot of trading with valley farmers, including the Boones, and had occasionally brought Dan'l and other Boone children small gifts. He had given Dan'l a small willow bow with stone-tipped arrows, together with a fancy worked quiver of beaver skin. Dan'l had been a good shot with the bow by the time he had reached his tenth birthday.

Dan'l smiled. "Your gift laid hunting in my heart, great chief," he said.

"The French have put a bounty on your head, Sheltowee," Yellow Eagle told him seriously. "It is a dishonor to you, and to my people."

"It is the French way," Dan'l said heavily.

"I have sent the word out. No brave of my

tribe may collect tribute for your death or injury. Even in battle."

Dan'l felt honored. "My heart is touched by yours," he said simply.

The pipe was back in the chief's hands now, and he puffed on it again, and again it was passed to Dan'l, who followed suit. Then Yellow Eagle got down to business.

"The white face has sent you to talk politics, Sheltowee," he said rather soberly.

Dan'l glanced toward the fellow called Medicine Eye, who was also originally an outsider, like Saucy Jack. He sat glaring at Dan'l with hostility.

Beside Dan'l, Iron Fist was impassive, hiding any feelings he had concerning the meeting.

"It comes to our council that Yellow Eagle prepares for war," Dan'l said quietly. "Like the great Shawnee tribes of the north and west. Our people are sad that they might lose the friendship of their red-face neighbors."

Yellow Eagle nodded. "Our brothers in the north have drawn a line on the ground, Sheltowee. They resist further invasion of their hunting grounds. I am advised to follow their lead. By Medicine Eye and others."

Dan'l glanced at Medicine Eye. "Great chief, I am asked to convey the message that my people and Shawnee, and your brother the Cherokee, can live in this valley together, in harmony."

"We cannot live in harmony with thieves and

murderers!" Medicine Eye suddenly blurted out, angrily.

Iron Fist glared at him. "Keep your silence, shaman!"

Yellow Eagle gave Medicine Eye a cold look, then turned to Dan'l. "Our feeling is, Sheltowee, that the lands you farm were taken from us without a treaty, and often by force. We have asked for help at your colonial capital, with no response."

Dan'l had heard of the emissary sent east.

"The ways of politicians are mysterious," Dan'l said.

"Agreed," Yellow Eagle told him.

"But we who live here will listen to your claims," Dan'l told him. "Maybe some payment—"

Yellow Eagle nodded now to Medicine Eye, and the latter replied to Dan'l. "It is too late for payments or promises of payment," he said harshly. "Our people want the valley back, white face. They want to stand tall like their brothers in the North, and regain their land. We advise you leave the valley, before there is armed conflict."

Dan'l looked at Yellow Eagle. "Is this your feeling, great chief?"

Yellow Eagle sighed heavily. "My people are aroused, Sheltowee. I must say what is in their hearts, and I must carry out their will. Yesterday Iron Fist killed a badger for me, and I cut its belly open. I removed the vital parts, and read the reflections in the pool of blood inside."

"And what did you see?" Dan'l asked him.

"I saw—death," Yellow Eagle said heavily. "Much death."

Iron Fist looked over at Dan'l. Years ago, when Yellow Eagle had stopped at the farm, he and Dan'l had played together while the men palavered over trade goods.

"You must know the seriousness of this," the chief said to Dan'l.

Dan'l nodded. "I understand. But I must advise what is in my heart, also, Yellow Eagle. It will be bad for the Shawnee if they take up the warpath. There are more white faces than ever before. They will answer with guns."

"They will be destroyed!" Medicine Eye said loudly.

Yellow Eagle ignored him. "I must be honest with you, Sheltowee. Affairs are spinning out of control. Take your family out of the valley. There will be trouble."

Dan'l took a deep breath in. "My thanks for the counsel, Yellow Eagle. But my family will probably not leave Yadkin. And the others neither."

"I understand their feelings," Yellow Eagle said sadly. He took the pipe up, and began cleaning ashes out of it. It was his sign that the meeting was finished.

Dan'l rose, and so did Iron Fist. "May peace come to us in these troubled times," Dan'l said.

"I will pray to the great spirits," Yellow Eagle replied.

Then it was over.

* * *

Later that same day, at Fort Cumberland, a young general arrived with a small entourage. His name was John Forbes, and he was a brigadier, newly promoted. He had come all the way from Boston to replace Colonel Jameson, new commander of the fort. Jameson knew of the visit, but not its purpose.

Forbes was brought into Jameson's office on that sunny late morning by an adjutant who could not hide his curiosity about Forbes's coming. A few moments later Jameson greeted Forbes very formally, and they seated themselves at Jameson's long desk, which had belonged to Braddock. The adjutant left them alone for privacy.

"So." Jameson smiled nicely, leaning back on his chair. He was in perfect military attire, and still had his arm proudly in a sling from his wound at Duquesne. He secretly hoped that Forbes had been sent to appoint him permanent commander of Fort Cumberland, with perhaps a promotion to brigadier. Braddock, he was certain, would have wanted it that way. "Have you come to discuss returning to Fort Duquesne perhaps, General?"

Forbes smiled pleasantly. He was just a bit older than the colonel, and a rather handsome fellow, with a fine-featured face and square jaw. He wore the usual powdered wig, and the red tunic with its gold braid, and a parade sword hung in a polished scabbard at his side.

"Not really, Colonel. I came to discuss the

command of this fort. I thought perhaps some-one at headquarters had told you."

Jameson smiled from behind his desk. He had been right. And they had thought him important enough to send a general to advise him of his new responsibility.

"I'm honored to receive you, sir. I'm glad they've finally understood what an important outpost this is."

"They apparently do," Forbes said blandly. "They've transferred me from the 32nd Foot to come here."

Jameson frowned. "Transferred?"

"Yes, I'm sorry you didn't receive prior notice. I'm to relieve you of command here." He reached into a pocket and produced a paper. "Maybe you'd like to read the orders."

The young colonel was scowling. "Relieve me of—"

"It's all there, in writing," Forbes said.

Jameson scanned the paper, and the scowl deepened. "I'll be damned," he finally said, dropping the paper onto his desk.

Forbes did not mind that Jameson had received the news in this way. He had heard that Jameson was a pompous upstart, arrogant like his old boss. "Is there something wrong, Colonel?"

"I . . . thought the post would be mine!"

"Yours?" Forbes smiled. "Oh, no, Colonel. You're perceived as one of the engineers of the debacle at Fort Duquesne, you see. An action that can only be described as a complete and abject failure."

"Debacle!" Jameson said hollowly. "That's easy to say, for one who wasn't there! To see the unprincipled tactics of the French, and the cowardice of our militia troops!"

"Cowardice?" Forbes said. "That's not the way it was reported to me, Colonel."

The junior officer rose and came around the desk, and for a moment forgot he was speaking to a general. "Reported to you?" he said loudly. "Have you been listening to the likes of that Colonel Washington, damn you!"

Forbes eyed him somberly. "Don't forget your rank, Colonel," he said evenly, quietly. "Get hold of yourself."

Jameson turned away angrily. "Son of a bitch!"

"The consensus is that you're not fit to command, Colonel," Forbes went on now, in a different voice. "You're to leave tomorrow, for Boston."

The colonel returned to his desk slowly, as if in a stupor. He threw himself onto his plush leather chair, and closed his eyes for a moment.

"Boston," he said heavily.

"Boston," Forbes told him. "I'm sure they'll find something honorable for you to do there. If we end up having real trouble with the colonials, maybe you'll even be given a command again. Out of necessity."

Jameson eyed him darkly. "General Braddock picked me personally for his staff," he said. "He had friends in high places. All the way up to the court of King George. And his friends will be my friends. I'll get by in Boston."

Forbes arched his brows. "I honestly hope you do. I'm just relieved you won't be here at Cumberland."

Jameson glared at him. "That makes the feeling mutual, General."

It was early the very next day, in Salisbury, when Dan'l and his family heard of the attack on the Bender farm, only ten miles away. A rider came past all flushed, and yelled that the Shawnee from a neighboring village to Yellow Eagle, mostly renegades who followed their own course, had attacked the farm less than an hour before.

"I'm going!" Dan'l told his father as he jumped aboard a saddled horse.

"Dan'l! Wait for some help!" his father called from the big barn nearby.

"I'm going now!" Dan'l replied, pulling his Kentucky long rifle from its saddle scabbard, looking it over, and thrusting it back in. "I'll be back soon as I can get here, Paw!"

"Be careful, son!"

It was less than a half-hour ride to the Bender place, at a gallop. Dan'l arrived on a hill overlooking the farm with his mount snorting and breathing hard, and looked down on the farm house and outbuildings. The Shawnee were gone, and the place was eerily quiet.

"Oh, God!" Dan'l said.

As he guided the horse on down the grade, he started seeing the results of the attack, and it was awful.

He first came upon the body of a girl child whose blond curls were gone. She had been knifed and scalped. Dan'l felt sick to his stomach.

He moved the horse on. Mrs. Bender lay in a pool of her own blood, not far from the house, her skirts up over her hips, exposing her private place to view, and she had been raped. Probably over and over. Her dress had been ripped open up above and one breast had been cut off, and Dan'l knew it would be cured like a cow udder to make a pouch. She too had been scalped, with the top of her head showing only raw meat. Her throat had been cut from ear to ear.

Dan'l swore under his breath. He moved on up to the house, and there was a boy in his teens riddled with arrows. Dan'l had talked with him about fishing, not long ago in town. Now he would never learn the fine points of that occupation.

Dan'l heard a rider behind him, and whirled with his gun aimed, but it was only the fellow who had ridden past the farm earlier, spreading the news of the massacre.

"Don't shoot! It's just me!" he yelled. His name was Frazier, and he lived alone about a mile to the south. He dismounted and came over to Dan'l, studying the corpses.

"My God! I knew it! I knew what it would be!"

"You're lucky they didn't see you too," Dan'l said.

They went on into the house, and Bender was there. He had been captured and brought in there, and nailed to an interior wall with spikes from Bender's workroom. Then he had been stripped to the waist and disemboweled. It was very messy.

"The goddamn heathens!" Frazier said thickly. "The soulless bastards!"

"We taught them a lot of this," Dan'l said heavily.

"They're butchers! We come in here and treated them just like white folks! Traded with them and lived with them! And look what it got us!"

"These Indians weren't from Yellow Eagle's village," Dan'l said, picking up a dropped piece of belt decoration. "They're the ones south of here. They never did accept us here in the valley. But there'll be more of this. Yellow Eagle has lost control out there at his village. The crazy ones are in power now." He had already reported that fact to the town council, and everybody was arming to the teeth.

"We'll go out there and wipe them all out!" Frazier said hotly. "They ain't doing this to our women and children!"

"You get some help to get this family buried," Dan'l told him. "I'll ride in and tell the council what happened."

"I already got somebody coming, including the law," Frazier told him. "I'll ride with you."

Dan'l was sorry to hear that because of Frazier's excited state. But they mounted their horses and Frazier rode into town beside him. When they got there, Frazier was yelling along the street at the top of his lungs.

"Shawnee at the Benders! They massacred the whole family!"

By the time they arrived at the meeting hall, every man in Salisbury was out on the street, some with guns, fear and hatred in their faces. Several council members were inside the meeting hall, and they also came out, as Dan'l and Frazier arrived at the place.

"What happened, Dan'l?" somebody called out.

"It was the Shawnee from Muddy Creek," he told the gathered throng. "They killed the Benders."

"They scalped the kids!" Frazier put in. "Mrs. Bender was raped! It was awful!"

The crowd reacted emotionally, muttering obscenities among themselves. Dan'l turned to Frazier. "Let me tell it."

Frazier looked at him wildly. "To hell with that! All of us here ain't Indian lovers!"

Dan'l frowned at him. He had not thought that anybody still held his early friendship with some local Indians up to ridicule, especially after Duquesne, and Scotborough.

"I just want it told the way it is," Dan'l said calmly. "All Shawnee ain't the same. If we react to this, we have to make sure we're talking about the right Indians."

"Aren't they all kind of related anyhow, Dan'l?" one of the councilmen said to him.

"Damn right they are!" Frazier yelled out. "I say we get us our guns and go pay them Shawnee a visit! At both places!"

"Revenge the Benders!" somebody from the small crowd yelled.

"Kill the Shawnee!"

"Death to Yellow Eagle and all redskins!"

"Kill every damn one of them!"

Will McAfee came forward from among the several councilmen. He was the one who had recruited Dan'l to go see Yellow Eagle, and who Dan'l had reported back to. "You told me that Yellow Eagle is getting ready to go on the war-path, Dan'l."

"That's right, but—"

"How do you know he isn't behind this? How do you know all of those at the farm were from Muddy Creek?"

"Well, I don't know for certain," Dan'l said. "But I know Yellow Eagle. He don't scalp kids."

"You said yourself," another councilman said, "that Yellow Eagle was being influenced by them savages from up north."

Before Dan'l could reply, a rider came galloping down the street toward them, and reined in amid a cloud of dust. Dan'l recognized him as a farmer from the north end of the valley.

"I just come past the Watkins place! It was attacked by Indians! I saw them riding off. That son of Yellow Eagle was with them!"

Dan'l came up close to him. "Iron Fist?"

"That's the one! Old Watkins got his head bashed in! The cabin was set afire, and there ain't much left of it!"

"What about the woman?" McAfee asked him.

"She's just setting out there on a stump, kind of dazed-like. That grandkid of theirs squalling in her arms."

"They ain't hurt?" Dan'l said.

"Didn't appear to be. I couldn't get her to come in. My missus is going to get her."

"Damn!" Dan'l said. "That sounds like Yellow Eagle, all right."

"Are you satisfied now, Dan'l?" someone asked acidly.

"This is terrible!" McAfee said loudly. "Yellow Eagle must have known about this when you were there with him."

"I don't think Yellow Eagle knew," Dan'l said. "He has people around him who want to run things themselves. I guess we'll never know if he gave his approval."

"It don't matter!" someone called out. "This has got to be answered!"

"He's right, Dan'l," McAfee told him. "We can't let this pass."

"Round up every able-bodied man in the county!" one man yelled out. "Get all our militia boys together! Dan'l here will go, won't you, Dan'l?"

Dan'l hesitated. "Yeah. I'll go."

"We'll wipe out the whole damn village!"

"Run the savages out of the colony!"

"Burn that damn Yellow Eagle at the stake!"

"We'll gather right here at dawn tomorrow," McAfee called out solemnly. "Every man should have a gun and a horse. Today, we have to get the word out. We'll go in force."

Dan'l stood there and listened to the shouting, and realized things were as far out of any real control now as they were in Yellow Eagle's village. It no longer mattered to these settlers whether the raids were directed by tribe leadership, or merely renegade actions. They were past concerning themselves about things like that.

Dan'l left before the crowd had dispersed, and rode on back to the farm. The news had already reached the family, and everybody was concerned. When Dan'l told them he had to ride with the other men on the raid tomorrow, Sarah could not understand why. But Boone knew without asking. He knew that Dan'l didn't want things to get out of hand, and it could make a difference if he were there.

Dan'l hardly slept that night. Two hours before dawn, his father rose with him and helped him saddle a roan stallion they kept for riding. Dan'l checked his rifle out, and shoved it into the saddle scabbard that was part of the mount's irons. It was still a half-hour before daylight when he waved good-bye to the elder Boone and rode off into the dark.

In Salisbury, men were gathering on the main street from all directions when Dan'l arrived. There must have been close to a hundred of

them there, he figured, and excitement rippled
through the morning air like sheet lightning.
McAfee saw Dan'l arrive, and when Dan'l dismounted, McAfee walked over to him.

"I won't be going, Dan'l," he said. "I'm past
the age for this kind of thing. I want you to report back to me. I know you don't want things
to get out of hand, and neither do I. We don't
need a bloodbath here. If you see the hot-heads
taking charge, try to cool them down."

Dan'l nodded, and sighed. "I wish this morning was over," he said heavily.

Frazier, the man who had been first on the
scene at the Bender farm, had taken charge of
the raid, it appeared, and Dan'l was concerned
about that. Frazier was a very emotional fellow,
and he had seen some pretty bad things at the
Benders. At just after dawn, he called the irreg-
ular company together, they all mounted up,
and he led them out of town, with Dan'l riding
just behind him.

It was just a half-hour ride to the area where
the village stood. The raid was to be on Yellow
Eagle alone, and not the Muddy Creek site, because the raiders thought all of it had originated
with Yellow Eagle anyway. The remnants at
Muddy Creek could be dealt with later.

A light fog was just lifting when the Indian
village came into view, across a broad meadow.
The first thing Dan'l noticed as he sat there in
his saddle, with horses neighing all around him
and men whispering harshly to each other, was
that the village appeared very much too quiet.

"Something's wrong," he said to Frazier. They had ridden out to a place in front of the massed riders.

"It looks all right to me, Quaker," Frazier said. He was a tall, lean fellow with hard eyes and a scar across his left ear, from a brawl as a young man years ago. He was breathing shallowly, in anticipation of killing Shawnee.

He turned to the men behind them. "Load up!" he called out.

"Maybe I ought to ride in there," Dan'l said, more to himself than to Frazier.

"The hell you will," Frazier said coldly to him. "If you ain't going to do your share of killing, Boone, just keep out of our way!"

Dan'l gave him a look, but Frazier was already loaded and primed. Each man also had a big knife or saber handy on his belt, because most would get only one or two shots from the clumsy guns. "All right!" Frazier shouted. "Let's kill us some Shawnee!"

In the next moment, they all thundered past Dan'l as he reluctantly primed his rifle. Then he was spurring his mount forward, and galloping in at the tail end of the raiders.

In moments they were all inside the village, racing their mounts through the rows of tipis and hutches, and Dan'l heard a lot of firing ahead of him. He kept looking for the braves of Yellow Eagle, who should have been running from their homes, fitting arrows to bows, and priming long guns. But none of that was happening.

175

As Dan'l focused in on what was really happening, he saw women running from their tipis, holding children, and yelling in Shawnee that they were surrendering to the raiders. But most of the raiders were not listening. Dan'l saw a woman go down, shot through the forehead, brains and blood everywhere, a baby that she had been carrying dropped in the dirt. A horse galloped over the child and crushed it under its hooves. Dan'l saw another woman go down, and another, and then they were being shot down and knifed all over the village. But not one male Shawnee was to be seen.

Suddenly Dan'l understood. He had heard about this tactic from up north. The men had found out about the raid at the last minute, too late to evacuate, so had left the women there when they ran off, hoping the settlers would not kill them. They had obviously been undermanned when the news had come to them.

"Wait!" Dan'l was shouting, as he reined in. He had not fired a shot. "The men are gone! There are only women and children here!"

Many of the men had already figured that out, and had put their guns down. But a few of them were still riding about the village, killing every woman who showed herself, and seeming to enjoy it. Dan'l saw yet another Shawnee woman run past a rider, only to be stabbed in the chest with a long saber. There were babies squalling in front of tipis, and Dan'l saw a couple more dead.

He rode up to the man who had just killed the

woman, and confronted him face to face. "Stop it, damn you! These are not Shawnee warriors!"

"What of it?" the fellow replied, wild-eyed. "They's Injuns, ain't they?"

Frazier sat on his horse nearby. He had shot a woman too, in the first moments of excitement, not really understanding what he was doing. But now he sat there dazed, realizing what was happening.

The wild-eyed one started past Dan'l toward a woman standing at the entrance of a wickiup. Dan'l caught his coat as he rode past, and yanked him off the horse, and it went thundering on down the lane of tipis and hutches. The fellow hit the ground on his back, and then was staring up at Dan'l as if Dan'l had suddenly lost his senses.

"What the hell's the matter with you!"

Dan'l shouted back at him. "We don't kill women and children, damn you!"

Another of the wild riders came up, and aimed a rifle at Dan'l's face. "What you doing, you son of a bitch!"

"Shoot the bastard!" a red-eyed fellow behind him called out. "He's in the way!"

The first rider thumbed the hammer back and re-aimed at Dan'l's head. "So long, Quaker!"

"Don't fire that gun!" Frazier's voice told them.

They all looked, and saw that he had drawn a cavalry pistol and had it primed and cocked, and was aiming it at the head of the man who held the gun. In that moment, Dan'l raised his own gun and cocked it.

"That's good advice," he growled.

Others had seen the confrontation, and the killing had stopped. Men were riding up to them, watching. Some, flushed in the face, looked suddenly dismayed at what had happened, even the ones doing the shooting.

"Hell, take it easy," the man with the rifle said. He lowered the muzzle and rested it on his saddlehorn. "They's just Injuns."

"Hold your fire!" Frazier called out. "Put your weapons away!"

He looked around the village street. There were quite a lot of dead, and it was very bloody. Babies were crying, and other women were moaning in grief outside their homes.

"My God," Dan'l muttered.

"What the hell did we do here!" Frazier said softly.

"Hell, they deserved what they got!" said the man Dan'l had pulled off his horse.

"You're lucky I didn't use this rifle on you," Dan'l said to him angrily.

"Hey, what the hell!" the man replied.

Frazier turned to the gathered force. "All right, they got away from us. They knew we were coming. Let's ride out of this butcher house and go try to find them."

They combed the area until noon, and saw a lot of tracks, but they never found one Shawnee brave. The Indians had outwitted them.

And now they had a real reason to go to war.

They had once again seen the white man at his worst.

Chapter Nine

CALL TO ARMS!
All able-bodied men not yet enlisted in the
Carolina Militia are urged to immediately
report to Sergeant Medford at the Salisbury
Meeting Hall, to respond to BLOODY MAS-
SACRES led by the French in Pennsylvania.
Bring rifle, powder, and lead. Monthly allot-
ment, food, and shelter provided. Reserve
troops await further orders.

Dan'l stood before the bulletin board and
read the flyer for the second time. He had already heard that General Forbes did not share
Braddock's dislike of colonial troops, and was
bent on enlarging the militia for a second campaign against Fort Duquesne. But he had also
spoken with Sergeant Medford on his arrival

back in Salisbury yesterday, and after a back-slapping reunion, had learned that the reserves would not be called up for at least another week.

Medford had also made a request of Dan'l. It seemed that Forbes was having difficulty getting supplies together, and Medford wondered if Dan'l would mind going west on a week-long hunt for camp meat for the troops, to be cut and dried for quick meals with hardtack and chicory coffee. Dan'l had agreed, and was getting ready to leave the next day. His younger brother Squire had obtained the permission of their father to go along, and would receive a portion of the payment received when it came from Fort Cumberland.

Dan'l liked the idea of having Squire along, because the brothers got along so well. Even though he was three years Dan'l's junior, Squire was a rather robust youngster who loved the woods almost as much as Dan'l, and Dan'l had taught him much about the wilderness that Squire had absorbed quickly.

Dan'l turned away from the bulletin now, and found that Corey Ruskin's old friend Nick was standing beside him. Dan'l glanced about to find the ever-present Little Red, but he was not there.

"What the hell do you want, Nick?" Dan'l growled at him. He had never had anything but trouble from those two, and he was in no mood for trading insults with some half-baked overgrown adolescent. Dan'l had become an adult very quickly, through what had happened to him in the past weeks, and especially the raid on Yellow Eagle. It had not been as bad as he thought, but five women were dead, and one child, done in by just a handful of men gone crazy. It was not like at Scotborough, where murder was ordered and performed by the man in charge.

Nick looked somehow different to Dan'l, standing there. His young face was somber, and he looked apologetic. "I done some thinking, Boone," he said.

Dan'l narrowed his eyes on him warily. "I didn't know you could," he said levelly.

Nick let a sour smile edge onto his square face. "I reckon I got that coming. But I ain't here to jawbone with you. I come to say . . . Hell, it was pretty dumb of me and Red to put Jack on you like that."

"I figured it was you," Dan'l said.

"I guess Jack got about what he deserved. But it could of been you."

Dan'l could not believe it. Nick Purvis was actually exhibiting some small concern for him. "If that's an apology, I accept," he said. "Now, I got to go talk to Medford."

"No, wait," Nick said quickly. He looked down. "Red and me, we split company. He wanted to go out and loot the Bender place. I wouldn't do it. We ain't speaking."

"Well, I'll be damned," Dan'l said.

"I'm a changed man," Nick said, averting his eyes. "I'm joining up, Quaker. I just decided."

"The militia?" Dan'l said.

"That's it. You and me will be at Cumberland together this time. Just like you and Corey was before. I know you didn't have nothing to do with his getting hisself killed. That was all horse pucky."

Dan'l looked him over, and studied his eyes. Maybe his face was not as hard as Ruskin's had been. And maybe there was just a hint of understanding behind his eyes.

Dan'l nodded to him. "All right, Nick. I'll be seeing you at Cumberland. You'll probably be lighting out of here early next week."

"And good luck on your hunting trip," Nick told him. Then, surprising Dan'l, he came up close to him. "The valley Indians is talking about that bounty on your head, Quaker. Watch your back."

Dan'l studied Nick's open, frank face. "Much obliged, Nick. I'll do that."

When Nick had gone, Dan'l found that his brief talk with him had somewhat lightened the heavy feeling inside him that he had had since the village raid.

Dan'l got some further instructions from Sergeant Medford before he left town that day, and was glad that his old sergeant would be going back to Duquesne with the troops. That evening before heading out for buffalo territory to the west, he and young Squire and their father sat out on the front stoop of their log house and discussed where the good areas were for hunting south and west of the valley. Then Dan'l turned in early to get plenty of rest.

In that rambling structure there were several bedrooms to accommodate the Boone children, and Dan'l and Squire usually slept in cot beds in the same room. But Squire had decided to sleep out on the porch that night, and Dan'l was in bed alone inside, in a tiny room off the main parlor. He had been asleep for three hours, and was having a small nightmare about Scotborough, seeing all those bloody corpses again, and Ethan tied to that stake, when the small noise came at the open window.

Dan'l slept like a panther. Sounds that many people would not have heard in their waking hours would disturb him and bring him fully awake in seconds—even an unusual odor that did not belong in that time and place. This night he experienced both at the same moment, and when he opened his eyes into a dark room, the Cherokee was standing over his bed with a razor-sharp tomahawk raised over his head.

The things that occurred next went so lightning-fast that it was all over in seconds. The war-painted face above him grew a wild, wide-eyed expression, and the big weapon descended toward Dan'l's face, to split it wide open.

Dan'l rolled instinctively to his right, off the edge of the cot, and the hatchet thunked heavily into the pillow where his head had lain an instant before, making goose feathers fly into the blackness.

Dan'l hit the floor and thrust his hand under

the pillow in one motion, and his hand came out with his own big skinning knife. The Indian pulled the tomahawk out of the bedding and raised it again above his head with renewed vigor. But in that instant, Dan'l turned his whole body and thrust the big knife into the Indian's abdomen.

The Cherokee gasped in abject surprise, his hard eyes widening, his jaw flying open. Dan'l pulled the knife back out, and only then did the Indian cry out in pain, in a hissing outburst. He turned then as if to leave through the window he had entered from, and circled around for a slow moment, then fell heavily to the floor. His leg kicked at the bedpost once, and he was dead.

Dan'l had never gotten to his feet. He lay there on his back now, propped on one elbow, breathing raggedly. In the next moment the door burst open, and Squire stood in the light from the next room.

"Dan'l, I thought I heard something—"

He stared down at the redskin on the plank floor, and swallowed hard. "Good Jesus!"

Dan'l rose. His knife was crimson-stained. He stood in long underwear, but bare to the waist, looking very physical, his long hair wild.

"Just a bounty hunter," he said quietly.

"In our own house, for God's sake!"

"We'll throw him down that dry well out at the back of the property," Dan'l said with such calm that he amazed Squire. "No need waking the others up." He wiped the blade clean on the

Cherokee's loincloth. "Then we'll try to get some sleep tonight."

Up at Fort Duquesne the next morning early, General Henri Duvall had just arrived at his small office when an aide came in with excitement showing in his lean face. Sun slanted in at a narrow window, casting a yellow bar across Duvall's desk.

"Yes, what is it?" Duvall said to his intruder. Duvall had been cleaning an Annely flintlock revolver, a relatively new weapon that held several shots at once, but still required priming for each shot. Duvall had just finished and had laid the pistol on the desk before him. It was an intricately worked, handsomely designed weapon.

"Mon General," the aide began, "I am sorry to report that we have a spy among us."

Duvall rose from his chair. "A spy?"

"Yes, sir. He was overheard asking several men about tactical plans. He came to us just recently, and speaks French with a slight accent. We checked his belongings, and found this."

He handed a small brass disc to Duvall, and Duvall regarded it closely. It had writing on it, and it identified its owner as a Corporal McLean of the British 5th Foot Regiment.

"Sacre bleu!" Duvall hissed out.

"It was caught up in the lining of a jacket he brought with him. I suspect he does not even know he still has it. He had packed some things

186

together, and we think he was intending to leave the fort shortly, to report back to Fort Cumberland."

Duvall's face had grown somber through the report. "Where is this fake Frenchman?" he said in a low voice.

"Waiting outside, General," the aide said. "Under guard."

Duvall pulled himself up to his full height. "Bring him in," he said.

A moment later the wary-looking McLean came into the room, accompanied by the aide and an armed soldier. He looked scared. He stood at attention before Duvall's desk, as Duvall looked him over arrogantly.

"This is the soldier, General," the aide said.

Duvall waved the guard away, and he left, closing the door behind him. The aide stood near the closed door, watching the suspect closely.

"So," Duvall said, coming around the desk. "You are Private Briand."

"Yes, sir," McLean said humbly.

"You are not!" Duvall yelled in his face.

McLean flinched under the verbal attack, but said nothing.

"Do you think you can come here and practice your cowardly sneaking about under our noses, and arouse no suspicion?" Duvall said to him.

"General, I don't understand!"

"You don't understand? Maybe this will clear

things up for you!" He held the brass tag up in McLean's face.

McLean blanched. "I have . . . never seen that before, General."

"Never seen it, you dirty liar!" Duvall fumed. "We found it in your belongings. After you unsuccessfully attempted to obtain classified information from my people. It *is* yours, McLean!"

McLean hesitated, and then sighed heavily. "Whatever you say, General."

"I say what you are!" Duvall said smugly. "A damned spy for that powdered-wig fop at Cumberland now who calls himself Forbes. Isn't it true?"

McLean knew the game was up. He averted his gaze to the floor. "I came to learn information for the British, yes. Your soldiers have done the same. There is no dishonor in it."

"There is cowardice and deception!" Duvall said harshly. "You are a thief, a liar, and a coward!"

McLean, a thin, rather tall fellow with sad eyes, just held Duvall's gaze and said nothing. Duvall went to his desk again, and picked up the pistol and loaded it slowly, taking a cloth and running it over the gun then.

"Did Forbes send you then?"

"I can't say, General."

"How many men is he gathering at Cumberland?"

"I wouldn't know, General."

"When does he intend to foolishly attack this proud fort again?"

"I know of no such plans, General."

"I can take him to the holding cell, General. We will find out what he knows," the aide said from the door.

Duvall primed the pistol, and came back around the desk. "That won't be necessary. I doubt that he knows anything that would help us. It would be a waste of precious time."

McLean relaxed some inside.

"Very well, General. I'll take him under custody, and we'll have a brief court-martial. A lawyer will be down from Pontchartrain next week and—"

Duvall had come up close to McLean again. He now raised the pistol to McLean's face, held it before his left eye, and squeezed the trigger.

There was an ear-ringing blast, the hair on the back of McLean's head blew out, and blood and matter hit the nearby wall, sticking to it wetly.

McLean went tripping backwards, arms flailing, jaw moving as if to utter some exclamation of surprise. He hit the same wall as his brain matter, then slid down it awkwardly, his limbs jerking as he went.

The aide gazed wide-eyed at the new corpse on the floor, then at Duvall.

"As I said, our time is precious," Duvall said, hefting the weight of the gun in his hand. He liked the feel of it, and figured it would be a nice addition to his arsenal of weaponry in battle.

"Yes, sir," the aide said quietly.

"This gun suits me, I believe," Duvall said, turning away from the body as if it were not there. He returned to his desk, laid the gun down, and sat down on his chair. "Haul that thing out of here. And tonight you may clean the wall."

"Yes, General."

The aide went to the bloody corpse, and started to bend over it.

"Incidentally," Duvall said.

"Oui, mon General?"

"This Boone fellow. Why is his head not atop the flagpole outside?"

The aide shrugged. "The word has been spread, General. Maybe we will get lucky, and he will return with General Forbes."

Duvall liked that idea. "Maybe so. But I am waiting, you understand."

"Of course, General."

"Now get this mess cleaned up," Duvall said.

By the evening of that day, Dan'l and Squire were over west near the border of the colony, and had entered the settlement of Dodge's Mill to spend the night.

Before they had left the family house early that morning, they had erased all evidence of the Indian's attack on Dan'l in the middle of the night. Dan'l did not want the family to worry over the incident. But they did confide to Boone Senior so he would know about it. He believed, like Dan'l, that nobody else in the house was in

190

danger. It was Dan'l they wanted, for the bounty Duvall offered, which was 20 British pounds.

Dan'l and Squire had already shot one buffalo, two deer, and a half-dozen rabbits in the area and on the way. Now they hoped to run onto more buffalo the next day, so they could take some big quantities of meat back, and also sell off the hides at the market in Salisbury. The dried meat of a half-dozen buffalo would feed a lot of hungry soldiers on the next march north.

Squire had been allowed to begin drinking hard liquor occasionally, so when Dan'l decided to walk down to the public house from the inn where they had bedded down, he took Squire along with him, having no suspicion that there could be trouble there.

When they arrived at the place, there were four other customers sitting at tables drinking, and a couple of fur traders throwing darts at the rear. They were clothed in Eastern dress, with dark, long-coated suits over frilly shirts, fancy knee leggings, and silver buckles on their shoes. Both men, Dan'l noticed, wore Mortimer pistols in their belts, across their bellies, so they showed past the open coats. They were men who bought furs from people like Dan'l, and then sold them on big markets back east for 200- or 300-percent profit. Most of them were arrogant dandies who looked down their noses at woodsmen, but they were also usually good with guns, so it was best not to have trouble with them.

Men like them, Dan'l knew, never joined the militia or ran for any office. They had no political beliefs, and did nothing to really civilize the wilderness. Their sole concern was profit, and how fast they could get rich.

Dan'l ordered a rum for each of them, and when the server brought it to their table, he recognized Dan'l.

"Hey, aren't you that Dan'l Boone? The one that's killed about a thousand Shawnee?"

A couple of other men at tables glanced over at Dan'l at that remark, and also one of the dandies at the rear.

Squire grinned, and Dan'l frowned. "I'm Boone, all right. But you got your facts wrong, mister."

He put some shillings down, and swigged some of the rum from a warm mug.

"One darn near killed him last night!" Squire said, widening the grin.

Dan'l gave his younger brother a fierce look, and the grin evaporated from Squire's lean face.

"Is that so?" the innkeeper said. "That must be some story!"

"It's all bog smoke," Dan'l said with a scowl.

"Didn't mean to pry," the fellow said. "It's just that folks been talking about you, Dan'l. Clear out here. We hear tell you got that French general so riled he put a bounty on your head."

Dan'l gave him a look. "Ain't you got something to do?"

The server got a hurt look, and turned and left

them. Squire met Dan'l's sober gaze. "Sorry, brother."

"Family business is private, Squire," Dan'l told him. "Don't forget that."

"I didn't mean nothing."

Just as he said that, one of the traders appeared beside their table. He was a little bigger than the other one, but both men were rather big and tough-looking. Dan'l noted with interest the lacy frills on the shirt bodice and sleeves, and the silken look of the pantaloon material.

"So you're Dan'l Boone," the big man said, in a patronizing voice.

Dan'l met his gaze. "You found him," he said.

The trader looked Dan'l over slowly. Dan'l was just average height, but was broadly built and heavily muscled under the rawhides, and had a very athletic look. His face was tanned and handsome, with a full mouth and straight nose. His deep blue eyes looked right through a man to the back of his head, and made some uneasy. At this age he was still unbearded, but he had a shock of long, sandy hair that had a sheen to it, and his hands bore callouses from farming, hunting, and trapping.

"I thought you'd be bigger," the man said. "And older."

"I am older," Dan'l told him. "Inside me."

The trader assimilated that, and now his partner came over to the table. "So this is the great Boone, heh? The one the Shawnee call Sheltowee?"

"He claims to be," the first one said with a

hard grin. "But I heard the real Dan'l Boone was tough. This one don't look tough at all to me."

Squire was looking scared. He noticed the first man had a thin scar that ran across his right cheek, and petered out in the beard of his jaw. The one that had just arrived was a slimmer man, and wore a gold earring in his right ear.

"You oughtn't pay attention to everything you hear," Dan'l said. "Now, will you boys let us drink our rum?"

The hefty man with the scar scowled at Dan'l. "You telling us to skedaddle, hunter?"

"The lad has cheek, by God," Earring offered.

"We don't want no trouble," young Squire put in, jerking a glance toward Dan'l.

"You hear that, partner?" the scarred one said. "These backwoods boys don't want trouble. They don't sound like Indian fighters to me."

"I'll bet this fellow is just calling himself Boone," Earring said. "So people will buy his drinks."

Dan'l looked up at them with a deadly look, and the thing in his chest was awake again. "Why don't you go sell a few squirrel skins to the French, boys? Then you can go buy yourself more of them little-girl shoes with the pretty buckles."

Suddenly the room was as quiet as a tomb. The server edged to the far end of a narrow counter, and two of the other customers rose and quietly left. The other two were back at a rear table. They just watched.

Earring looked quickly at the scarred fellow to see his reaction to the comment of Dan'l, and his partner's face was reddened.

He drew the Mortimer pistol at his belt, and Earring followed suit. The scarred one was breathing rather shallowly.

"I'm going to blow your damned face off!" the big one said in an urgent voice.

Dan'l swigged some more rum. Young Squire sat there wide-eyed, wondering what to do next. Earring aimed his gun at Dan'l too. They did not seem interested in Squire.

"Don't do no shooting in here, boys!" came a plea from the proprietor. "Take it outside!"

"Get up and take it like a man," the scarred one said to Dan'l, ignoring the fellow behind the counter.

Dan'l had been thinking about the predicament. He had known when they left home that there might be moments like this, since he almost never took a long gun into a business establishment. So he had brought an extra weapon besides his hunting knife. It was a ceremonial tomahawk given to him by a Cherokee trader as an offering of good faith, when Dan'l was in his teens. It now hung on his belt, attached by a rawhide thong. He now edged his right hand down to the weapon and released a catch that held it in place.

"Maybe you didn't hear him, hunter," Earring growled.

"You boys ought to think this over," Squire

said in his high voice. "This ain't right."

But Dan'l was ready now. "If you say so, boys," he said flatly.

In the next moment he rose abruptly to a crouching position, and grabbed the table and turned it up on end. The mugs went crashing to the floor, and Earring stumbled backwards a step. Dan'l and Squire fell into full crouches behind the table just as the scarred fellow took aim and fired at Dan'l.

There was a deafening explosion in the confines of the room, and the hot lead smashed into the thick wood of the tabletop just in front of Dan'l's face. Dan'l's arm was already coming up in a wide throwing arc, though, and now he hurled the tomahawk at his attacker. The weapon turned over just once, and buried itself in the trader's forehead, splitting it open.

The trader's mouth flew ajar, and he fell backwards, hitting the floor spread-eagled, all four limbs flailing and thrashing.

Earring was shocked. He quickly aimed his own gun at the now-exposed Dan'l, and the room shook again with a loud shot, as Dan'l rolled away from the line of fire. The lead cracked flooring beside his head. Earring now fumbled to reprime, and Dan'l tried to get at his knife, but was lying on it. He grabbed a broken table leg instead, and just as the second trader aimed at him a second time, he hurled the thick club and it hit the trader in the side of the head.

Earring went down, and Dan'l scrambled to get his legs under him, knowing the gun was still ready to fire. But then young Squire was there, hurling himself on top of Earring, and plunging his own knife into Earring's heart.

The gun fired into the ceiling, harmlessly, and Earring quivered all over and died beside his partner.

As the two other customers watched wide-eyed, the two hunters cleaned their weapons on their victims' silky clothing, and replaced them to their belts. Dan'l threw two coins onto the nearest upright table, glanced toward the pale-faced owner, and started toward the door with Squire.

"That tomahawk ain't bad balanced, but I think I could add some to the handle," Dan'l was saying, as if nothing had happened. "But that blade of yours needs some stone."

Then they were gone out the door. The owner looked over toward the customers who sat frozen in place, and then at the dead bodies on the floor.

"Jesus Christ in heaven! You seen it, boys. You just seen Dan'l Boone in action!"

"Amen," one of them replied.

Chapter Ten

The next day, Dan'l and Squire searched that whole area for buffalo, and found none. But then they rode south, to where Dan'l had found a herd on a previous trip.

Dan'l was riding the roan stallion from the farm, an animal he would come to like and take as his own, and Squire was mounted on a chestnut mare. Both animals had hunting experience, and the stallion had been on two buffalo hunts.

It was almost mid-afternoon when their luck changed. They crested a hill and looked west, and saw the dark shapes in tight formation, for as far as the eye could see. Bulls, cows, and calves, all grazing quietly, as if they could do that until the end of time. Dan'l savored the scene for a long moment; then he and Squire dismounted and crawled on their bellies down the incline, until they were just 50 yards from the close edge of the herd.

They were both sweating and dirt-streaked when they arrived behind scrub cover, rifles in hand. The nearest animals were a little skittery now, and a couple of bulls snorted and looked right at them, but did not see them. Dan'l loaded and primed, and Squire took a bit longer, but was soon ready. Spced in reloading was very important now, because after the first shots, the herd would scatter, and second shots would be at a greater distance.

Dan'l got up onto his knee, and Squire did likewise. Dan'l picked out a big bull quite close to them, and Squire chose a cow that had plenty of meat on it. Dan'l nodded, and whispered, "On three."

The count started then, and both guns roared out in the tranquil meadow. Both targeted animals went down like stones, raising dust.

The next moments were hectic. Buffalo were stampeding in all directions, some coming right at the hunters. Dan'l and Squire were frantically reloading, and it required almost half a minute, including priming. A big cow buffalo came charging right past the brush clump they were kneeling behind, and almost knocked Squire over. Now the nearest animal was a hundred yards distant, and moving. Dan'l raised his gun first, but waited for Squire. They both fired again, the guns making their ears ring. Dan'l's animal went down in a heap. Squire's ran for

50 yards, and then collapsed onto its side.

Suddenly, a large segment of the herd turned and headed right for the shooters, in a frenzied stampede. Dan'l realized that the shooting was over in that moment, and that now they had to think about saving their lives.

"Get down!" he yelled at his brother. "Lie flat behind that log!"

Squire dived behind a fallen log, and covered his head with his hands, and Dan'l flattened himself behind a mound of dirt with brush atop it. In just seconds the herd was all around them, the thundering hooves shaking the ground and drowning out all other sound for miles. The great heads and wide horns looked mountainous to Squire. Hooves thudded beside him and all around him as the buffalo jumped the log that partially protected him. Over behind the mound of dirt, Dan'l felt a hoof tear at his sleeve, and another crashed into dirt beside his head.

Then they were gone, as quickly as they had come, disappearing over another hill behind the two brothers. In a short time they would have forgotten why they were running, and would quiet down to grazing again.

On the meadow before Dan'l and Squire lay the four dead buffalo, scattered over a couple hundred yards. Dan'l rose to his feet, and brushed dirt from his face. Squire got up, badly shaken.

"Damn!" he said in a shaky voice.

"You all right?" Dan'l asked him.

Squire nodded weakly. "I think so."

"Now you see why buffalo are dangerous," Dan'l said. He looked back to the crest of the hill where they had dismounted, and the horses were still there, tethered to stumps, nervous but in place.

"Come on," Dan'l said. "We got some work ahead of us."

They went and got the horses, led them to the nearest animal, the bull Dan'l had brought down, and staked them out there. Dan'l had decided on hunting on foot because he had Squire with him, but sometimes, especially if there were several experienced hunters present, he had ridden into the herd on horseback, firing and reloading as he kept the horse within the running herd, musketballs in his mouth, powder horn on his chest, ramrod clutched against rifle barrel. It was a wild ride, with the sound of hooves so loud you could not hear gunfire, and men had been killed doing it, falling under the plummeting hooves.

The next three hours were spent skinning the four downed buffalo, and cutting big chunks of meat off them. Dan'l skinned head and all because the eastern markets liked them that way. There was no attempt to move an animal to a better spot, to skin it. The big bull they started on weighed over a ton, and you did not try to move that much weight. Dan'l, with Squire's help, slit the skin of the bull all the way down the belly from the throat to the root of the tail, and down the inside of each leg to the knee.

After that he tied a rope to the animal and pulled it onto its stomach by hitching the stallion to the rope. Finally, he got Squire to stake the animal's head to the ground by driving a wagon rod through the nose. Now he was ready to skin the animal the easy way, by using his own mount. He tied a hitch of rope to a thick wad of hide on the back of the neck, fastened the other end to the roan's saddlehorn, and then guided the stallion away and to the rear, and the skin neatly ripped off the corpse as the horse moved away.

Squire had not seen that method before, and he stood in awe as the whole skin came off in one operation.

"I'll be damned," he said, his hands and knife covered with drying blood.

"You learn shortcuts after you done this a while," Dan'l grinned at him.

They did the other three animals the same way, and Dan'l allowed Squire to try one himself. He did it clumsily, but he managed it. Dan'l decided his brother was going to be a fine hunter.

They cut a lot of meat in the next hour or two. They wrapped it in beaver skins, and would let it hang and dry in camp that night. Dan'l also scraped the skins and folded them for carrying back with them. The militia did not want them, but they would bring a good price in Salisbury, and the family always needed good robe-quality furs too.

As they sat on the ground and cut meat off

the last of the animals, Squire began asking Dan'l questions about the war.

"Paw says you got this feud going with some French officer," he said as he cut at a loin with his skinning knife.

Dan'l looked over at him. His hands and clothing were crimson-stained. "You ain't got no concern with the war," he said soberly.

"Everybody's talking about it," Squire said. "Is that Frenchman the one that ordered Ethan's death?"

Dan'l looked over at his innocent face. "How much do you know about that?" he said quickly.

Squire shrugged. "Not much. That's about all."

Dan'l sighed. "Yep. He ordered Ethan's execution. By burning."

"God!" Squire said.

"He was shot before it could happen," Dan'l said, watching Squire's face.

"Good," Squire said. "That's good, Dan'l."

He did not know, Dan'l decided. "That man can't go on living," he said after a long moment. "If somebody don't send him to hell, there ain't no use having one."

Squire looked over at his brother, and studied his face.

"His name is Duvall," Dan'l concluded, rolling the name on his tongue and making a face as if the taste of it was bitter.

"Is that why you're going back with the militia?" Squire finally asked him.

"It's one reason," Dan'l admitted. He took the

wide-brimmed dark hat off his head for a moment, and wiped sweat from his brow.

"Maybe you could use some help," Squire said.

"Huh?"

"I'm old enough, they'd take me."

"The militia?"

"Why not? I want to go, Dan'l. I want to go to Duquesne with you. You saw me in Dodge's Mill. I can handle myself."

Dan'l looked over at that innocent boy's face, and remembered Corey Ruskin being burned alive beside his ammunition wagon.

"Listen to me, Squire," he said somberly. "War ain't no game for kids to play. People die out there on these marches. You ain't old enough."

"I ain't no kid!" Squire said hotly.

"I know that. You can handle a gun, I know. You got a lot of savvy for your age, because of what you done with me. But you ain't no soldier. And you could get killed trying to be one."

"Hell," Squire said, cutting savagely with the knife. "What if Paw said I could go?"

"It wouldn't make no difference," Dan'l said pointedly. "But he wouldn't, you can bank on it."

"Hell," Squire said. But he knew that was the end of it.

They packed all the meat and skins aboard a travois Dan'l made from willow limbs, like the Cherokee did, and the horses took turns hauling it. That night, they camped in a stand of white oak, in a tiny clearing among the trees. They ate dried jerky and hardtack, and drank real coffee. When they were finished, and the sun was setting behind some distant hills, they heard the riders come up into the trees just a short distance away.

Dan'l heard them arrive, and started for his tethered horse, but a voice called out to him.

"Arretez, monsieur!"

Dan'l looked and saw the man in buckskins holding a long gun on him. Squire had just risen from a low campfire, and was also quite some distance from either horse. They both stared hard at the newcomers, seeing there were three in all, all dressed like hunters. They were dismounting from their horses now, and two of them held guns on the Boones.

Dan'l realized that these were French trappers, poaching in territory that was considered British. He shook his head slightly, wondering what else could go wrong on this hunting trip.

"Who are you?" he said easily.

"That is none of your business, *monsieur*," the first trapper replied in accented English. He came forward into the firelight, and he was bearded and rough-looking. His two companions, not as tall but broad-looking, and also bearded, came on past Dan'l and Squire and looked the camp over, and saw the skins hanging from a tree and the chunks of meat skewered on broken limbs.

"Ah," one said in satisfaction.

The tall one and the other one holding a gun came and stood so they flanked the two brothers. The tall one spoke in French to the third man, and he went to his own mount and came back with two lengths of rope. He stepped behind Dan'l and began binding Dan'l's hands together behind him. Dan'l objected.

"What the hell is going on?" he complained.

The fellow made no reply, nor did any of them. When Dan'l was bound, Squire was tied up next. Their feet were left free.

"Go sit down on your ground sheet by the fire," the tall man told them.

Dan'l turned to Squire, and nodded to him that he should obey. They had little choice. Dan'l was blaming himself already for not hearing the intruders earlier. It was because he was so tired from the hunt, he knew. But that was no excuse. Now maybe he had gotten them both killed.

The tall man sat down on a stump across the fire from them, and poured himself a tin cup of coffee and drank of it. One of the others was going through their saddlebags, while the third was looking the meat and skins over. Nobody said anything further to them.

"You can have the skins," Dan'l said to the tall fellow. "Just leave us the meat."

Squire gave him a curious look. The tall man picked up a burning stick from the fire, and threw it at Dan'l. It hit him on the neck as he ducked away, and then fell to the ground beside him.

206

"Damn it!" he growled, feeling the stinging on his neck.

"You will not speak unless spoken to," the tall fellow said.

Squire's young eyes flashed fire. "You'll all go to jail for this!"

The man looking the meat over came and swung the stock of his musket against Squire's head, knocking him over. He saw bright lights inside him, and needles of pain jabbed into his head.

"You bastards!" Dan'l said quietly.

The tall one laughed in his throat, and swigged more of Dan'l's coffee. Squire struggled to sit up again.

The one looking through the saddlebags came over to the fire, too. "They are from Salisbury," he said in French, which Dan'l understood. "I think they're Boones. This one would be the one that was at Duquesne." He gestured toward Dan'l arrogantly.

"Well, well," the tall one said to Dan'l. "So. We have caught ourselves a prize, *oui?*"

"I don't know what you're talking about," Dan'l lied.

"He is talking about the bounty," the fellow who had hit Squire across the side of the head said. "You know all about bounties, is it not so, Boone?"

Dan'l settled down inside himself, and did not respond. He looked over at Squire, and hoped he was all right.

"The skins aren't much," the last man said

again. "But the meat looks good. Then there is their horses, and saddlery."

"The bounty adds up to more than all of that," the tall man said to the others. "This is our lucky night, it seems."

"We can shoot the young one," the man who was looking through Dan'l's saddle wallet said. He pulled out a gun tool and threw it onto the ground. "We can't get anything for him."

The one who had inspected the skins came over and looked down at Squire. He wore an Indian-made belt on his waist, and he was known as Cherokee. He drew a small-caliber military pistol from that belt now, took a moment to prime and cock it, and aimed it at Squire's forehead and squeezed the trigger.

As Dan'l stopped breathing, and Squire sucked his breath in sharply, there was a metallic click from the gun. It had misfired.

Squire began breathing harshly, and Dan'l felt his heart pummeling his chest.

Cherokee swore in French, and examined the pistol. As that happened, the tall fellow came and looked down at Squire. "I don't know. He is a Boone. We might as well take him too. Maybe the army would like two heads to decorate its forts."

"Two are not worth the trouble," the second, brawny Frenchman who had assessed the skins said.

Cherokee's pistol was reprimed. "I agree," he said. "Let us see if this works now." He aimed again at Squire.

The tall fellow stepped over and knocked his arm down. "If we take both in, we will win favor at Duquesne. We may gain an exclusive contract. Put the pistol away!"

Cherokee grumbled some in French, but returned the pistol to his belt. The brawny one threw Dan'l's saddle wallet into the fire. "I frankly do not care to win favor at Duquesne. This is complicated. I would shoot them both and sell their goods at Dodge's Mill. Then we could get back to what we are out here for. Hunting."

The tall man shook his head. "That is exactly why you need somebody to do your thinking for you," he said caustically. "We are heading north anyway. We will sell everything to the military, who pay top prices. The bounty will be a bonus."

Both Dan'l and Squire had sat silent through all of that. Now Dan'l spoke up. "My brother's under bounty too," he said.

They all turned to him. Squire, still recovering from nearly being killed, looked over at Dan'l quizzically.

"Is that right?" the tall fellow said.

"He was at Scotborough with me," Dan'l lied. "Duvall wants both of us."

The tall man turned to Cherokee. "There. You see?"

"I see he is trying to keep his brother alive," Cherokee said flatly.

The tall man nodded soberly. "Perhaps. But we will presume the young one has some value to us. He will have none with a bullet in his head."

The tall hunter ordered Cherokee to tie Dan'l and Squire back-to-back then, with a third rope around their torsos, and after some brief preparations, he and Cherokee lay down on ground sheets, leaving the brawny fellow to keep the first watch over them.

Within a half-hour the two Frenchmen were asleep, and the brawny one was nodding sleepily under a tree not far away. The fire was guttering out, with just coals burning in the blackness. Dan'l and Squire sat back-to-back beside the fire, on the opposite side from the sleepers. A hot coal popped and crackled occasionally, and somewhere in the night an owl hooted out its nocturnal call.

Dan'l had been working on his wrist knot almost from the moment the two hunters had lain down to sleep. Now the rope was finally loosening, and Squire was able to help, pulling down on the rope that was behind him.

The brawny fellow let his head fall down onto his chest. Dan'l struggled openly with the rope for a moment, and suddenly his hands came free. He turned his head and gave Squire a signal to be perfectly quiet.

The man on guard grunted, and his head snapped up and he focused on the Boones. He adjusted the Charleville flintlock that lay across his knees, and took a deep breath. Dan'l waited, like a cougar. Finally the guard settled down again, and his head began nodding as sleep tried to overcome him. His head fell down again, and Dan'l brought his arms forward, found the knot that bound him to Squire, and carefully untied it. The rope dropped to the ground. He quickly turned and worked on Squire's wrist knot. In just moments, they were both free.

The man at the tree had dozed off. The two on the far side of the fire were snoring lightly. Dan'l gestured toward the tall man, and the musket that lay on the near edge of his ground sheet, within his reach. Squire acknowledged him, and edged around the fire. Dan'l turned and crawled soundlessly to the brawny man under the tree, as skillfully as any Shawnee. When he arrived there, the fellow was still dozing lightly. He turned and signaled to Squire, and they both went for the guns at the same moment.

Dan'l snatched the Charleville from the brawny fellow's grasp, and then was on his feet, the guard letting out a small outcry of surprise and coming wide awake. At the fire, Squire had the other long gun in hand and was cocking it. The tall hunter came awake at that same moment.

The next few seconds were bloody. The brawny fellow reached desperately for the pistol at his belt, and Dan'l squeezed the trigger of the Charleville. The yellow explosion ripped the tranquillity of the night, and the lead nailed the Frenchman to the tree. The hunter looked down at his chest, bewildered, and then went stiff.

The tall man uttered an obscenity and reached for the third musket, belonging to the man called Cherokee. Squire fired the tall man's musket and blasted half of his face away.

The last hunter was wide awake now, and sitting up to face his attackers. While Squire quickly tried to reload the musket with his own ball and powder, Cherokee jumped to his feet and went for his pistol, the one he had almost killed Squire with earlier. In just a moment, he would get another chance.

But Dan'l was already charging across the small distance between them, musket in hand. He came through the fire like a charging bull, kicking up hot coals that flew into the black sky, and just as Cherokee got the handgun cocked and was aiming it at Dan'l's chest, Dan'l hit him bodily, knocking him off his feet. They went down together, but then Dan'l was up on his knees and swinging the musket like a club. It came down with great force onto the face of Cherokee, and staved it in just as he fired the pistol. The shot tugged at Dan'l's collar, and then Dan'l was swinging the gun again, connecting with the other man's head. The animal had exploded into him again, and now he was hitting over and over with the long gun.

When he finally stopped, the Frenchman's head was a bloody, pulpy mess.

He rose and stood over the corpse, and threw the big gun down. "What do you think of that bounty now, you bastard!" he gasped out.

Squire came over to the dead Frenchman and

kicked him in the side. "You damned murderer!"

Dan'l looked around. The tall one had lost half his head, and the brawny one was still staring, unbelieving, at his own chest, and seeing nothing. There was blood everywhere.

Squire looked down at his hands, and found that they were shaking. "Damn that Duvall!" he said huskily.

Dan'l walked tiredly over to the tree where the skins and drying meat hung. "They didn't hurt our goods," he said. "We'll take their horses and irons, and I see they had a few skins. We'll sell it all at Salisbury. I'll donate my share to the militia."

Squire caught his gaze. "You can have it all," he said.

"It will help when the war starts up again."

"You sure we ain't in the war now?" Squire grinned.

Dan'l returned it, and clapped his brother on the shoulder. "Come on. Let's drag these bodies out of camp and try to get some sleep. We got a big day ahead of us tomorrow."

Chapter Eleven

Dan'l and Squire made a long trek the next day, and arrived at Salisbury with all of their meat and skins intact. They also had the horses and gear of the French trappers, and gave them over as contraband to Sergeant Medford. Medford praised them for their work, and Dan'l was paid for the meat. The hides were sold later on the open market at Salisbury, and brought good prices.

Later that same day of their arrival, after Dan'l had delivered his younger brother safely home, Dan'l attended a town meeting at the request of several councilmen. The meeting was about to get started when Dan'l arrived. When he walked into the big hall, there was scattered applause from the young men present. Dan'l nodded to them, but otherwise ignored it.

The council, consisting of seven men, sat at a table on a raised platform at the head of the room, and other citizens sat on straight chairs throughout the room. Dan'l took a seat about halfway back, and noted that Nick Purvis was nearby. Nick nodded to him, and he returned it.

The head councilman was a man named Atkins, and he knew the Boone family well, and had always liked Dan'l. He stood now, behind the long table, and announced Dan'l's arrival.

"As you see, gentlemen, Dan'l Boone has just arrived. I hear he's brought a lot of dried meat in for the militia, and I think we owe him a special thanks."

There was general applause now, and Dan'l was embarrassed. He rose briefly. "It waren't nothing at all," he said. "Just plain hunting, and young Squire did a lot of it."

Atkins sat back down. "Dan'l, it'll be a few days before you're called back to active duty, according to Sergeant Medford. Some of the boys here are wondering if we should mount another raid on Yellow Eagle's village. If they did, they'd want you to lead it."

There was some murmuring of approval of the idea, in the assemblage. Nick was one of those voicing his agreement. Dan'l was still standing. He turned to look at some of the faces present, and saw that they were mainly young men who had always mistrusted the local Indians, and who wanted to get rid of them for

215

good. A couple of them had killed women on that other occasion.

"They'll hit us pretty soon!" one of them said loudly now. "We might just as well go after them first!"

Dan'l sighed heavily. "You want to kill another couple of squaws, Daniels?"

The mood of the room changed. There was some low muttering, and Atkins gaveled the room quiet.

"All right, let's have order. I know Dan'l was rightly upset about what happened that other time. Nobody here wants to see women and kids caught up in the fighting, not even Daniels, I'm sure. If we went again, Dan'l, with you leading the raid, I don't think that kind of thing could repeat itself."

"That's right," somebody said.

"We'd make sure the braves hadn't snuck off this time," came another voice.

"You boys talked about it too much before," Dan'l said, slowly. "Word got back to Yellow Eagle. That ain't the way to fight no war. Ask Sergeant Medford."

"We learned our lesson the last time," a young man said.

Dan'l looked over at him. He was sitting just beyond Nick. Nick had not said a word.

"We went in and just started shooting, not caring what we was shooting at," Dan'l told them. "I heard from a Cherokee friendly that one of them women was the squaw of Iron Fist. He's still mourning her loss. While that's going on, you think we got the right to go in there again? You want to prove to the red man that we're just savages, worse than them?"

"They killed the Bender woman and her baby!"

Dan'l turned to the fellow who had called out. "That wasn't directed by Yellow Eagle, and you know that. That was some Muddy Creek renegades."

"What the hell's the difference!" somebody else called out to him.

"It might not make no mind to you," Dan'l retorted. "But they ain't all the same to me."

"Maybe you known them too well," came another voice.

"Now, now, boys," Atkins said from the council table. The other council members, most of them older men, had not spoken a word. "We all know Dan'l realizes where his loyalties lie. And a lot of us in this room have befriended an Indian or two in our time. You all know how well Dan'l fought at Duquesne. I'd guess he had to take down an Indian or two there."

"Hear, hear," an old councilman put in.

A farmer from Dan'l's end of the valley stood up. "Anybody says words again this boy ain't hardly right in the head." He looked around the assemblage, scowling.

"That's damn right," Nick Purvis agreed.

Dan'l looked over at him, surprised.

The farmer continued. "I think we leave it up to Dan'l whether it's time to make a move. He knows the situation better than any of us here."

A couple of them voiced their agreement with that. Up at the council table, Atkins focused on Dan'l. "All right. Dan'l, what do you say?"

"I don't think Yellow Eagle's showed his hand yet," Dan'l said slowly. "Maybe he'll play a waiting game. If any of you boys want to fight Indians, get in the militia and go to Port Duquesne with us. You'll get a bellyful."

"The new recruits is leaving tomorrow!" Nick suddenly said.

Dan'l's answer was obviously not what a lot of those present wanted to hear. There was a lot of grumbling throughout the assemblage.

"Well, the council can accept that, for now," Atkins announced to the room, after conferring with his colleagues. "Any big disagreements?"

"I think we're making a big mistake, just sitting on our hands and waiting," the one called Daniels said. He rose and stormed out of the building. A couple others followed him, but most accepted the council's decision.

Several minutes later, the meeting dispersed.

That same afternoon, up at Fort Duquesne, General Duvall was preparing for a second campaign against the fort, by Braddock's successor. His troops were receiving target practice every day, even on Sundays, and were being trained in hand-to-hand combat. Duvall had also sent officers to the village of Chief Blackfish, to train his braves in the use of the musket. Duvall was resolved to defeat the Fort Cumberland garrison so finally that he would never have trouble from that direction again.

Duvall had a map of the surrounding area spread out on his desk, studying it for tactical advantages, when his aide came in, the same one who had brought the spy McLean to him a few days before.

"There is a messenger, General."

"What?" Duvall said, straightening up from the map. "From whom?"

"From General Forbes, sir. He came under a white flag."

"A white . . ." Duvall looked puzzled. "Do you mean, an Englishman?"

"Yes, sir. From Fort Cumberland. We almost shot him when he rode up to the gate."

"I'll be damned," Duvall said, musing, furrowing his almost transparent brow. His long face grew a curious look. "How quaint!"

"Shall I bring him in, sir?"

"Yes, by all means," Duvall said, coming around the desk expectantly.

A moment later a British corporal was ushered in, in proper military attire despite his hard ride. His red uniform was immaculate, his buttons all polished brightly. He saluted smartly.

"General Duvall," he said.

Duvall came and looked him over. He despised all Englishmen, particularly the ones wearing the uniform of King George. "And your name?" he asked in good English.

"Ashburton, sir. Corporal Ashburton." He had been hand-picked by one of Forbes's top aides because of his superior record. He had not been with Braddock on the first campaign, and had no idea what kind of man he would be delivering his message to.

Duvall looked him over arrogantly. "And you have a message from your general?"

"Yes, sir."

"Well, where is it?"

"It is not written down, sir. I must speak it to you."

"Well, then do it, you fool!" Duvall said curtly.

The corporal's face flushed slightly. "The message is that reparations must be paid for unwarranted attacks on English settlements in this area. If such can be arranged, it may be that we can negotiate the future of Fort Duquesne."

Color rose slowly into Duvall's usually rather pallid face. "Reparations?" he said icily. "Negotiate my fort's future?"

"That is the message, General," the redcoat said.

Duvall thought to himself that Forbes was counting his victory before any battle had even been fought.

"May I take a reply back to General Forbes?" the corporal asked him.

Duvall glared at him, very angry suddenly. "Yes, you may, Corporal. Tell him he should remember Braddock. Tell him, 'Calamities often come to the English in bunches nowadays.'"

The soldier stood there. "Is that all, General?"

"Yes, damn you, that is all!" Duvall said. He turned back to his aide. "Arrange for this man to receive twenty lashes before his departure."

"General?" the aide said.

"For bringing this arrogant message here!" Duvall said emotionally.

Shock crept onto the redcoat's face.

"He may not be able to ride after twenty lashes, General," the aide said to Duvall.

"I don't care if he has to crawl back to Cumberland," Duvall grated out now. "See to it."

The corporal was breathing shallowly. "General Forbes will not like this, General."

Duvall allowed a harsh smile to move his narrow face. "Good," he said.

Dan'l was still having bad dreams. That night at home in bed, he tossed and turned, and kept seeing the women of Yellow Eagle, lying in their own blood, their bodies ravaged by hot lead. He woke up twice in a sweat, wishing the night was over. He also was sleeping more lightly now, because of the nocturnal attack on him by the Cherokee renegade. Sergeant Medford had advised him that Dan'l and other reserve militiamen would be heading back to Fort Cumberland in a few days, and Dan'l wished they were already gone. He could do a little more hunting locally for Medford, but there was nothing else to do but wait.

At least, that was what he thought.

After that restless night in his own bed, he and the family received a surprise the following morning.

It all happened about a half-hour after dawn,

when Sarah had eggs frying in the kitchen and Squire Senior had just returned from milking in the barn. The family was gathering at the long kitchen table. There were Dan'l's two younger brothers, Squire and Edward, both just in their teens, his older sister Elizabeth, and little Baby Hannah, in addition to Dan'l and his parents. Dan'l had just come into the kitchen, and was standing and drinking a hot cup of coffee when Boone came in from the barn.

"I could of swore I heard something up on the hill back of the house," he said to Dan'l. "I wonder if that bear cub is back, ready to cause us more trouble."

Dan'l turned warily to his father, and Squire, seated at the table, watched his brother's face. Elizabeth was helping her mother make breakfast, and Edward and Hannah were waiting to be served, Hannah on a special chair, making a fuss because she was hungry.

"What kind of noise, Paw?" Dan'l asked him.

Boone hunched his broad shoulders. "Just a rustling, I guess. It waren't much."

Dan'l put the coffee cup down, went to the nearby window, and unlatched a shutter and shoved it open. Cool outside air flooded in, and he peered into the dusky dawn.

"They ain't no bird sounds," he said.

Everybody turned toward him. He squinted down, looking out toward the hill, and thought he saw a shadow move out there.

"Paw, brothers. Maybe you better get the guns, just in—"

222

An iron-tipped arrow hissed in through the opening, sliced a cut on Dan'l's right ear as it flew past, and then narrowly missed Elizabeth and Squire, who had stood up, as it traversed the entire room and crashed into dishes stacked on a shelf on the far side.

Dan'l slammed the shutter closed. "Shawnee!" he yelled.

The next moments were bedlam. Chairs overturned, a skillet fell on the floor, women screamed. The male Boones rushed to gun racks, and loaded long rifles. Outside, there were war whoops of Shawnee, and they were riding in circles around the house, firing guns and arrows.

"Elizabeth! Sarah! Get in the big bedroom!" Boone shouted at the women.

Sarah had already grabbed little Hannah, and now she obeyed her husband's command. But Elizabeth stood firm.

"I can shoot a gun, Paw. You taught me."

Boone hesitated. "All right. Dan'l, get her that small-caliber musket off the wall there!"

Dan'l loaded the gun for Elizabeth, and then opened up three windows of the long house so Edward and Squire could respond to the attack. He and his father stood at the kitchen window, and began firing at the riders outside. Light was springing into the sky, and Dan'l could see a couple of Shawnee that he recognized, and one of them was Iron Fist, Yellow Eagle's heir apparent. Iron Fist was wearing the seven feathers of a chieftain, and Dan'l realized immediately he had taken leadership of Yellow Eagle's people, and had decided to lead them against the valley settlers, urged on by the advisors from the north, where Duvall was wreaking havoc with Blackfish's warrior army.

Dan'l had now fired twice, and knocked two riders from their ponies. Gunfire split wood beside his head, and arrows were flying and thudding into the house, some with flaming tips. Dan'l could see the nearby cornfield now, and Shawnee were trampling the growing crop, destroying it. They had also set two outbuildings on fire.

Elizabeth came running into the kitchen. "I hit one! I need more ammunition, Dan'l! Where is it?"

"No, put it down!" Dan'l told her. "Bring lead and powder to your brothers and Paw! Now!"

His father was reloading, next to him, when a Shawnee fired at him from just outside the window and struck him in the left shoulder. He was spun off his feet, and hit the floor hard, near Elizabeth. She screamed loudly. "Paw!"

"I'm . . . all right!" he replied. "Get Dan'l some powder!"

Another arrow, flaming, shot in through the same window and sizzled past Elizabeth so close she could feel the heat from it. It thudded into a wall cabinet, and she went and pulled it out, dousing the fire with her apron.

Dan'l had reloaded again, and shot another Indian off his mount. Iron Fist came into view, saw the shot, and turned his mount to face

Dan'l, who was busy reloading. Iron Fist, who had played with Dan'l as a small boy, now raised his arm defiantly, with a lance in his fist, and shouted something unintelligible at Dan'l, then hurled the lance right at his head. Dan'l ducked low, and the long weapon hurtled past him and into the interior, impaling itself into the kitchen table.

At other windows, both young Squire and Edward had fired into the attackers. Squire had killed one Indian, and Edward had wounded another. But there were too many of them out there. Dan'l was worried that soon they would be inside.

Just as he figured things looked blackest, though, Iron Fist yelled a command, and the Indians started riding off, firing last shots as they went.

A few more shots followed them from the house, and then it was over. Everybody inside just stood at the various windows and watched them disappear over the hills in the distance.

Then Boone yelled at his family. "The fires!" he called out.

While Sarah and Elizabeth tended Boone's shoulder wound, which was not serious, Dan'l and his brothers raced out to the barn and two outbuildings. A fire that had started at the barn was quickly doused, but one outbuilding was lost. No serious fire had been started at the house.

Dan'l had blood on his collar from his ear, but it was just a scratch. He helped the women tend his father, and soon Boone had a thick bandage on his shoulder, and young Squire had ridden off to Salisbury for the local doctor.

"The council was right!" Sarah said tearfully, clutching Hannah to her, as they all sat around the kitchen table later. "We can't trust the valley Indians no more!"

Dan'l shook his head. "If I didn't tell them not to go after Yellow Eagle, this might not happen."

His father looked over at him. Elizabeth was trying to clean up the kitchen, and young Edward was still studying the nearby landscape through a window.

"This waren't your fault, Dan'l," Boone told his son. "We didn't have no reason to go there till now. You done the right thing. It's Iron Fist that's got to live with this. Not you."

"I was figuring what was in Yellow Eagle's head," Dan'l said. Blood was now caking dry on his ear. He looked at his father's bandage, and saw the crimson stain coming through the layers of cloth. "But it's Iron Fist we got to deal with now. It's a whole different thing."

"They'll go now," Boone said.

Dan'l caught his look. "And I'll go with them."

"Oh, God!" Sarah said.

There was a second big town meeting that afternoon, when word got out about the attack of the Shawnee. Two other farms near the Boones had been hit too, and two men were dead.

The settlers were up in arms.

"Now what do you say about your Shawnee friends, Boone?" one young hot-head called out to Dan'l after the meeting had begun.

Dan'l sat at the rear of the seating, and he could see a lot of hostile faces glaring at him.

Atkins pounded a gavel for order. A couple of the council members were absent, because they were afraid to leave their homes.

"Now there's two men dead, and your own daddy wounded!" another man said loudly.

"Now, boys," Atkins calmed them. "Dan'l advised us based on what he knew at the time. He couldn't know about Yellow Eagle."

They had had news, just before the meeting, that Yellow Eagle was dead. He had apparently had an unexpected heart attack, and Iron Fist had been elected the new chief of the valley Shawnee. His father's death had hardened him even more, it was reported by a Cherokee friendly, and he had declared war on all settlers in the Yadkin Valley.

"I'm sorry it worked out this way, boys," Dan'l said, standing to address the gathering. It was mostly young men, with a few older males and a few women. Most of them had their guns with them. "Iron Fist was always more of a fighter than his paw. I reckon he wants his land back."

"*His* land!" somebody said heatedly. "This valley was just a damned wilderness when we come here! Now we got enough crops going to feed us *and* the damned red man!"

"We got boys out rounding up every available manjack in the valley!" a robust young man told

227

Dan'l. "We're going tomorrow, whether you come or not!"

Dan'l set his jaw. "Oh, I'm going," he said.

"You by God better not get in our way, Boone!" an older man told him. "We're going to kill us some Injuns. We're going to wipe them out, by Jesus!"

There was a chorus of assents, and Dan'l waited until it had all died down, then addressed the council.

"The Shawnee deserve to be paid back. But they don't deserve what I saw the last time we went there. We don't want to act worse than them we think of as savages."

"I think the council can agree with that," Atkins said to him. "Any objections?"

There was some minor grumbling from the gathering, but nobody spoke up.

"Then I say we go teach Iron Fist a lesson," Dan'l concluded.

There was an outburst of boisterous approval, and cheering. When it subsided, Dan'l spoke one more time.

"You can't talk about this with no one outside this room, except maybe your wives," he said. "We got to keep this quiet this time, till it happens. We ought to leave in the night, so we're there before dawn, in cover of dark."

More sporadic exclamations of agreement.

"Then I'll see you all here tomorrow morning," Dan'l said. "Say, about four?"

That was fine with all concerned.

The plans were made.

Dan'l did not sleep much that night. He told his father and young Squire why he would be rising at three a.m., and both of them decided to go. Dan'l had to argue with his father for over an hour, reminding him how important he was to Sarah and the children, until finally Boone relented, but only because his shoulder wound had not healed.

Young Squire told Dan'l he was going no matter what Dan'l and their father wanted, and it was only when Dan'l advised him that he would prevent him physically if he had to that Squire gave it up. Dan'l told them that they were both needed to defend the farm anyway, and that one soldier in the family at a time was enough. In fact, he reasoned, if the attack on Iron Fist was not successful, he might not be able to go off to Fort Cumberland. If the family remained in any substantial danger, his first duty was to them.

Getting-up time seemed to come about a half-hour after Dan'l went to bed that night, and then he was dressing hurriedly and getting his Kentucky rifle and ammunition ready to go. By four, he was in Salisbury, and joining the milling throng there in front of the Meeting Hall.

Dan'l was surprised at the number of men who came. It was twice the size of the last vigilante group that went on the Yellow Eagle raid, and they were all armed to the teeth. Some men had three guns of varying kinds, so they could get as many shots in as possible before having to stop and reload.

Since Dan'l knew the routes that would attract less attention, it was agreed that he would lead the raid, and he did not like the responsibility. He could depend on militia reserves to fight with some discipline, but new recruits like Nick Purvis were already gone off to Cumberland with Sergeant Medford, and many of the others were just farmers with their own individual ideas of how to fight an Indian war.

This time they approached the village from the far side, away from Salisbury, and it was plain from the beginning that they had succeeded in surprising the Shawnee on this occasion. The braves' horses were all tethered in a corral at the north side of the settlement, and there was a sleepy, quiet look about the place. They had arrived while it was still dark, and the only sounds from their group were the neighs of their mounts, as they sensed the excitement in the air.

The men wanted to go in immediately, but Dan'l held them up. "We want to see what we're shooting at this time," he told them. "And we want to see who's shooting at us, and from where."

Patience had almost run out when light finally flooded slowly into the eastern sky, behind them. "Come on, Boone!" a farmer whispered harshly into his ear. "Their sentries will spot us pretty quick now!"

Dan'l agreed. "Yes. Let's go in."

Upon a hand signal from Dan'l, the company of riders, over a hundred men in all, spurred their mounts and thundered into the village for the second time.

This time it was very different. A sentry saw them coming, and let out a signal cry, and suddenly the village was alive with braves as they rode in, and there was heavy firing on both sides.

The only thing Dan'l had seen that was comparable to the slaughter that ensued was at Fort Duquesne, and at Scotborough. This, though, was the opposite of Scotborough. This time it was the settlers who were wreaking havoc on the Shawnee. Guns roared, arrows sliced through the air, and tomahawks flew to their human targets. The gunsmoke was so thick after the first few moments that it was difficult to breathe in it. Shawnee were going down all over the village, and settlers were being knocked off their horses and sliced up with sharp blades, and their skulls were being split open.

But it was the Shawnee who were suffering most, because they had been caught off guard by the attack. Settlers avoided going after women this time, because of Dan'l, but a few were hit. Dan'l killed an Indian every time he fired, and like many of his comrades, had to dismount finally to be able to reload with less awkwardness. When he got on the ground, though, he was more vulnerable from all sides, and had to defend himself from vicious attacks by several Shawnee, clubbing them down with the stock of his rifle.

After the first few minutes, it was clear that

231

the Shawnee were being overwhelmed this time, and many began running. They started disappearing into a woods behind the village, a few at a time, and the ones who could not escape were losing heart. It was becoming a slaughter.

Dan'l kept looking for Iron Fist, but could not immediately find him. Then, just after he had given up on reloading the rifle and had begun to fight hand-to-hand with his hunting knife, shoving it into the belly of an attacking brave, Iron Fist came out of nowhere.

Dan'l saw him hurtling through the air at him, big and magnificent, war paint frightening, muscular torso gleaming with a fine dew of sweat. He had a fancy ceremonial tomahawk in his hand and was swinging it toward Dan'l's head.

Dan'l caught the hand and then went down under the brutal assault. When they were children, he and Iron Fist often wrestled in play, and they were about equal in physical strength. Now, rolling on the ground again with Iron Fist, Dan'l wondered how it had come to this. Iron Fist rolled on top of him, anger flashing in his dark eyes.

"You killed our women, Sheltowee! Now you must die!" he snarled in Shawnee between his teeth.

"It was not I who killed your women!" Dan'l gritted out, "I tried to stop it! But you attacked my family, at our home, where we received you as friends!"

"The days of friendship are gone!"

Iron Fist broke free of Dan'l's grasp, and brought the hatchet down. Dan'l ducked away, and the blade buried itself in the ground beside his head. A brave came running up, and stood over them, and aimed a lance at Dan'l's chest.

"No!" Iron Fist yelled. "Go away!"

The perplexed brave stood there for a moment, then turned and re-entered the fray, running toward a mounted settler.

"It is you and me, Sheltowee!" Iron Fist grated out, as he retrieved the hatchet from the hard ground.

Dan'l broke Iron Fist's grip on his right hand, and swung the long knife at the Indian's throat, but Iron Fist blocked the blow with the tomahawk. They rolled over and over again, kicking up dust, grunting and sweating. Finally Dan'l landed on top, and he had Iron Fist pinned to the dirt. With his strong right arm, he slowly brought the point of the knife's blade down toward Iron Fist's heart.

A settler rode up, still mounted, and aimed his musket at Iron Fist's head.

"Stop!" Dan'l yelled.

The fellow shrugged, aimed the gun at an onrushing Indian, and shot him down. Then he was defending himself from another attack.

Iron Fist grinned, but then the grin slowly disappeared as Dan'l's strength edged the blade toward his chest. When it arrived there, Dan'l stopped. Around them, the fighting was about over. The reamining Shawnee had surrendered to the settlers, and Iron Fist looked about and saw what had happened.

His handsome face became straight-lined. "Go ahead, old friend. Kill me."

Now several settlers came and stood around them, waiting to see the end of the struggle between them. They were all carrying primed rifles.

Dan'l looked down into the face of Iron Fist.

"Kill me, so I may join my ancestors in honor, and look my father in the eye!"

"Hell, let him up!" a settler called out in sour disdain. "We'll kick his ass out of here along with the rest of them! This valley is ours, by God!"

Dan'l saw the look in Iron Fist's face. There was nothing left for him now but humiliation. His eyes pleaded with Dan'l.

Dan'l shoved the knife on into his heart.

Iron Fist's body stiffened in Dan'l's grasp, and then relaxed in the rictus of death.

Dan'l drew the blade back out, and looked at it as if he had never seen the weapon before.

"Jesus!" someone muttered.

"I'll be damned!"

When Dan'l rose off Iron Fist, the man nearest to him was surprised to see moisture in Dan'l's eyes.

"Now let's get these braves rounded up," Dan'l said in a cracking voice.

The settler beside him nodded. "Whatever you say, Boone," he said quietly.

Chapter Twelve

During the next week, Dan'l and other settlers escorted the remaining Shawnee out of the Yadkin Valley. Dan'l was part of the operation for only three days, however, because his reserve unit had been called back into action, and he was obliged to return to Fort Cumberland.

Word spread quickly about Dan'l's killing of Iron Fist, and some took it all the wrong way. Radical elements of the settlers, who thought the only good Indian was a dead one, came up to Dan'l in his brief couple of visits into Salisbury, and made attempts to befriend him, and were surprised when they received a cold snub from him.

The day before he was to leave for Cumberland, when he was getting his gear ready for his departure, Dan'l received a surprise visit from an old friend, John Findley. Findley was the soldier who had riveted Dan'l's attention with stories of the wilds of Kentucky, on that first march to Duquesne.

He appeared in the yard on a tattered-ear mule that morning, while Dan'l and his father were out beside the house, splitting cut lengths of wood for their two fireplaces. Dan'l looked up from his work and recognized Findley immediately.

He wiped a hand across his brow. "Well, what do you know!"

Findley, looking half-bear and half-man, climbed off the mule with a grin. He wore a coonskin cap and rawhides, and carried a long gun slung over his shoulder. Squire Boone focused on him with wary interest, rubbing his healing shoulder.

"Morning, Dan'l. Glad to catch you here."

Dan'l went over, caught Findley's hand, and pumped it hard. "Damn, I thought I'd never see you again, John!" He turned to Squire Boone. "Paw, this is John Findley, the feller I talked about. He's been to Kentucky."

Boone offered his hand, and Findley shook it. "Pleased to meet up with you, John," Boone smiled. "Dan'l here seemed plumb taken with you when he come home from Duquesne."

"It's Kentucky he's taken with." Findley grinned.

"Can you stop in for a late breakfast?" Dan'l asked him. "Maw's got some eggs left in there just awaiting."

236

Findley liked that idea. "Can't say I want to turn that down," he said.

Inside the house, Sarah and Elizabeth greeted Findley warmly, and fixed him some eggs and buttered bread, while Dan'l and his father sat down to a hot cup of coffee. Young Squire was in town, and Dan'l was glad. He did not want his younger brother's head filled with wondrous tales of distant places just yet. After the men got settled down to the kitchen table, Sarah and Elizabeth discreetly disappeared into another part of the house, so the men could talk man talk.

Findley put the breakfast down with dispatch, while Dan'l and Boone watched him eat. In between mouthfuls, Findley would ask how things were in Salisbury, and they mentioned recent developments with the Shawnee.

Findley finally finished, and wiped a sleeve across his mouth. He was wearing a full beard now, and his hair was wild, and Dan'l liked the looks of him. He had left his rifle out on the mule, but he still wore two skinning knives on his belt, one on each hip.

"I just come back from Kentucky, Dan'l," he said then. "It was even better than before."

"I hear tell there's more game than a man can aim a rifle at," Boone Senior said.

Findley looked over at him. "You can't have no idea, Mr. Boone. One day I found myself in the middle of a buffalo herd so big I couldn't see the edge of it in any direction. A man could get rich just selling hides and robes. A few has

237

tried, but ain't none of them come back. The Shawnee defend the area ferociously."

"You have any trouble?" Dan'l asked him.

Findley looked at his eager face. "There was four of us started the hunt. It was only me what come back."

Boone Senior gave Dan'l a look.

"They attacked our camp one night," Findley said. "A half-dozen of them. I killed one before I saw we was overwhelmed. I slipped into the woods and they lost me. Later, I could hear them killing the last two of my group. There was a lot of yelling."

They were all silent for a moment.

"When I come back the next day, the bodies was still there. Except for the heads."

Another long silence.

"There was other parts cut off too. Before they killed them. Well, I was just glad I skedaddled."

Squire Boone looked over at his son, but said nothing.

"It's Indians like that, Dan'l, that Duvall is recruiting," Findley added after a moment. "Hell, I ain't going back in there for a while. The French is got them all riled."

"What's next for you, John?" Dan'l asked soberly.

"Oh, I'm heading into Tennessee. I got some money behind me this time. Some people what want to buy land out there. I thought you might want to come along."

Dan'l looked at the table.

His father just sat there, hoping that his son would accept the invitation. He did not like the idea that he was heading back to Fort Cumberland the next day.

"I'd like to, John. I really would."

Findley hunched broad shoulders. "Well?"

"But I got to go back to Duquesne."

Findley sighed. "It's still Duvall, is it?"

"It's still Duvall. Us Boones don't forget the killing of kin. Ain't that right, Paw?"

Boone laced his thick fingers together, on the tabletop. "I know I told you that once, Dan'l. But I waren't talking about something like this. You got to fight a whole army to get to Duvall. I say, leave him to the Devil."

"With all due respect, Mr. Boone"—Findley smiled wryly—"I think maybe he *is* the Devil."

Dan'l regarded his friend balefully.

"I heard some things when I come past there," Findley went on. "He just about wiped out settlements in western Pennsylvania and Ohio. English settlements, that is. He's talking about driving all of us into the ocean. You have to hand it to him, he's got grit."

Dan'l gave him a cool look.

"Well. I mean, if the Devil's got any due."

"I hear tell General Forbes will be different," Dan'l said to them. "I'm counting on that."

Findley rubbed a hand through his beard, scratching and scraping in it. "Forbes sent a courier to him the other day. I heard it from a friendly."

"What for?" Dan'l asked.

239

"Word is, he wanted to talk reparations. But Duvall wouldn't have none of it."

"Good," Dan'l said quietly.

"The bastard punished the courier," Findley added. "Sent the poor devil back to Forbes half-dead."

Dan'l sat there and absorbed that, and felt the old anger eating at his insides. "That demon from hell!" he said.

"I reckon he'd like eventually to take Fort Cumberland," his father put in.

Dan'l looked up. "Sergeant Medford said he tried to get more troops down from Detroit. To get up to regiment strength. But he ain't convinced nobody he needs them."

"If they ever give that bastard all he wants," Findley conjectured, "he'll be down on the colonies like locusts on a cornfield."

"The man is a menace," Boone said to them. "But that don't mean he's your personal responsibility, Dan'l," he added.

"I thought of getting out from the militia," Dan'l admitted. "When Iron Fist come that day. I figured maybe I was needed more here than at Duquesne. But the Shawnee ain't no threat here in the valley now."

"You can do as much for Carolina going with me," Findley argued, "as going back north under another British officer, maybe to get yourself killed because of brass foolishness."

"I told him the same," Boone said, looking older than usual sitting there.

"The colony can get along without trekking

for a while," Dan'l said to Findley. "Not that I think you're doing wrong to go. But for me, John, I ain't got no choice. As long as that killer is alive, this family is dishonored."

Findley grunted. "Even if Forbes takes Duquesne, they'll end up in some gentlemen's agreement, Dan'l. And Duvall will be sent back to Detroit some kind of French hero. If there is such a thing."

When Dan'l spoke again, they both noticed the change in his face, and particularly his eyes. "If that happened, I'd go there after him," he said slowly. "I'll follow him back to hell, if I have to."

"Well," Findley said, glancing at Dan'l's father. "I guess it's settled, then."

"I reckon so," Dan'l told him.

That same afternoon, Brigadier General John Forbes called into his new office the recently promoted Colonel Luther Dunbar, who was now the commandant of the combined Carolina and Virginia militias, the position George Washington had held under Braddock on the first Duquesne campaign.

Dunbar was an older man than Washington, but had served under him on that same campaign, and had battle experience. He had stood with Washington in criticizing Braddock's tactics in combat, and now had a much more sympathetic ear in General Forbes.

"You wanted to speak with me further about our upcoming campaign, Colonel," Forbes said to him after they had settled onto chairs at Forbes's long desk. His rather handsome face looked somber in the sun from the nearby window.

Dunbar was a heavy man, with pudgy, awkward-looking hands and a farmer's ruddy face. But he had shown himself to be a brave and competent fighter. He wore a plain, dark uniform of militia officers, and held a tri-corner hat on his knee.

"Yes, sir. First of all, I understand General Duvall has rejected your overture for peace with reparations."

Forbes's young face went dark. "That son of a bitch. He damn near killed my courier."

"I was sorry to hear that, sir."

"I hope we manage to capture that blackguard," Forbes said angrily. "The impudent scoundrel has gone too bloody far this time. He's not dealing with Braddock, by God!"

"Then you intend to march soon?"

"In two days time I expect all our reserves to be here, including the ones from the South. We'll leave immediately upon their mustering in."

A little thrill of raw pleasure skittered up Dunbar's back. He had been looking forward to this ever since his return from the first campaign. "Very good, General."

"We ought to have nearly a regiment. Enough for a jolly good show, wouldn't you say?"

"Yes, sir. Unless we squander our riches, as Braddock did."

"You need have no fear of that, Colonel."

Dunbar leaned forward on his chair. "You said you'd listen to your colonial commanders, General. Well, this is my advice. Fight in the Indian way."

Forbes smiled. "Don't say that within earshot of my junior officers, Colonel. Most of them would be outraged to think we could learn anything from savages."

"I know that people like Braddock think it's cowardly to sneak around in the woods and ambush the enemy, instead of meeting him face-to-face. But we've frankly come to admire the tactic, General. It's damn smart. The Indians have no gentlemen's agreements in war. But that doesn't make them cowards. Some of the bravest men I've ever met are Shawnee or Cherokee."

"Colonel Washington told Braddock about the same things," Forbes said. "There's a good chap, incidentally. Are you quite certain he can't be persuaded to join us again?"

"I spoke with him personally, General. He says he won't fight under British command again. I think it goes beyond Braddock and Fort Duquesne. He and other Virginians are unhappy with King George."

"Unhappy with their king?" Forbes said, raising his eyebrows. "I love the arrogance of it."

Dunbar joined in Forbes's wry smile. "Many colonials are arrogant, by English standards," he admitted. "We've had to make our own way over here for too long, General, to be obsequious toward a European monarch. I hope it doesn't offend you."

Forbes widened the smile. "I rather like it. Now, Dunbar, how would you conduct this march, if you were in charge?"

Dunbar was surprised at the question. He had not thought Forbes would really want colonial advice, despite his earlier assurances that he would accept it.

Dunbar rose, walked to a map on a side wall, and took up a pointer from a narrow shelf below it. He put the end of the stick on Fort Cumberland.

"We're only a couple of days from Duquesne," he began. "I think we may properly take the open road through the first day's march. That will gain us time, and save the men from fatigue. We will probably get about here the first night, where Braddock encamped."

"Yes, that's what I figured."

"We should place sentries all around the encampment that night. Well out, maybe a half-mile. The next day, we should leave the road, dividing our force on either side of it, in the woods that follow it. We should rejoin our forces as a fighting unit only when we stand before Fort Duquesne."

"Our men are not accustomed to long marches through heavy forest," Forbes reminded him.

"*Your* men are not," Dunbar said. "Our colonial troops are. We'll lead the way, cutting trails. Our people would also be more alert to ambush, because they've experienced it."

Forbes just sat there, listening. Dunbar had been right. Colonials were arrogant.

"This is no reflection on British troops, General. There are no braver, harder-fighting troops anywhere. But they haven't lived here in the colonies, most of them."

"I hear you, Colonel."

"During that second day, we should also have scouts out ahead of us, and flanking our troops. I mean, men who know the woods and the Indians. We have some down in the Yadkin Valley area that would be very good. One I have in mind was with Braddock on the first campaign. His name is Boone. Dan'l Boone."

"This man is a colonial officer?" Forbes asked.

"No, no, General. He's barely a man, just out of his teens. But the Indians know him from Carolina into Ohio. He's been hunting and trapping alongside them since he was a boy. He was at Scotborough when Duvall sacked the settlement, and Boone shot the general's horse out from under him, and then got close enough at Duquesne to actually try to kill Duvall."

"I say, bloody good!"

"Duvall put a bounty out on him. Every damned Shawnee under Duvall's command will be trying to raise his scalp if he goes with us. But I hear he'll be here tomorrow or the next day."

Forbes sat back and stared out through the

sunny window. "What did you have in mind for this Boone?"

"He drove an ammunition wagon before. But he's voiced an interest in scouting, according to Sergeant Medford in Salisbury. I'd like to put him in charge of a small scouting unit. Let him pick his own men."

Forbes turned to him. "Any young man who exhibits this much fighting spirit should be rewarded, Colonel. You have my permission to form a party of scouts, headed by this Boone. And I'd like to meet him when he arrives."

"I'll bring him in, General."

Dunbar put the pointer down, and came and stood beside Forbes's desk. "Well, General?"

Forbes looked up at him. "I've been privately studying colonial militia techniques, Colonel. I like what I've seen, and I like what you've suggested here. Prepare to implement your ideas all the way."

Forbes rose from behind the desk, looking very military in his red tunic and gold braid. "I'm going to get that bastard Duvall, Dunbar. Our resolve has been sicklied over with old European habits that don't work over here. Now it will be different!"

Dunbar merely smiled, saluted, and turned and left.

The general had exceeded his grandest expectations.

Private Sam Cahill had been one of the wagon drivers who had gone to Duquesne on that first campaign with Dan'l and Corey Ruskin, and he and Dan'l were the only two drivers of munitions wagons who had survived the battle. Cahill was going back to Cumberland too, and had asked Dan'l if they might travel together, and Dan'l had agreed. Nick Purvis was already there.

On the morning after John Findley's visit with him, Dan'l left for Fort Cumberland with Cahill.

They went on foot, because of the rough terrain for mounts, and because Dan'l had decided to try an easier route north by making use of a small tributary of the Potomac, which ran errantly toward the fort.

They were gone an hour before dawn on that chill morning, and were into deep forest by sunup. Cahill was not a woodsman, and depended almost entirely on Dan'l as his guide. Dan'l had preferred to go alone, as was his habit, but Cahill had so obviously needed someone to travel with, Dan'l had agreed to take him along.

Young Squire had asked to travel with Dan'l to the fort too, even though he had been refused permission to join up by their father. But Dan'l would not take him. He was concerned that, once at the fort, Squire would have applied pressure to Dan'l to allow him to enlist. So the lad was left behind, very disappointed and a bit angry.

Dan'l had said good-bye to his parents and siblings the night before, but both Squire Senior and Sarah had risen to see him off in the darkness, and to wish him luck.

Dan'l could not believe it was less than a month since he had been pulled into this war by the loss of Ethan at Scotborough. It seemed like a year. He hoped fervently that this would be the end of it, at least for him, and that he could return to trapping and exploring western territories, which were his only goals.

They traveled all day through deep woods, on animal trails, and Dan'l avoided Shawnee trails carefully. He knew they were dangerous, and particularly for him. When the two men got on the river, that would have its danger too, but at least ambush was difficult on a swiftly moving stream.

They camped on the bank of that stream that night, with crickets and frogs making a racket all around them, and bear tracks only 30 yards away. Cahill was surprised when Dan'l told him they could not both sleep. He insisted they take watches of two hours each, until dawn. Cahill agreed grumblingly.

Cahill was a tall, lean farmer who knew a lot about horses and cattle and pigs, but very little about the wilderness. He wanted to build a fire to cook over, and Dan'l would not allow it. He pulled a mouth harp from his pocket, and Dan'l told him he could not play it. By the time they settled in for the night, with Dan'l taking the first watch, Cahill was in a bad mood, and not even talking to Dan'l.

The night was uneventful, except when Cahill woke Dan'l at just past midnight, scared to death because of sounds he had heard in the nearby woods. Dan'l went to investigate, and found more bear tracks.

"Holy God! He was that close?" Cahill said.

"You don't have to worry over it," Dan'l told him. "Ain't no bear going to attack you with that rifle on your knee. They seen plenty guns around here."

Cahill was not convinced, but finally the night passed without incident, and by an hour after dawn, they had walked downriver to a tiny fishing camp run by an old-time Cherokee. He was a friend of Dan'l from years ago, and agreed to sell Dan'l a birch-bark canoe that had just been resealed and rebuilt for just a few shillings.

The old Indian stood tall beside them on the riverbank that early morning. "A hunter of men came asking about you, Sheltowee," he said in a hollow, bass voice. "Yesterday."

"From Blackfish?" Dan'l asked.

"He was Shawnee," was the reply. "He wanted to know if you had passed this way. I think he wants your scalp, my friend."

Dan'l grunted. "Him and a lot of others."

"The leaves shook on the elders last night, Sheltowee. A sign of much trouble, much conflict. You will be in it."

"Yes," Dan'l said.

"Be careful," the Indian told him. "The moon is in its last phase. A time for dying."

"I'll go with care. Thanks for the canoe."

A few minutes later, Dan'l and Cahill were on the river.

Dan'l was at the back of the canoe, to guide it through the narrow river. They went silently, with the only sounds from their paddles dipping in the water. Occasionally a bird would shriek out a warning cry from the bank. Dan'l kept his gaze fixed on one bank and then the other, watching and waiting. But there was no sign of human life.

The river became more narrow in late morning, and rapids formed under them. White water regularly surrounded the small craft, and it was all Dan'l could do at times to keep it erect. Cahill was little help, and Dan'l had to do all the work to keep the canoe away from rocks and overhanging limbs.

Finally, the place arrived that Dan'l knew about, but had never traversed. They could hear the roar a half-mile in advance, and then they were entering an area where the river dropped down, cascading over rocks in shallow falls, and boulders and white water were suddenly all around them, much more ferocious than before.

Dan'l was paddling fast, and his Quaker hat flew off and was lost, and suddenly it was just white spray around them, and he could not see to steer the canoe.

"Keep it right!" he yelled at the top of his lungs. "There's less rocks over there!"

"I can't make it turn!" Cahill yelled back.

"Paddle on the left side!" Dan'l yelled again. He could hardly see Cahill now. Mist and spray were everywhere, and the violent roar of the water.

They crashed into a boulder, and Dan'l could hear the splitting of the canoe's bow. They careened on down the narrow gorge, and skidded along the side of another rock.

"If we lose the canoe, swim to the right bank!" Dan'l yelled loudly at Cahill.

"I can't swim!" Cahill yelled back.

"What!"

"Never could swim!"

In the next moment, the canoe went over on its side, after striking another half-submerged boulder obliquely. Both Dan'l and Cahill were in the water, tumbling head over feet, trying to get their heads above water so they would not drown.

Dan'l got himself righted, and briefly got a glimpse of Cahill downstream from him, in the boiling white stuff. Then Cahill's head went under, and Dan'l lost sight of him. Dan'l could have swum for the nearby bank, but he wanted to try to save Cahill. He swam after him, trying to keep his head above the surface, searching the river with his eyes, but seeing nothing.

"Sam! Where are you?"

Now Dan'l was coming out the far end of the white-water tunnel, and the water was calmer. He dog-paddled on downstream, shouting Cahill's name.

"Sam? Are you down there?" He looked again downstream.

Nothing. Not a glimpse of another body in the

water. Now Dan'l was in a calm part of the river, and the banks were farther away. He looked around for the canoe, and saw the remains of it floating over by the nearest bank. It looked useless.

Dan'l finally saw something sticking above the surface downstream a short distance. He swam on down there, and when he arrived at the object beside a branch protruding from the water, he saw it was Cahill's head and chest.

"Sam!" Dan'l said, swallowing hard.

He came up to the floating Cahill, who was snagged on the branch, and released his still form. Cahill's eyes were closed, and he did not seem to be breathing. Dan'l swam with the limp form to the nearest bank, and dragged both of them ashore, onto a mud spit. He lay there getting his breath back for a moment, and saw that the canoe was ashore too, downstream. He might be able to salvage some supplies, as well as the guns, which were secured to the small craft.

Cahill looked dead. Dan'l straddled him, shoved on his chest, and got no result. In desperation, he turned Cahill over onto his stomach, and began kneading at his back. He pried Cahill's jaw open, and resumed his rhythmic shoving against his rib cage.

Suddenly, and entirely unexpectedly, a gusher of river water flowed from Cahill's open mouth, and then he was alive and coughing spasmodically.

After much violent coughing, Cahill was

breathing raggedly, and his eyelids fluttered open. Dan'l turned him over onto his back again, and Cahill looked up at him.

"I was . . . gone, wasn't I?"

"You waren't breathing," Dan'l said.

"Much . . . obliged, Dan'l."

"You're a damn fool," Dan'l said. "To go on a river, and can't swim."

"Yeah."

Dan'l let Cahill recover for an hour or so, and retrieved the guns and some food from the busted canoe. Dan'l then half-carried Cahill downstream to a small settlement on the river, also lugging guns and food on his back. Cahill was deposited with a local family with the idea that Dan'l would leave him there for recuperation. But by the time Dan'l had arranged for a second canoe to go the final distance, Cahill was up and on his feet.

"I guess I didn't swallow much. My lungs burn, but I'm okay, Dan'l."

"You ain't in no condition," Dan'l told him.

"I want to go," Cahill insisted. "I want to be at Fort Duquesne."

Dan'l grinned at him. He liked that. "All right. I'll make a pallet for you in the canoe. You can rest some more on the way there. They say there ain't no more white water between here and the fort."

"Hell," Cahill smiled. "I was looking forward to some more excitement."

Chapter Thirteen

They arrived at Fort Cumberland after dark, several hours later than planned. Dan'l reported for both of them to Sergeant Medford, in the tent camp within the fort's walls. He had already taken Cahill to the dispensary for medication, and left him there.

Medford was in charge of the Salisbury area contingent once again, and Nick Purvis had already been billeted in the same company. Medford had just about given up on Dan'l's coming, and had reported his absence to Colonel Dunbar, when Dan'l appeared in his company headquarters tent. Medford was alone, having just dismissed a corporal who was making out a muster roll for the men.

"Well, look who's here!" Medford said, grinning. "We thought you decided to go back to trapping, Dan'l."

"Not as long as that bastard Frenchman is alive," Dan'l said.

Medford laughed quietly. "Yeah."

Dan'l told him about the trouble on the river, and Cahill. "But I think he'll be all right tomorrow."

"Good. Cause we're marching at six in the morning."

Dan'l was surprised. He had just barely made it. "I'm glad I got here."

"We are too. Cahill will get another wagon, he's a good driver and we need him. But you're going to take on a new job."

Dan'l looked perplexed. "Oh?"

"I think the general is still working. Come on, Dan'l, he wanted to meet you."

Dan'l was surprised. He was not accustomed to being summoned by generals. They left the tent and walked past Colonel Dunbar's small headquarters tent, and Dan'l was introduced to him.

"Good to have you with us, Boone," Dunbar told him. He was in underwear to his waist, and had to pull a tunic on. Dan'l thought he looked overweight. But he seemed like a pleasant fellow.

"Let's see if General Forbes has a minute, all right?"

"Fine with me, Colonel."

Medford went with them to the white-washed

building at the end of the compound, where oil lanterns still glowed from all windows. They went inside, were passed by an orderly, and found themselves standing before Forbes's desk. The general, looking very young to Dan'l, was poring over a map that took up most of the desk. He looked up and recognized Dunbar immediately.

"Yes, Colonel?"

"I have Private Boone here, General, and his sergeant."

"Ah, yes. Jolly good, laddy." He came around the desk, and Dan'l saw he was rather tall and elegant-looking. Dan'l felt somewhat humbled in his presence. Forbes stuck his hand out, and Dan'l noted the kerchief in his sleeve, with its lace edge. "I've heard a lot about you, chappie."

Dan'l tried a weak smile. He still had mud on his rawhides, and was hatless, with wild-looking hair. He took the general's hand in his, and it just lay there, with no attempt at a grip. Forbes's world was a strange one to frontiersman Dan'l.

"My honor, General," he managed.

"He just came in off the river, General," Medford said. "He and his partner almost drowned. But they'll both be all right."

"Capital!" Forbes exclaimed, seeming in good cheer. "Please be at ease, gentlemen."

They relaxed, and he returned to his desk and sat on the edge of it. His tunic was unbuttoned, and he looked tired. "I've been talking with Colonel Dunbar, Sergeant. Boone."

Medford and Dan'l exchanged a quick glance.

"He has convinced me of the need for more scouts on our march to Duquesne." He looked directly at Dan'l. "I want you to be in charge of such an operation, Private."

Medford had not understood the import of the meeting in all its details. He smiled widely at Dan'l. Dunbar did too.

"Thanks, General," Dan'l said, very surprised. "I just thought I'd be driving a wagon again."

"No, you're much too valuable for that," Forbes told him. "You know the woods. You know our adversaries. Is that correct?"

Dan'l hesitated. "I reckon so, General."

"Colonel Dunbar thinks we need two or three men out in front of the column, and a couple on each flank. I want you to pick these men, Private."

Dan'l nodded to him. "Yes, General."

"Sergeant Medford here can help you if perchance you need it. But I want the final decisions to be yours, and yours alone."

"Understood," Medford said for them.

Dan'l took all that in, and studied his hands for a long moment. "You don't care who I pick?"

"Not at all," Forbes said.

"When I was here under Braddock, General, I saw we had several Shawnee doing kitchen work."

"They're still here, Private Boone. They're friendlies."

"There was a couple I took to. I'd want to take them along."

257

Forbes looked shocked. He looked over at Dunbar, who was momentarily embarrassed. Medford was grinning.

"Private," Dunbar began. "I don't think the general anticipated that—"

"No, Colonel. Let him explain," Forbes said.

Dan'l looked from one face to the other. "They know this country better than any of us. They know how Blackfish's braves think."

Forbes nodded, and sighed. "There are some men here who criticize me—and my predecessor—for having Indians on the post. They think we may all have our throats cut in our sleep!" He laughed a soft laugh.

"You can imagine the reaction if we tell them we'll use Shawnee braves—our traditional enemies—to lead us to Fort Duquesne," Colonel Dunbar explained to Dan'l.

Dan'l chose his next words carefully. "Shawnees been fighting each other since the beginning of time, Colonel. And the Cherokee. They all got different ideas of how the world ought to be, just like us."

They were all silent.

"These Shawnee you got here come from the east. They're used to white folks, and try to get along. They ain't nothing like Blackfish's people, and them farther west."

"General," Dunbar said. "I don't think it's a good idea. We have the men to consider, and their attitudes. Our colonials will probably be more shocked by the notion than your own troops."

Dan'l was surprised by the lack of support from his own commander. But now Sergeant Medford spoke up.

"Begging your pardon, Colonel. Our people been living with these savages for some time. They know there are good and bad red men. I think the idea is a good one."

Dan'l saw how Dunbar had been backed up against a wall, so he quickly intervened. "I know how the colonel feels. My own family was just attacked by Shawnee. One of them was a friend from when we was boys."

Dunbar was pleased with that admission.

"Then what are you saying, Private?" Forbes asked him.

"I think we should use the very best people we got available," he said carefully again. "General Duvall will, you can bet on it. But we don't want to get the troops riled neither. Let me have just two, to ride out front with me. The other four can be picked from colonial troops, and I'll do that with the sergeant's help."

Forbes was pleased with that solution. He rose off the desk. "Is that all right, Colonel?"

Dunbar paused, then nodded. "I think it's a good compromise." He looked over at Dan'l in a new way.

Medford was grinning again.

"Then that's the way it shall be," Forbes told them. Let's get on it tonight, Private, there's a good chap!"

Dan'l saluted in the sloppy, militia way, and

Forbes smiled at it. "All right, gentlemen. You're dismissed."

Dan'l went right from the general's office then to the kitchen tent at the south side of the big parade ground, where there were also still lamps burning. Inside he found four of the so-called "civilized" Shawnee that had been hired some time ago to do menial work that private soldiers disliked. Two of them were older men, in middle age, and on Dan'l's last visit he had spoken at length with them, and had enjoyed their company. One was called Standing Bear, because of his husky build, and the other White Patch, because of a shock of white hair running through his scalp brush at the front.

Standing Bear was getting soft, and was a bit overweight from good living at the fort. He had a round, genial face and gentle eyes, and a rather subservient manner. But Dan'l noticed the remains of a great warrior in him. White Patch was a few years younger, and well built, and very knowledgeable about the goings-on at the fort. He knew of Dan'l's reputation and made it clear he respected his talents as a woodsman. When Dan'l had left on the first march to Duquesne, White Patch had given him a stone amulet for good luck, which Dan'l still carried in his belt pouch.

When Dan'l came over to them that evening, the other two red men understood the need for privacy, and left the tent. Dan'l sat down at a long table with the two Shawnee, and put his offer before them. Their assignment would be for the march to Duquesne only, but they would receive scouts' pay, which was much better than what they were receiving at the fort.

They both considered the offer for a long time. Dan'l knew it was a big decision for a Shawnee, even one from the eastern tribes, to fight with the white man against other Shawnee. It just was not done. In fact, even working at this fort was considered a dishonor by some back home.

"Why do you come to us, Sheltowee?" Standing Bear asked Dan'l finally in Shawnee. "You have many soldiers with guide experience."

Dan'l acknowledged with a nod. "Yes. But they do not know these forests as you do. Nor do they know the braves of Blackfish as you do."

Standing Bear thought about that.

"Our people will not like this," White Patch said.

"Some of our people will allow themselves to starve, not to work for the English," Standing Bear said. "But we have always thought that to be foolish."

White Patch looked at him. They were from the same village, east of Cumberland. In that village, as in most Shawnee villages, the English were looked upon as adversaries, as well as the settlers under their rule. The French, on the other hand, who were largely hunters and trappers and did not settle the land, were tolerated by Shawnee and other tribes alike, and at this time were looked upon as allies against colonial advancement into traditional hunting grounds of the red men.

Dan'l knew all that, but he nevertheless said, "Your brothers work and fight for the French. Once they have pushed the English colonials out of here, they will bring in their own settlers who will want to farm the hunting grounds."

White Patch sighed. "This is true. I have seen it in the bones." He referred to the practice of seeing into the future by shaking animal bones and dropping them onto a ground sheet, to study how they fell.

Standing Bear exchanged a long look with his companion, and then turned to Dan'l. "We will do scouting for the General Forbes. And for you, Sheltowee."

Dan'l was pleased. "You will answer to no one but me. Is that satisfactory?"

"It is the only acceptable way," Standing Bear said.

"You will both ride out in front of the column, with me. You will be issued rifles. Are you trained in their use?"

"Yes, Sheltowee," White Patch assured him.

"I will see you at militia headquarters an hour before dawn tomorrow morning," Dan'l said.

Before he spread his ground sheet that night, he had two visitors to the tent he had been assigned to with three other militiamen. Nick Purvis came first. Dan'l knew he had a lot of woods experience, and asked him to volunteer as a scout. Nick did.

"I'd be pleasured, Dan'l."

"You'll be working under my charge."

"That suits me down to the ground."

"It will be good soldiering with you, Nick."

The thing was, Dan'l really meant it. He held no grudge because of the way Nick and Corey Ruskin had treated him at one time. He figured Nick had really changed, and he felt a man ought to be allowed to grow up and leave behind him his mistakes of youth. It was also good having somebody from Salisbury close by.

Sergeant Medford came past just before Dan'l was getting ready to lie down, and called Dan'l out of the tent, to speak with him in private.

"I thought you might want to know this before you turned in tonight. Colonel Dunbar just promoted you to corporal."

Dan'l stared hard at the sergeant. He had never expected any rank at all to be given to him, no matter what responsibilities he shouldered. The news was a complete shock.

"He did that?"

Medford grinned happily. "And well deserved too, Dan'l. Congratulations, and best wishes to you tomorrow. You ain't under my wing now. You report directly to Colonel Dunbar. You see him at his tent tomorrow morning."

Dan'l was still reacting to the news. "All right, Sergeant."

"See you on the march." Then Medford disappeared into the night.

It was pitch black when the troops were awakened the next morning. Dan'l was already

263

wide awake, though, his brain spinning with all the new developments. He checked at the wagon compound and found Sam Cahill there, getting his team into traces. Cahill looked good. Dan'l wished him luck, and found Medford outside Dunbar's headquarters tent.

"I picked out four other scouts, Sergeant," he said. He recited some names to him, including that of Nick. Medford listened, and pursed his lips. "I see they're people from the Yadkin Valley. You know them all?"

"I do," Dan'l said. "And I think they all got the savvy to do the job, Sergeant."

"Fine. You got them," Medford said. "I'll tell them to report to you, Corporal Boone."

Dan'l smiled. "Much obliged."

By daylight, the regimental column was on its way. Once again, it was an enormous, unwieldy mass of fighting men, mixed regulars and militia, and on this leg of the journey, Forbes had decided to let the regulars lead the way. Four abreast, they left the fort in military formation, looking much more formidable than they really were. Shined shoes, polished buttons, and bright red coats made them look like an unbeatable force, but Dan'l had already learned that that was not true. In their fore was the band, playing a slow march, with drums rolling. It was a real spectacle. Behind the regulars came the odd assortment of militia soldiers, wearing work clothing and farm wear, a few in buckskins, and hats of all kinds, including some coonskin caps.

Dan'l Boone #1: A River Run Red

Dan'l had checked in with Colonel Dunbar, and had been given instructions to deploy his scouts as he saw fit, and Dan'l did so. He put two militiamen on each flank of the long column, riding well off the road, and after the column got out of sight of the fort, he took his two Shawnee and rode up past General Forbes on his black stallion and his top officers on their prancing mounts, to a position a half-mile ahead of the column. He and all his scouts had been issued horses for the duration, and saddle scabbards for their long guns. The Indians had the British Brown Bess, as did three of his other people. Nick had brought his own Heinrich from Salisbury, and Dan'l still had his Kentucky rifle, which shot long and accurately, and which could knock a bear head over heels at a hundred yards.

The morning was warm, and the column slowed to a crawl in the heat, equipment clanging, feet kicking up dust. But Dan'l and his scouts saw and heard none of that. They were in a world of their own, watching and waiting for trouble: dismounting to check spoor, gazing into the distance to glimpse some reflection of light off a chunk of metal.

But there was nothing. In late morning, Dan'l decided to deploy his two Shawnee out on flanking positions ahead of the column, and he kept to the road. But about midday, he rode off to the left of the column, looking around, keeping his eyes and ears open. For a while, he was off by himself.

It was during that time that he came to the hanging foot bridge over a small chasm, with a stream at its bottom.

Dan'l squinted in the sun, looking across the chasm to the opposite side. He could see nothing, but he felt the hair rise on the nape of his neck. He looked the bridge over. It was one of those swinging hemp affairs thrown up by the Indians, with rope sides and thick branches for a floor. It was just three feet wide and looked very unsteady.

It was the only place for miles to cross over.

Dan'l started across it.

He moved carefully, the bridge swinging underfoot. His rifle was slung over his shoulder, but loaded and primed. He took a misstep, making the bridge swing badly, and a lance came singing past his head, narrowly missing him.

Dan'l looked up, and saw that three war-painted Shawnee had emerged from the trees on the far side of the narrow chasm. One had just hurled the lance at him, and a second one was preparing at that moment to do the same.

Dan'l released his grip on the bridge ropes and almost lost his balance. He cocked the rifle awkwardly, and fired toward the second lance-thrower, beating him. The musketball struck the Indian just beside the heart, exploding the aorta and breaking a posterior rib, then pulling the fellow off his feet and dumping him in a heap on the ground.

The third Shawnee stepped onto the far end of the bridge, holding a tomahawk in one hand.

He seemed very practiced on the flimsy structure, and advanced slowly toward Dan'l while the first Indian watched from the precipice. Dan'l began reloading. The Shawnee was 30 feet away. Twenty. Dan'l reprimed, and cocked the long gun.

The Shawnee was ten feet away, and now hurled himself at Dan'l. Dan'l squeezed the trigger of the big gun and it roared a second time, right in the Indian's face. The lead smashed his nose and drove sharp splinters of bone into his brain pan with the lead of the ball, creating crazy lights and images in the man's skull as he fell backwards, then went over the edge of the bridge.

His grip on it jerked the bridge sidewise and almost turned the whole apparatus over. Dan'l almost fell off, but clung on tightly as he watched the Indian plummet a hundred feet to rocks below, at the edge of the winding stream down there.

The bridge gradually stopped swaying, and righted itself, and Dan'l was obliged to sling the gun over his shoulder again, to have both hands for balance. Now the last Shawnee stepped onto the far side.

"Sheltowee!" he gritted out, as if he had just realized whom he was facing.

"The same," Dan'l said grimly. "Come to collect the bounty, Blackfish squaw?"

The Indian's face darkened with the insult, and he advanced onto the bridge: 25 feet, 15. Dan'l drew the big knife from his belt, to defend against a second tomahawk.

"Your last day of the world has arrived, white face," the Shawnee advised him. "You will not cross this bridge alive."

Dan'l's eyes were narrowed in resolve. "Black-fish himself could not prevent me," he growled. "I am Sheltowee!"

"Your mother mated with a beast from hell!" the Shawnee hissed at him. "Now I will send you back there!"

Those were the last words spoken between them. The bridge moved and swayed in a slight breeze, and Dan'l realized this would not be like fighting on solid ground. The Indian came to within five feet, and began feinting with his weapon.

Dan'l parried each feint with the big blade, and then the Indian, his face brightly painted, his dark eyes fierce, lunged at Dan'l.

Dan'l ducked away from the tomahawk, and thrust with the long knife. The Shawnee caught Dan'l's wrist and stopped the thrust, and they were face-to-face, and Dan'l could smell the Indian strong in his nostrils, and see the hatred in his eyes. The Indian struggled hard, obviously not caring if they both fell to their deaths below. The bridge swayed and twisted as they struggled hand-to-hand, and then Dan'l saw the opening. He broke his right hand free and thrust hard again, and the knife sank into the other man's torso to the hilt.

The Indian's eyes saucered, and he stared into Dan'l's eyes. "Damn you—Sheltowee!" he snarled in a grating voice. Then he fell to his right, and Dan'l lifted him over the rope guard and off the bridge.

As the second body plummeted into the chasm, Dan'l almost went over too. He fell off the structure as it turned over, and then he was hanging in mid-air from its ropes, underneath it. He looked down and saw the two bodies down there.

Slowly, hand over hand, he moved along the flimsy structure from beneath it, his whole body hanging in the air. His strong hand grabbed at one purchase after another, and he closed the distance to the far bank.

He almost lost his grip. The bank came closer.

Dan'l grabbed onto a post at its far end, a cut tree trunk that supported the structure. He drew himself up on that post, until he was lying flat on the edge of the small cliff, panting and breathless.

He had made it.

He rolled over onto his back, and stared at the sky for a long moment. Scouting appeared even more dangerous than he had imagined.

Just as he was climbing back onto his feet, White Patch appeared on the far side of the bridge, coming out from a clump of trees there. He looked across at Dan'l, and then at the bodies in the gorge.

"Sheltowee! You are not hurt?"

"No. I'm all right," Dan'l said.

"I found your trail and followed it. I feared you were too far off the main trail."

Dan'l grinned. "You were right. Come, I'll hold the bridge steady while you cross. Then we'll rejoin the column."

White Patch shook his head slowly. "You will make our ancestral spirits pleased to do so," he answered.

The rest of that day was uneventful. Dan'l reported the Shawnee attack to Colonel Dunbar when the column stopped for a midday meal, and Dunbar gave Dan'l permission to make a small camp out in front of the main encampment that night, to keep a better watch on things. Dan'l would also establish two other small camps on either flank, and Nick would be in one of them. Dan'l told Nick.

"I'd like to make camp with you, Dan'l," Nick said to him, after Dan'l had dismissed the others from their midday meeting. "That private you put me with rags on me all the time. We don't rightly get along, I reckon."

Dan'l looked into his square face. Every time he looked at Nick nowadays he thought of Corey Ruskin, and how he had burnt to death when his wagon was attacked. Dan'l could not get it out of his head that maybe if he had acted more quickly, he could have saved Corey.

"Our camp will be the most dangerous one," Dan'l told him. "You sure you want that, Nick?"

"Hell, it's going to get might scary tomorrow anyway. For all of us."

Dan'l agreed. "Well, I can send Standing Bear out to your partner. You can camp with us tonight, and stick with us tomorrow if you want. It don't matter a lot."

"I think I'd like that, Dan'l," Nick said.

By dark, the entire column had settled down for the night, expecting to reach Fort Duquesne late the next day. Forbes planned to attack the fort early the following morning.

Dan'l reported to Dunbar once more that evening, and was amazed at how big the encampment looked in the dark, stretching along the road for a mile and spread out in the trees on either side of it. In accord with Dunbar's recommendations, Forbes had ordered sentries to stand guard well away from the encampment, in pairs, and had stationed others close up, in addition to the three scout camps. When Dan'l was assured that everything was secure, he rode back to his own small camp, a couple of miles up the road, where White Patch and Nick Purvis awaited him.

When Dan'l arrived back there, where their camp sat hidden off the road in thick trees, he was greeted with a surprise.

"We been robbed!" Nick greeted him.

Dan'l dismounted and looked over at White Patch. "It is true, Sheltowee," he said in English, because Nick was with them.

"What happened?" Dan'l asked.

Nick sighed. "White Patch went looking for firewood. He told me to stay here, but I didn't. I heard a sound, and went into the woods looking for what made it. I was gone longer than I thought, I reckon. When I come back, our mounts was gone. And White Patch's musket."

"Hell," Dan'l said.

"It's my mistake. I'm right sorry, Dan'l."

"They cannot be far away," White Patch said. He had donned war paint, and looked ferocious, standing there in the dim light from a low campfire.

Dan'l nodded. "I'm going after them."

"Let me go too," Nick pleaded with him. "I caused the trouble."

White Patch saw Dan'l's reluctance. "It is fair," he offered, even though he wanted to go.

"All right," Dan'l said. "You stay here, White Patch. If you have any trouble, give our crow call, and we'll hurry back. We'll be back as soon as we can."

"Be cautious," White Patch told him.

Dan'l circled the campsite and found the tracks immediately. White Patch was impressed. He himself was not that good. Many Shawnee and Cherokee would not even attempt to track an animal or human after dark. But there was strong moonlight tonight, and that would help.

Dan'l headed off into the trees, away from the main road. His gun was loaded, primed, and cocked. Nick was carrying his Heinrich rifle. He followed closely behind Dan'l, and let Dan'l do all the tracking.

Dan'l plodded along, watching the ground and the underbrush. A heel impression here. A broken branch there. He went carefully, and no word was spoken between them. At one point,

Dan'l almost lost the trail. Then he found a crushed leaf underfoot. So it went, for most of an hour.

Then he held up his hand for Nick to stop.

Nick came up beside him, and Dan'l pointed into the trees. Nick could see nothing at first. There was no fire, no tent. Then he made out a shadowy figure through the trees. He nodded understanding to Dan'l.

Dan'l made some gestures he hoped Nick would understand. It would have been easier with White Patch. Nick would go directly in on them, after he had given Dan'l time to circle around to the other side.

Dan'l went off into the darkness, picking his way carefully. One loud snap of a twig, and they would be compromised. He went in complete silence, in a large circle, and finally he was around to the far side of the encampment. He sneaked up close to the small clearing, and could see them sitting on a log, their ground sheets near them. He could hear their soft talking in Shawnee. He moved a few feet farther, and saw the dark shadows of four horses—two of theirs, and two of White Patch and Nick. Dan'l could hear the quiet laughter between them now, as they discussed the success of their small raid. They were probably planning on returning to kill the white faces in their sleep. Just the two of them.

Dan'l waited until he could make out Nick's shadowy form beyond the clearing. He did not want them shooting into each other. He had had little time to instruct Nick, and hoped Nick knew what to do when the moment came.

There would be no time for white flags, or discussion.

Dan'l made certain his Kentucky rifle was still cocked, and then raised it toward the two sitting Indians. Then he called out, in an owl-hoot cry.

The Shawnee both jumped to their feet, which was what Dan'l wanted. He fired the big gun, and the nearest Shawnee was hit in the jaw, the far side of his head torn away. He did a somersault like an acrobat, while Nick's gun exploded in a yellow flash from the far side. The shot hit the other Indian in the high chest and spun him off his feet.

Dan'l rushed in now, and Nick did too.

"We got them! By Jesus, we got them!"

Dan'l did not even look at him. He saw that the man Nick had shot was still alive. He bent over him with his knife, and slit the Shawnee's throat from ear to ear.

The Shawnee quivered for a moment, and expired.

Nick stared down at him in amazement.

Dan'l rose, cleaned the blade on Nick's shirt, and replaced it to his belt.

"Hey, what the hell!" Nick said.

Dan'l came and spoke into his face. "Your life might depend on killing with the first shot. Remember it!"

Then he walked off into the night, gathering horses as he went.

Nick followed quietly. He had learned his first lesson from Dan'l.

And it was an important one.

Chapter Fourteen

Early the next morning, General Forbes gave orders that that day's march would be quite different from the preceding one. When he told his officers that the colonials would be in the fore, and would be the first troops to arrive before the fort at Duquesne, a couple of his officers were outraged. He had kept the news from them until the last moment.

"But, General! The colonials aren't trained regulars! You can't take the initial confrontation away from our own troops!"

But Forbes would not listen. He received further resistance when he insisted all troops leave the roadway and resume their march in the cover of the woods. Finally, after Dan'l suggested it to Dunbar, Dunbar recommended a different route that would take longer to get there, and that idea too was disliked by the officers under Forbes. But the column took that smaller road.

By seven o'clock the confusion was straightened out, and Forbes's orders were followed. The march to Duquesne continued, but in a very different way from that of Braddock on the first campaign.

Dan'l kept Nick Purvis with him up front, and the three of them, including White Patch, rode in spread formation, with Nick taking the open roadway because the Indian and Dan'l knew the woods better. Standing Bear and the other scouts rode farther out, on the flanks, watching for ambushes.

It was another rather hot day, and by the time the column stopped just past noon, fatigue was becoming a factor. Forbes allowed a bit longer for the midday meal, and Dan'l rode west to see whether Standing Bear and his partner had seen anything. He sent Nick east for the same purpose, and left White Patch at the road, well out ahead of the troops.

It did not take Dan'l long to find his two scouts, and when he did, the sight shocked him.

They were both dead.

Dan'l first saw them at a hundred yards off, and knew immediately what he was looking at. In a small clearing, they both lay on the ground. They had been staked out, on their backs, and worked on with knives.

Dan'l rode up and dismounted, grim-faced.

Both men were stripped to the waist, and had been carefully flayed. Standing Bear had had his fingers cut off, one by one, and his eyes poked out. The militia soldier whom Nick could not get along with had had his arms and legs shot with arrows, but not the torso. So he would last longer.

"Goddamn it!" Dan'l said, standing there.

He scanned the trees for any sign that the attackers were still about, but there was nothing. Then, for the next half-hour he circled the place, reading sign. He had to make sure this was not a large contingent bent on attacking Forbes's main force. But there were tracks of only four men, on foot. A scouting party, maybe under Duvall's orders. They would report back to Fort Duquesne, and Duvall and Blackfish would know of the British advance, and where they were. Maybe, even, the size of the regiment, since one of the dead men might have talked under torture.

When Dan'l rode back to the main column, they were just readying to continue the day's march through the forest. Dunbar received Dan'l, and Sergeant Medford was there too. When Dan'l had told them what happened, it was Medford who spoke up first.

"I'm damn sorry, Dan'l. Now you know what it means to command."

"I keep thinking of what I could have done if I'd got there sooner," Dan'l said heavily.

"We know, Dan'l," Dunbar said. "I'll report the loss to Forbes. We'll be getting pretty close this afternoon, so let us know of anything you see. Or even feel."

"We'll do it, Colonel," Dan'l told him.

At Fort Duquesne, a colonel in full dress uniform came into Henri Duvall's office with a report from their scouts. His ruddy face was flushed, his blue eyes full of excitement.

"Yes, Colonel? What have our scouts reported?" Duvall asked him easily. He appeared very relaxed, very much in command of things. He had his men massed inside the fort, and outside it, and they were all ready to move out. Surrounding the fort were close to a hundred Shawnee, all under Chief Blackfish's command.

"Our Shawnee have encountered scouts from Forbes's regiment, General. Just the other side of Berry Creek."

Duvall rose from his desk, and stared down at a map that lay open there. "Ah. They're almost here."

"They have also seen large numbers of troops coming through the forest, off the main road. They could not tell how many, but it was many."

Duvall smiled wanly. "Well. Forbes has learned something from Braddock's failure. The British are not completely stupid after all."

"One of our spies says the colonials are responsible for the change in tactics," the colonel told him. "There is a colonel named Dunbar, who fought with Braddock."

"I remember the name."

"There is also a scouting party this time. Led

by a Salisbury man. Boone, I think his name is."

Duvall's face clouded over. "Ah! Now I understand the tactics! That damnable trapper again!"

"Sir?"

Duvall clapped his hands behind his back, and strode to the nearby window. "It is a long story, Colonel. Because you are recently down from Detroit, you do not know it. But suffice it to say that this Boone has been a thorn in my side for weeks now. I have a bounty on his head. You might remind your men of that."

"Yes, sir."

"Also, tell them I am doubling the amount of the bounty."

"I shall do so." A quizzical frown. "But isn't this fellow just a private soldier, General?"

Duvall turned to him. "*Oui*, Colonel. But this damned farmer-turned-hunter has become a nettle caught in my boot! Now he has shown the British how to fight us. There is no end to it. Until his head decorates my flagpole!"

The colonel regarded his general warily. "As you say, General."

"We have lost the advantage of ambush," Duvall told him. "But I suspect that Forbes will want to rest his troops when he arrives here, and attack tomorrow morning. We will not allow that to happen. We will attack his column this evening."

The colonel was surprised. "But Chief Blackfish is expecting more braves to arrive through the night, Colonel. We won't be at full strength."

"A few Shawnee one way or the other are not going to make the difference between victory and defeat," Duvall said curtly. "Go get Blackfish, and bring him here. I want to prepare at once for an assault."

The colonel stood there for a moment, wondering whether to speak. "General."

"Yes?" Duvall asked impatiently.

"We could also just let them come. Defend the fort from inside. We could hold out for weeks against a siege. And I suspect Forbes doesn't have the provisions to last that long."

"Hold out!" Duvall said loudly. "This garrison does not *hold out*, Colonel! We have cleaned the British out of this area with aggressive action, with offensive strategy. Not by hoping to hold out! Do you understand me?"

The colonel was chagrined. "Yes, sir!"

"This fort has never been defended from inside! It is not the French way! If you favor that mode of fighting, I recommend you relieve yourself of command, Colonel, before the battle begins!"

"No, sir. It was just an alternative suggestion." A bead of sweat popped out on his upper lip.

"I do not want to hear of holding out, or defending against a siege," Duvall concluded. "We will go meet the enemy on our home terrain, and defeat it before it has any opportunity to destroy this stronghold of our royal forces!"

"I understand, General."

The meeting was finished.

* * *

Out in the forest several miles from the fort, General Forbes gave the order for the long column to halt.

It was still divided into two parts, one on each side of the road leading to Duquesne, as it advanced toward its objective. Now the order was passed through the ranks that the small army would rest here and reform, making an encampment that would spread through the forest for some distance. Then tomorrow morning early, they would mount their attack on Fort Duquesne.

Scouts were called in, and sentries were stationed all around, in force. Fires were built, and headquarters tents were unbundled. But then, as all of it was just getting under way, Dan'l rode into the melee from up in front of the column.

He found Dunbar immediately. Dunbar was conferring under a tree with General Forbes and a British colonel. Dan'l dismounted from his militia-issue mount, a gray gelding, and came over to the threesome.

"Ah. Corporal Boone," Forbes said.

Dunbar and the other colonel turned to confront Dan'l. Dan'l saluted in the casual manner of the militia. "General. Colonel Dunbar. I sent White Patch up to the fort this afternoon. He just arrived back."

"Yes?" Dunbar said.

"The French are mustering out in front of the fort, Colonel. The Shawnee are preparing their horses and weapons. It appears the enemy will attack us today."

"Damn!" Forbes said heavily. "That's bloody bad news!"

The British colonel made a face. "General. I don't think the French are prepared to fight today. Why should we take the word of a damned Shawnee who was working in our kitchen until a couple of days ago?"

Dan'l was angry suddenly. "That Shawnee just risked his life for this regiment!" he said heatedly. "I trust him to tell us the truth!"

"Balderdash!" the colonel said, laughing softly. "Last week he was probably lying about the amount of salt he used for the stew! I know these people, General. They'll say anything, to make you think they're doing their job properly."

Dunbar was reacting angrily now too. "Corporal Boone picked these men with care, Colonel," he said tautly. "I don't see any motivation for lying."

"Motivation?" the English colonel said. "Why, just to show he did something important, like a fishwife telling tales! Or better yet, because his real loyalty is with Blackfish and his brother Shawnee!"

"You know damn little about the Shawnee, Colonel," Dan'l said flatly, "if you think that White Patch has any loyalty to the likes of Blackfish!"

"Why, you impudent farmer!" the colonel sputtered.

"Now, now, gentlemen." Forbes smiled. "We don't need dissension among ourselves. I'm sure the corporal can understand the colonel's apprehension about the Shawnee in general."

Dunbar nudged Dan'l, and Dan'l reluctantly nodded. "Yes, sir," he said quietly.

"What the corporal means, Colonel," Dunbar now spoke up, "is that it's hard to know about a whole people by observing a few men working in a kitchen."

"They're all damned savages!" the colonel blurted out. "Who will kill, cheat, or lie for money. It's they we'll be fighting soon, by Jesus!"

General Forbes soothed him again. "That's all somewhat true, Colonel," he said. "But I agree with Colonel Dunbar in one respect. There would be little motivation for our scout to exaggerate the situation to us. I think we had better prepare as if—"

His conclusion was interrupted by a rider dusting up to a stop very near them, and dismounting hurriedly. It was Nick Purvis, whom Dan'l had left up in the fore with White Patch.

"Dan'l! Colonel Dunbar! The French is on the move! They're coming right at us! They's a lot of Shawnee, and it looks like our forces is equal matched!"

Dan'l turned back to them with a sober look. "Well?"

"Damn!" Dunbar said.

The English colonel looked very flustered. "I wouldn't have thought it!"

Forbes rubbed his chin. "Call the men to ranks, gentlemen. We're going to meet this attack in a manner suggested by Colonel Dunbar. We'll take several companies of regulars right up the road, and draw the enemy into our advance. But we'll have most of our troops out on the flanks, in the woods. When we're engaged here, drawing the French and also their Shawnee in on us, then we'll hit them from both flanks."

"Damn!" Dan'l exclaimed excitedly.

Dunbar looked at him and grinned. "I think you've devised a plan that has a high chance of success, General," he said.

The other colonel felt left out. "Well," he blustered, "let's bloody well get at it then!"

Dan'l turned to Nick. "Let's get back at the head of the column."

Within a half-hour, with plenty of light left in the sky, the column was on the move again. British regulars marched down the road, four abreast, with some militia mixed in. Just like under Braddock. Drums rolled ominously, and the heavy tramping of footfalls on the ground could be heard for a half-mile in all directions. Wagons rumbled along behind the first troops, but some were held back, in the trees. Out on both flanks, in deep woods and out of sight of the main column, marched two columns of troops in almost absolute silence. Some regulars, but mostly colonials, who knew this kind of fighting better.

Dan'l's scouts were strung out ahead of all

three columns, with Dan'l, Nick, and White Patch a few hundred yards out in front of the main column.

It was they who saw the advancing French uniforms first. They were marching along the road openly, but Dan'l could see glimpses of many Shawnee flanking them in the trees, some on horseback, and some on foot. Blue-uniformed officers rode out in front of the column, looking very military. Dan'l looked for Duvall, but did not see him.

"Nick, ride out to the right flank, and say we come on the enemy!"

"I'm off, Dan'l!" Nick replied, his young, square face full of excitement. He paused for a moment. "Thanks for making me a part of this, Quaker!"

Dan'l smiled. "Get going, farm boy!"

Dan'l sent White Patch over to the left flank, and the Indian rode off quietly, trying to keep out of sight of the advancing army. Then Dan'l rode back to his officers.

He reported to Dunbar, and moments later the word had been passed back from company to company. Muskets and rifles were loaded and primed, and new bayonets from Boston were fixed. Officers drew sabers, and flourished them.

Excitement was running high.

Once they were ready to move forward, they marched on with more caution. Forbes was out front, watching the road for signs of the enemy. Dunbar and the British colonel rode beside him, and Dan'l was right behind them. While they were so deployed, a hot chunk of lead punched into the English colonel's chest, and only then did they hear the explosion of the gun, from the nearby woods. The colonel fell from his horse like a stone.

"We're under attack!" Forbes called out, stunned. "Take cover and return fire!"

Now French troops rounded a bend in the road, and there were a lot of them, in massed formation. Others could be seen in the trees lining the road, and Shawnee were suddenly everywhere, yelling and firing guns and arrows.

"Fire!" Dunbar was yelling. "Fire at will!"

Under fixed orders, many of those troops on the road ran for quick cover of the trees, unlike the way they had been told to fight under Braddock. Other platoons stayed on the roadway, returning fire openly to the French and Shawnee, and killing many in the first volley.

Then, also under previous orders, the men on the road fell back, as if they were being overwhelmed. The French and Shawnee, seeing this, charged forward under officers' orders, and kept firing as they came. Dan'l was with those retreating, and he got a shot off in the first volley, and killed a French officer immediately. Down the road a small distance, with the Shawnee closing in now for hand-to-hand, he fired a second time and the big .72-caliber ball took two Indians down. He kept scanning the enemy troops for Duvall, and Blackfish, and saw neither.

Now the French and their allies were shoving the British and colonials back at a fast pace, and Shawnees were coming in on the column with their hand weapons. Dan'l saw a lot of troops go down under the brutal assault, and then he spotted Duvall in the midst of his troops, waving his saber.

"Attack! Attack! Push them back to Cumberland!"

Dan'l started to ride toward his nemesis, but the opposition was too great. Lead whistled past him, and a ball tore a hole in a coonskin cap the militia had issued him when he lost the Quaker broad-brimmed hat. The cap was now knocked off his head, and his long hair flowed wildly as he wheeled his mount and rode off to the left flank, into the woods.

He encountered more Shawnee there, and he knocked two of them off their mounts by charging into them. One was trampled by his mount, and the other was shot by a colonial soldier. Dan'l rode forward then, hoping to flank Duvall, and now the columns in the trees were closing in on the French on the road.

In moments, the main force of the French was attacked on both flanks, and they found themselves surrounded on three sides. Dan'l could see it all happening, out on the road. Bayonets had been issued widely by both sides this time, and the British were using them with great efficiency in hand-to-hand combat. They were being thrust into chests, bellies, and limbs. There was more blood than if only lead had been fired. There was bewilderment among the French, then panic, and then they were running for the fort behind them, in wild disarray.

Dunbar's tactics, and Dan'l's, had worked.

Dan'l rode back onto the road, and caught a glimpse of General Duvall, riding among his troops, trying to keep them from running.

"Stay and fight, damn you!" Stay and fight them!"

A blue-uniformed soldier ran past him, and Duvall swung his saber, and the fellow's head flew off his shoulders and hit the ground near Duvall, the eyes still open in astonishment.

Dan'l rode back out onto the open road. A French officer came at him with a saber, and Dan'l parried the swing at his head with the barrel of his gun. Then he fired the gun into the officer's face, blowing him completely off his mount. Dan'l looked up ahead, and saw Duvall still atop a black horse, cutting British soldiers down with his saber, in the thick of the battle. Just behind him was Chief Blackfish, exhorting his braves to kill English. As Dan'l spurred his mount forward toward them, Nick Purvis came riding out of the trees toward them from the far side of the road, and Chief Blackfish aimed a rifle at him and fired.

Dan'l saw Nick hit by the lead, in the side. He was just hanging on his saddle. Duvall rode past him and decapitated him in one stroke of the saber.

"No, goddamn it!" Dan'l cried out.

Both Duvall and Blackfish heard the cry, and

saw Dan'l riding toward Duvall, in a gallop. A French soldier shot at Dan'l as he came, and hit him in the thigh. Dan'l hardly felt it. He spurred his horse into the middle of the battle, and arrived at Duvall's position in just seconds.

"You! Damn you!" Duvall hissed.

"You demon from Hades!" Dan'l yelled at him.

Neither man got to use a weapon against the other, though. A Shawnee came and aimed a gun in Dan'l's face, between Duvall and Dan'l, and when he tried to fire it, it hung fire. Then Duvall was being pushed back by British soldiers, and had to turn his horse about and move back toward the fort.

The French were being overwhelmed now. Blackfish waved a lance in the air, a signal for his people to back off, and then he looked over at Dan'l, who had jumped off his horse to kill a French soldier with his knife.

"You have won, Sheltowee!" Blackfish shouted at him. "Your name will live in Shawnee legend!"

Dan'l had blood running down his left leg, and he had been cut on the arm, and he felt as if he could not move another step forward. But Blackfish was right. They had won the day.

The Shawnee chieftain had wheeled his horse now, and was riding back toward the fort, along with most of his warriors. The British and colonials were yelling and killing with every moment that passed, coming past Dan'l now in great numbers, pursuing the fleeing enemy.

Dan'l saw Forbes among them, looking like a white knight, savoring his victory, flushed in the face.

Now Dan'l had time to go over and look down at Nick Purvis's dismembered corpse. Soldiers were jumping over the body in their emotional attack, and Dan'l was almost knocked down. Dan'l felt a heaviness in his chest. In the end, he had come to actually like the Salisbury bully who had said he had reformed.

In another short time, Forbes recalled his troops with bugle calls, and the entire regiment gathered before the fort. The straggling French had retreated behind its tall stockade walls, but Dan'l knew there were not a lot of them left. The army of Blackfish had dispersed into the woods, and Dan'l was certain that most of them were on their way home.

The victory had been complete.

The Cumberland men were firing guns and yelling, out in front of the closed-gated fort, waving rifles and muskets.

White Patch limped out of the woods, leading his horse. He had been shot in the leg with an arrow, and whereas Dan'l's wound was superficial, his was deep.

He stopped beside Dan'l, smiling. "We did well, Sheltowee."

Dan'l returned the smile, wearily. "We did."

"I will thank you for Standing Bear. You gave us the chance to prove ourselves in battle."

Dan'l remembered the way the other Shawnee had given his life, and was sobered. "I hope his spirit rests quietly," he said.

Suddenly General Forbes appeared from out of the midst of his troops, riding his dark stallion. He looked magnificent, Dan'l thought.

"Reform your ranks! Rejoin your own companies!" His clear voice came over the smoke-filled air.

"We're going in!"

Chapter Fifteen

It was well after dark when Forbes's troops had reorganized themselves into companies, and had surrounded the fort.

The general had passed the word along that there would be no sleep that night. The siege would begin immediately, and they would attack before morning.

Dan'l had gathered his remaining scouts around him, and they had had a light meal on the edge of the woods, just behind the front-ranked troops facing the fort. After that, Dan'l had walked back through the jubilant colonials until he found Colonal Dunbar's headquarters tent, and Sergeant Medford was there, conferring with Dunbar and two other colonial officers. Medford had his right arm in a sling, and Dunbar's left hand was bandaged. Neither one seemed to notice his wounds. Dan'l had had his thigh bandaged also, and walked with a slight limp.

"By George, there's the scout master!" Dunbar said loudly when Dan'l came up to them. "Fine job you did for us, Boone!"

"Much obliged, Colonel," Dan'l managed. "Looks like we all got banged up a mite."

"It's all part of the job, lad," Dunbar grinned.

"Pleased to see you made it, Dan'l," Medford said.

Dan'l sighed. "Nick Purvis didn't," he said soberly. "The burial detail is taking care of him right now."

"I'm real sorry, Dan'l," Medford told him. "I saw him go down. Sam Cahill done some fine fighting, though. Thanks to you."

"We lost quite a lot of people," Dunbar said. "But we ran Frenchy home, didn't we?"

"We didn't get Duvall yet," Dan'l said.

"We will, by God," Dunbar said.

"When are we going in, Colonel?"

"Well, we got the dead and injured to take care of. That ought to take past midnight. Forbes is bringing our small cannon up that we hauled here on one of the wagons. Matter of fact, I think your Cahill hauled it. Forbes is going to raze the fort."

That pleased Dan'l.

"The general wants to attack in the wee hours. They might not expect it. That means very few of us are going to get any sleep tonight."

"That suits me fine," Dan'l said.

"Look," Medford said. "Here comes our light cannon now."

A wagon rolled up past them, with a single small cannon strapped to its bed. On the buckboard, Sam Cahill waved to Dan'l.

"Hey, Quaker! See you in the fort!"

Dan'l smiled. It was gratifying to see Cahill sitting on that wagon, looking dirt-smeared and weary, but alive and doing an important job for their side.

"Give 'em hell, Sam!"

The wagon rumbled on forward, and Dan'l felt a little better about losing Nick Purvis.

Dan'l was returned to his original unit, under Medford, for this final phase of the battle. By midnight, units had been reformed, and a British regular unit was placed up front behind the cannon, because one of the regular colonels had insisted. But just behind that was Medford's militia company, with Dan'l in it. Guns were cleaned, and midnight meals eaten. Ammunition was distributed, and sabers and knives were sharpened.

At just past two in the morning, the light cannon began firing exploding rounds into the fort.

That continued for almost two hours, with bright yellow explosions lighting the night, and pummeling the ears of those up front. Fires were set inside the fort by the cannonade, and holes were torn in the wall and the big gate. French soldiers fired their muskets and rifles from parapets atop the wall, but Forbes had positioned his troops just out of range. There was no return fire from the attackers, except for the cannon.

Finally, Forbes concentrated the cannon fire on the gate, and it was slowly ripped to pieces. At just after four o'clock, he came forward on his stallion and waved his saber in the air.

"All right, men! We're going in!"

Moments later, the air rang with shouts of "Charge! Charge!"

The British company of regulars rose and ran forward toward the shattered gate. But halfway there, they were caught in a withering, blistering hail of hot lead that cut them down one after another. Men were hit in the chest, the face, the limbs. It was butchery. Only a few survived in that first rush, and they huddled fearful on the ground, still under the fire of the French.

The officer in charge of Medford's company rose and waved his saber in the air. "All right, boys! It's our turn! Before those regulars are wiped out! Before the Frenchies get reloaded!"

Medford was up too. "Ready, boys! Charge!"

Dan'l was up and running with the first of them, in charge of the second platoon. But he was limping on the shot leg, and could not keep up front, and that saved him. About half of the first line of militia was cut down, but the rest kept running toward the gate, yelling at the top of their lungs. Dan'l ran with them. A chunk of lead ripped his right sleeve, and another sizzled past his head. Then the first men were at the gate, and in hand-to-hand combat with the defenders. Dan'l came up behind them, and ran on into the fort.

French soldiers were everywhere, firing at the attackers. But more and more militia poured into the opening now, and British regulars behind them.

Dan'l had fired and reloaded twice, killing two French soldiers. But then there was no further time to load. The big knife came out, and he ran, limping, at a soldier loading, and stabbed him through.

It was wild in Fort Duquesne in those moments. Dan'l for the first time looked around the compound, and what he saw shocked him. He had known that a few of Forbes's people had been captured, and now he saw what had been done with them. Their heads decorated poles all around the compound, blood dripping from the necks, some eyes bulging, staring at the fighting but seeing nothing.

"Damn that demon!" Dan'l growled.

A French soldier swung the butt of a musket at Dan'l's head, and he ducked aside and stabbed into the fellow's chest. The soldier went down at his feet, dying.

The odors of gunsmoke and rich blood were thick in his nostrils, and guns still cracked out their deadly messages all around the compound. But the French were going down fast now, with more British and militia coming into the fort.

Dan'l looked toward the headquarters building at the far side of the fort, and saw Henri

Duvall standing there with three officers, looking very grim.

"There you are, damn you!" he grated out angrily.

But Duvall quickly turned and disappeared into the building, with his aides. Dan'l ran toward the building, shouting as he went. "It's Duvall! Get after him!"

Several men rushed the door to the building with him, and he was surprised to see that one of them was Sam Cahill.

"I'm with you, Dan'l!" he said above the melee.

They broke the door in, and rushed into the building, and two French soldiers fired on them. Two of the militiamen were hit, but not Dan'l or Cahill. Cahill was fully loaded, and killed one of the defenders with one well-placed shot.

"Don't kill the other one!" Dan'l yelled.

He ran into another room, and then was in Duvall's private office. There was no one there. Cahill met him coming back out.

"We can't find him, Dan'l."

"He isn't here!" Dan'l replied. He hit his first into the nearby doorjamb. "There must be a back door out of here!"

"I'll go look," Cahill told him. He diappeared into another part of the building, taking a second militiaman with him.

Dan'l went over to the second French soldier, who was being held against a white-washed wall by two militiamen. The fellow looked very frightened.

"Where is Duvall?" Dan'l asked the fellow.

"I don't speak English," the soldier said in French.

Dan'l repeated the question in good French.

The soldier hung his head. "He is gone."

"Where?"

The soldier did not reply. Dan'l took his knife out, and held it to the man's throat. It bit into flesh there, and a small worm of crimson inched onto the soldier's throat.

"Tell me how he got out," Dan'l said in a low voice, "or I'll by God cut you up like a goddamn prairie buffalo."

He meant it.

The soldier looked into his eyes, and licked suddenly dry lips. "You're Boone, aren't you?"

"That ain't an answer," Dan'l growled.

This soldier just happened to be one of the many who had not liked Duvall's many cruelties. He felt he owed him little loyalty. He took a deep breath in. "There is a storage room. At the back of this building."

"What's he saying?" a militiaman asked.

"Go ahead," Dan'l said.

"In that room, there is a small gate that leads outside the fort."

"Damn," Dan'l muttered.

"The general took that exit, I am certain," the soldier concluded. "With several of his officers."

"Can you show us the exit gate?"

"Oui, monsieur."

"Will you?" Dan'l said.

A hesitation. "Yes."

Cahill had just arrived back. "I can't find anything, Dan'l."

"Come with us," Dan'l said to him. He jabbed his knife onto the French soldier's side. "Take us. And you had better not be lying, soldier."

They were led through a corridor then, the four of them, and to a large dining room. At the rear of it was a kitchen, and behind that was the tiny storage room. A door behind a cupboard stood partially open, and it led through a small space in the compound to a closed, small gate in the wall of the fort.

Dan'l moved forward and yanked the small gate open, and looked out onto a clearing toward thick woods behind the fort. Most British troops had been withdrawn from the rear when the attack began, but there were four soldiers lying dead in the grass close by, killed by Duvall and his officers, who had run out on their men, leaving them to face annihilation without leadership.

Dan'l looked out beyond the four dead soldiers, and saw something else. The last of Duvall's three underlings was just taking a last look toward the fort, on horseback, and then disappeared into the woods.

"That's them!" Dan'l said excitedly. He turned and saw a small detachment of British troops, mixed in with some colonials, still being held back as reserves, at the side of the big fort. "Come on!" he called to the others.

When he arrived at the contingent, he saw that the colonials were a remnant of Medford's company. There were three officers on horseback.

"Sergeant!" Dan'l called out to Medford. "Duvall is riding off to the North with three of his officers! Let me go after them!"

Medford looked toward the woods, and toward his superior officers. They had heard the request too. The lieutenant in charge nodded his head, and told his comrades to dismount. They followed orders, and the lieutenant led his chestnut stallion over to Dan'l.

"Sorry they got past us, Boone. We all know your special interest in Duvall. Take these mounts."

Dan'l smiled. "Much obliged."

Sam Cahill and a tall, lean colonial took the other horses, and the fourth man stayed behind with Medford's platoon. In a moment the three men were mounted.

"Good luck, Dan'l!" Medford said to him.

Then they rode off in the direction Duvall and his people had taken.

Duvall had a small head start on Dan'l, and a big advantage. Duvall could ride as hard as the forest would allow him, but Dan'l had to go carefully, tracking Duvall's every twist and turn, so the threesome would not lose the trail.

That went on like that for three hours, while the sky brightened and a sunny morning unfolded. By mid-morning, Duvall had a big lead on his pursuers, and figured on losing them entirely by noon.

Duvall's party stopped briefly on the crest of a wooded ridge, and one of Duvall's subordinates took a long glass out and peered through the monocular to see if he could spot anybody behind them in the valley they had just come through.

"There is nobody in sight, General," the colonel told him. He was Duvall's top aide. His left arm had a bloody tourniquet applied to it, above the elbow.

"*Tres bien*," Duvall said tiredly. "Maybe we have lost them. We will continue toward Pontchartrain du Detroit. I will persuade the commander there to help us raise another regiment, and we will return to Duquesne."

"*Certainemente*," the wounded officer agreed.

A second one, a younger, rather thin fellow, was the one who had disappeared into the woods last, when Dan'l had spotted him. "General."

Duvall looked over at him impatiently. The general's shirt was open at the collar, and his blue tunic was torn. He had never lost a fort before, or even a battle. He was still trying to grasp the meaning of what had happened on this bloody morning, and the previous day. "Yes, Major?"

"I believe it is the one called Sheltowee that saw us leaving the fort."

Duvall's face changed so dramatically that it was as if he had become a different person. His mouth turned down, his eyes flashed hot fire, his cheeks crimsoned.

"What!"

"The one called Boone by his people, sir."

"That damn son of a bitch!" Duvall sputtered. "That crazy man! Will nobody rid me of this maniac!"

The wounded colonel sighed. "He is our pursuer. And he will not quit, General. He will follow us to Detroit."

Duvall had little trouble accepting that conclusion. His mount, catching his nervousness, neighed quietly.

"You're right. Blackfish says he is the best tracker on the frontier. There is no point trying to lose him. We must stand and make a fight. We will lay an ambush."

The second colonel, the one who had supervised the whipping of Forbes's messenger, now spoke up. "This is as good a place as any, General. We command high ground. And we have the trees behind us for cover. They will ride right into our fire when they crest this ridge."

Duvall thought for a moment. "Yes. I like it," he said.

The young major caught his eye. "General. I'll ride back and find them, with your permission. I'll lie in wait for them, and pick Boone off before he gets here."

"They will kill you," Duvall said bluntly. "And you will have ruined our little surprise. No, I want to see Boone's face when he goes down."

"Then let us prepare," the wounded colonel said.

At that very moment, Dan'l and his two riders were just a mile away, and closing fast. Duvall's group had slowed, and Dan'l had kept his people going beyond their ordinary endurance. When they reined in on a hillcrest, the third man complained to Dan'l.

He was a fellow from near Salisbury named Dunham, and he was very fatigued. They had ridden for several hours without any rest.

"Damn it, Boone! We ain't catching them! They're probably halfway to Detroit by now. I say we turn around. To hell with Duvall!"

Dan'l was still bareheaded, and he looked very wild at the moment. He was fatigued too, and his leg ached from his wound. But he was not going to let Duvall slip from his grasp. Not now. Not after getting this close.

"No, they're not, Dunham," he said heavily. "The trail is getting fresher with every mile we cover. They're just up there ahead somewhere. Maybe over the next ridge."

Dunham looked over at Cahill. "What do you say, Sam?"

Cahill regarded him balefully. "Dan'l outranks us, Dunham. Anyway. This boy saved my skin, on the river coming to Cumberland. I won't leave him out here by hisself now."

"Well, you're a damn fool!" Dunham said. He was a short fellow who was almost bald under a dark hat. He owned a small herd of cattle in the Yadkin Valley. "I don't care what rank you hold, Boone. I'm heading back to Duquesne. Where we're needed."

"You can't do that," Cahill said. "We need you here more, Dunham."

Dan'l shook his head. He was wishing he had brought somebody else. "Let him go," he said, after a moment.

Cahill looked over at him.

"A man ain't no good for fighting if his heart ain't in it," Dan'l said. "Go on, Dunham. Tell them we'll be back soon. After we catch that butcher."

Dunham sat there on his horse. "No hard feelings?" he said.

Dan'l shook his head. "Get going, Dunham."

Dunham wheeled his mount and rode off, with Dan'l and Cahill looking after him. Now it was two against Duvall's people. Dan'l still had no idea how many they would face.

"Let's ride," he said after a long moment.

What Dan'l also did not know was that the next ridge held the enemy, and that he was just a half-hour ride away from an ambush.

During that half-hour, as they rode through trees and meadows in the low land before the next ridge, Dan'l and Cahill loaded their weapons and got their powder horns and ammunition bags in handy places for further use.

Cahill rode without complaint. His tall, skinny figure slumped in the saddle, and his very bony face sagged with fatigue, but he knew Dan'l was right. Duquesne was only half a victory without bringing Duvall to justice. And somebody had to go after him.

They crested the ridge where Duvall and his three officers waited not long before midday. Dan'l knew they were getting very close, because of the moisture still in the hoofprints of the French officers' horses and in the mud at their edges.

Up on the ridge, crouching behind scattered boulders and tree stumps, out in the open, the trees behind them, Duvall and his people knew Dan'l was climbing the ridge, because the young major had seen them coming. They waited tensely, knowing there were only two men coming up that hill and they would have the element of surprise.

Duvall had made a mistake, though. He had tethered their mounts just 50 yards away, in the trees, and as Dan'l and Cahill approached the crest of the rise, still on horseback, one of Duvall's horses whinnied softly.

Cahill did not even hear the sound, but Dan'l reined in immediately. "Whoa, hold it," he said softly.

Cahill stopped his horse, and looked over at Dan'l.

"They're here," Dan'l told him. "On top of this ridge. Probably waiting for us."

Cahill swallowed back his fear. "Now what?" he said.

"We surround them." Dan'l grinned wryly.

Cahill laughed. "Anything you say, Dan'l."

Dan'l told Cahill to circle the rise, and come

up on the left flank of their ambushers. Dan'l would go to the right. Cahill would not shoot until Dan'l did, or until they were discovered.

They dismounted quietly, and Dan'l saw that there were unloaded muskets aboard the horses, in saddle scabbards. He and Cahill loaded them too, and slung their rifles on their shoulders. Each would have two shots before reloading.

"Let's go," Dan'l said then.

Cahill disappeared around the hill's curve, and Dan'l moved quietly through underbrush around the opposite way. He had to skirt a bramble patch, and crawl through some very thick shrubs, and he became dirty and sweaty. But now he could hear quiet voices on top of the ridge. He crawled the last few yards uphill, and finally stuck his head up over a clump of thick bushes.

There they were. Four of them, in a loose semi-circle facing the front of the hill. Duvall, one over from the end, crouched behind a low boulder. On Dan'l's side of him was the wounded colonel, and beyond Duvall were the other officers.

Waiting.

To blow Dan'l's head off.

Dan'l waited until he was certain that Cahill had them flanked from the other side. He unslung the Kentucky rifle from his shoulder, and laid it beside him on the ground, cocked and ready. Then he cocked the musket, a British

Brown Bess, and aimed it toward the tight little group in the clearing.

He knew they would never surrender to him. But he knew that Dunbar and Medford would expect him to give them the chance. He raised up onto one knee, and called out.

"Over here, boys!"

The wounded colonel reacted first, but they all turned in surprise. The colonel did not hesitate. He aimed an Annely revolver at Dan'l's face, ready to fire. Dan'l beat him, and the musket roared out its deadly message. The colonel was blown off his feet, a hole in him from belly to back.

"Damn you!" Duvall was yelling. "You damn half-beast! Now you die!"

Duvall fired with a Charleville musket, and Dan'l reached down for his rifle at the same time. The hot ball of lead creased the top of his skull and knocked him on his back.

Dan'l lay there dazed and bleeding from the scalp. His right hand felt for the rifle, but could not locate it. Out on the hilltop, the other colonel had exchanged fire with Cahill, and lost. He had gone down in a heap, and now the young major fired at Cahill from behind a low stump, and hit him in the side, breaking a floating rib. Cahill was knocked backwards, but did not lose his footing. He now fired the rifle that was already loaded, and hit the major in the Adam's apple, breaking his neck and killing him instantly.

Dan'l still had the fired musket at his side. He

grabbed at it again, giving up on the rifle. He unclipped a bayonet from its barrel and affixed it to its end just as Duvall came upon him, looking crazed with emotion.

Duvall was now carrying an Annely revolver, and he had aimed it at Dan'l's head.

"Now, Monsieur Boone!" he breathed out raggedly. "I send you to hell!"

Just as his finger squeezed on the trigger, Dan'l swung the long gun in an arc and released it as the bayonet end came around. The musket flew through the air like a lance, directly at Duvall's heart. When it reached him, it impaled him on the bayonet, the blade passing completely through him and protruding wickedly from his back.

The revolver went off, and dug up dirt beside Dan'l's head.

Duvall just stood there then, not quite understanding what had happened to him. Grabbing at the musket as if it were his life.

"You . . ."

Dan'l raised up onto his elbows, his head swirling from the shallow scalp wound. He saw two Duvalls for a moment, both standing over him in their torn blue tunics. There was no arrogance in the general's face in that timeless moment. Only the blank stare into his non-existent future.

Then he fell heavily beside Dan'l, hitting the ground with a heavy thud, lying on his side, still holding the musket that protruded from his chest and back.

Cahill came staggering up to them, looking like he might collapse at any moment. He was holding his side, and blood seeped between his fingers.

Duvall was not quite dead. The cold iron had not penetrated his heart, but had passed through him just beside it. He lay gasping, his face turning an odd color. Dan'l struggled to get up onto one knee, fell back down, and got up again. He pulled his long, razor-sharp knife from its sheath.

Cahill furrowed his brow.

Dan'l leaned forward, and grabbed Duvall's hair in a tight grip. Duvall's mouth flew open, and his jaw worked. But only an odd sound came out. Dan'l put the blade to his head, preparing to scalping him. He turned his face to the sunny sky, and let out a Shawnee war cry that echoed loudly in the surrounding hills. Then he bent to take Duvall's scalp, as he had taken the Shawnee's scalp on that long march back from Duquesne, that first time.

"No, Dan'l!" Cahill called out.

Dan'l glanced at him, then bent back to his task. He sank the blade into Duvall's scalp.

But then Cahill was there, grabbing at his arm, preventing him. Dan'l looked up savagely. "You don't know what he did!"

"Yes, I do," Cahill said, his lean face showing real fear of Dan'l now. He still held Dan'l's wrist.

Dan'l jerked away violently. "Then you know how important this is! Ethan's spirit must rest quietly!"

309

Cahill knelt beside him. "It does, Dan'l."

Dan'l stared hard at him.

"Forbes wouldn't want this. The Sarge wouldn't want it. Maybe most important, Ethan wouldn't want it."

Dan'l looked into his eyes, and as the animal-thing inside him crawled back into that place where it came from, he understood that what Cahill said was true.

He took the knife away from Duvall, and in that moment, Duvall shuddered once, and died there.

Dan'l looked down on the butcher of Duquesne, and realized there would have been no satisfaction in it anyway. Scalps were taken from brave enemies. Not black-hearted murderers.

"Thanks, Cahill," he said finally.

Cahill grinned, then made a grimace. "I owed you one, partner."

Dan'l retrieved his Kentucky rifle, then scanned the hilltop clearing. All of Duvall's officers were dead.

They had followed Duvall to hell.

"You get hit bad?" Dan'l asked Cahill.

"It's just a nick," Cahill told him. He gestured toward their horses, down on the hillside. "I guess we ought to get these underground. There's a shovel on my mount's irons."

Dan'l clapped him on the shoulder, and they began heading for the horses. "It'll be a common grave," Dan'l said soberly. "Deep, Cahill.

310

And I want it covered so good not even a Shaw-nee can find it."

Cahill eyed him curiously.

"Maybe they'll forget him if they can't find him," Dan'l explained. "I don't want him dug up by the Frenchies and made no goddamn hero."

Cahill understood. "We'll see to it," he said. "Then maybe I can get back to farming the Yad-kin."

Dan'l saw some deep woods in his head, and a sparkling stream, and smelled the redolence of the forest's fragrances, and he realized he was getting a glimpse of his future.

But he did not express any of that to Cahill. "Just about anything would beat this," he grinned.

Cahill nodded, but did not reply.

Dan'l had said it all.